Praise for

Chess

I can see why the author uses the game of chess as a comparison. The strategy and give and take in the relationships is similar to the moves each piece must take in a game of chess...I love that they author created such unique characters with their own personalities...if you are looking for well written characters with good personalities and fun dialogue that have lots of sexy fun, this is a great choice!
~ *MM Good Book Reviews*

Chess and erotica are two totally different things, right? One is all about the strategy and the other is all about the doing. At first glance, mixing the two sounded pretty out there to me. But you know what? In the context of this foursome, each of the three members of the existing threesome struggling for a position in the face of a new member of their household, the analogy actually works...
~ *QMO Books*

CHESS
Volume One

Opening Moves

Middle Game

SEAN MICHAEL

Chess Volume One
ISBN # 978-1-78184-529-5
©Copyright Sean Michael 2012
Cover Art by Posh Gosh ©Copyright 2012
Interior text design by Claire Siemaszkiewicz
Total-E-Bound Publishing

Published in 2012 by Total-E-Bound Publishing, Think Tank, Ruston Way, Lincoln, LN6 7FL, United Kingdom.

OPENING
MOVES

Dedication

As always, for my readers.

Prologue

God, he was bored.

Like intensely, crazy bored.

Jason kept his eyes on the spot on the ceiling where the stain stopped. Being perfectly motionless was the whole trick of life modelling, but even so... The last thing he needed to do was sit and think about how his only remaining client at the gym had just dropped him and his rent was two months past due.

What was he going to do? He could live in his car for a little while, but winter was coming. Hell, it was already bearing down—he could feel it in the mornings when he went out to run. God knew this was not the place to be homeless when the winter came.

And without training clients the gym wouldn't let him in.

And he couldn't get more clients without a gym.

Fucking economy.

Fucking money.

Fucking Jack Winters dropping his prices at the fitness centre so far that nobody private could compete, not after paying the gym its cut.

The life modelling gig was the last thing he had left and, at forty bucks a night, it wasn't going to help. Not at all.

The night's session was almost over when two guys came in — one big, dark and quiet, the other slender, blond and bouncy. "Hey, Knight!"

"Hey, you hooligans." A guy from the back stood and stretched. "I'm out of here, Ginger. You good?"

Ginger Peters, the instructor, who had to be thirty months pregnant, smiled. "Yeah. I'll get Jason to help me to my car. In fact, time's up, everyone. Thanks, Jason, for sitting."

Jason sat up, grabbed his robe and tried to smile. "Sure."

The taller one of the guys who'd just arrived leaned into his painter friend. "Is that him, Knight?"

"Mm-hmm." The artist — Knight — grinned, the smile slow but not sweet at all. "Approve, Bish-love?"

"I just might. You have a good eye."

"Well, duh." The guy called Knight grabbed his palette pad, scribbled on it, then rolled it up.

Jason tried hard not to pay attention, not to anybody, but it was tough. Really tough.

Especially when the fierce-looking dude walked up to him and pressed the paper into his hand. "For you, stud. Enjoy."

Then the trio just…walked away.

The blond looked back just as they got to the door, gave him a warm, inviting smile, then they were gone.

Ginger smiled at Jason. "Keep that."

"Huh?"

"Chris Knight's one of the up-and-coming artists. It'll be worth a fortune one day."

His fingers clenched around the roll. "No shit?"

"You have my word."

Jason shook his head. "No way. Why's he here then?"

"I hear he likes to go incognito, take the beginner courses and have some fun. More than one teacher's ripped him to shreds only to backpedal when they found out who he was."

"Weird. I'll get dressed, hon, then carry your stuff."

Artists were strange.

He got back to his clothes, put on his jeans, T-shirt, hoodie, tennis shoes. Only then did he look at his picture. It was him, but…

He was…

Erect. God. And there were hands and cocks and mouths on him and…

Jesus.

Oh, God.

He stared, stunned, his fingers curling as he shook his head. Fucking pervert. They said there wasn't anything sexual about posing like this.

Nothing.

But this was…

God.

He shook his head, swallowed hard. He just needed to throw this trash away, go home.

Bleach his brain.

At the bottom of the picture was a scribble— *Interested in a job? Come to the Z'va coffee house. Tonight.*

No way.

No.

Fucking.

Way.

Pervert.

Chapter One

Rook bounced as they headed towards the Z'va coffee house, walking between Knight and Bishop, his two favourite people in all the world. "He was a stud, Knight. He really was."

"I told you." Knight winked at him, goosed him gently. "O ye of little faith and large penis."

He jumped at the goosing and rounded on Knight, his ire fading as he played the words back. "His was pretty impressive, too. You think it was just a shower? Or a grower, too?"

"That I don't know. He's never sprung wood in class." Knight winked.

"That's a damn shame." Rook stepped back between them and looped a hand each through Knight's and Bishop's arms. He loved touching them. Hell, he loved them, plain and simple. "So. I know I'm not the only one who wants to do him six ways to Sunday."

Bish snorted. "Or get done by him."

"Sure. I'm easy." He was. As both his lovers well knew.

"He might say no... You do realise this, dear boys." Knight could be such a turd.

"You wouldn't have suggested it if you believed that."

Knight nodded, hips bumping his. "He's got a great ass and the rumours are he's unattached. A little gym bunny."

"I didn't get a good look at his ass, but the rest of him was vavavavoom!"

"I saw his ass," put in Bishop. "It was great."

"I need a cup of coffee. I told him where we'd be. We're sticking with the original plan, boys?"

They'd made similar offers before—four times. No one'd ever said yes. Of course, Knight hadn't picked before.

A boy. A man. A lover. Someone for them to play with at will. They'd started talking about it late one night—the three of them naked and lazy, sprawled. Knight had been teasing Bish about getting a houseboy, someone they could touch, drive crazy. Boss around a little. Play with.

That had been Knight's phrase. Play with.

Rook nodded eagerly and Bishop grunted an affirmative.

Rook tried not to get excited, but damn. It wasn't easy.

They piled into the shop, waved at Rick and Les. "The usual, boys?"

"Please. You and Bish go sit, I'll get it." He pulled his wallet out and sauntered up to the counter.

Rick grinned at him and Les made the black coffee, the mocha latte, and the triple espresso with a shot of caramel. "We haven't seen you three in almost a week. I was going to send a search party."

"If you promise it'll be full of studs, it'll be another week before we're back."

"Shit, I can't afford that! Knight keeps me in business!"

He pouted. "Too bad. I guess we'll have to keep finding our own studs."

He handed over a twenty and waved away the offered change. Grabbing the tray, he headed to the table Knight and Bishop had chosen. Knight was straddling a chair backwards, Bishop's hands on his lean shoulders, rubbing hard. Knight looked tired, but each touch seemed to make that sexy body to relax. Rook licked his lips. Who needed a search party of hotties when he had his two very own personal studs to love on?

The look on Knight's face was pure bliss—lips parted, surrounded by goatee and moustache, the hair black as pitch.

"No orgasming in the coffee shop—they'll throw us out again," Rook teased, putting their coffees down on the table.

"Shh. He's rubbing. Don't distract him."

He grinned at Bishop, who just smiled back. "I'll do you when we get home."

It was probably for the best—he'd never met a massage he didn't want to turn into more. Especially when Bish was the one dishing out the massage—you could feel the love in every touch.

Knight moaned, the sound like liquid sex. "Bish has the best hands."

"He does." Rook was getting hard. Between the look on Knight's face and the memories of what exactly those hands could get up to...

He sat down and pulled his chair up to the table. Bish could make you beg, make you scream, make you hurt in ways that felt so fucking good after... And after... He never ever doubted that Bish loved him.

He tried not to whimper—he already had a reputation for being easy, so the last thing he needed was to get all hot and bothered by *memories*.

Knight met his gaze, near-black eyes dazed. "Tell me when you see him."

Not if.

When.

That had him even more jazzed. Knight really believed this guy was going to show up, was going to at least listen to their proposition. He bit his lower lip and nodded, eyes going automatically to the door.

Bishop was murmuring softly to Knight. Rook couldn't hear the words, but it didn't matter. He knew the tone, knew the need. Knew that, no matter what the stud said to their offer, Knight was going to get worked over tonight and he was going to get to enjoy all the benefits.

Fuck, his life was good.

He took a sip of his espresso, humming at the sweetness of the caramel.

One eye half on the door, he gave most of his attention to his lovers.

Knight's high cheekbones were painted a rosy red, his eyes closed. The man had the longest damn eyelashes he'd ever seen. Ever.

Rook wished, all of a sudden, that they were at home. Oh, he wanted to meet the stud, to make the offer and have it accepted, but he also wanted to pounce, to suck Knight's cock and then do whatever Bish ordered him to do. He wanted to hear Knight beg, to see Bish in those tight leather pants, in the black leather gloves...

His cock pushed hard against his jeans and he barely bit back a moan. Bish gave him a knowing, loving look, hazel eyes hooded.

He barely saw Bish's tongue flick out, touch Knight's ear.

He licked his lips, ready to leap up and suggest they go home, when the door opened and the stud from the art class walked in.

"Psst. Guys. Look." He nodded in the direction of the door.

Bish backed off, and Knight's eyes opened. "Go ask the pretty boy what he wants to drink, Rook-love. Then bring him over."

"Anything for my Knight." He let his hand trail along Knight's shoulders before he went over to the cutie.

"Hey there. What can I get you?"

"I don't drink coffee. A small non-fat chai, please?" The guy pulled out a wrinkled five from his pocket.

Rook wrapped his fingers over the hand with the five. "I've got it, sugar. Why don't you go sit with Knight and Bishop?" He nodded towards his lovers.

"Knight and Bishop. Those are cool names."

"Yeah, they're cool guys, too. I'm Rook, by the way." He held out his hand.

"Jason Myer." The handshake was firm, strong.

"Hi, Jason, it's great to meet you." He waved at the guys behind the counter. "Large non-fat chai for my friend, please."

It felt good when Jason relaxed a little bit, took a deep breath. "Thank you. I... You're not in the drawing class, huh?"

"Hell, no. I can't even draw stick figures!" He laughed, paid for Jason's drink and grabbed four of the café's huge cookies at the same time.

"Me neither. I'm a personal trainer, not an artist."

"Oh, cool! Bish is at the gym a lot." He grinned and patted his belly. "I'm there just enough."

Jason smiled back at him and...whoa. Yeah. That was why Knight'd picked him. Yummy.

Bish was going to eat this one alive.

He gave Jason his best flirty look, grabbed the guy's drink and led him over to Knight and Bish. "Guys, this is Jason Myer — personal trainer and studly model."

"Hey, stud. Have a seat. You like my portrait?" Knight wasn't looking all dazed now — no, the man was sharp and on fire.

"It was... I thought I should return it."

"Oh, honey, why would you do that?" Rook frowned.

"It's very...personal, and she said it was worth something, that you were there just to observe."

Knight waved one hand. "Nonsense. I drew it for you."

"There you go." Rook waited for Jason to sit in the booth and then slipped in beside him, sitting close. "It's yours."

Jason looked at Rook wide-eyed, then wrapped his hands around his mug. "So, your note said something about a job?"

Rook and Bish both looked at Knight, grinning. Rook even bounced in place a little.

"Yeah. I overheard your conversation about your situation at the gym and the boys and I are interested in hiring someone."

Jason's head tilted. "As a trainer?"

"Not precisely, no, although training is very much involved."

Bish smiled. "Yes, training is important. Are you good at taking orders, Jason?"

"I follow directions really well. I didn't lose my clients because I'm bad at my job. I just can't compete with the big houses, price-wise."

"That sucks." Rook put his hand on Jason's thigh and squeezed, giving him a sympathetic look.

Those big muscles leapt and jerked. "Thank you. So…what are you hiring for?"

Knight looked over, grinned and winked. "We want someone to play with. For a year."

"Wh…what? Play?"

Look at that shocked, innocent face. Rook was going to cream his jeans.

Knight's smile went purely wicked. "Yes, dear boy. Play. Hard."

Rook squeezed Jason's thigh again. "One year with us and you'll be set for life."

"Play… You mean… You're talking about sex, right? But…I'm not gay. I don't do men."

Rook could answer that one easily. "Oh, honey, that's okay. You don't have to do any of us — we'll be doing you."

Bish chuckled. "We might let you do Rook a time or two. He likes it. A lot."

"This is true." Knight leaned across the table, met Jason's eyes. "Look, you don't have to decide tonight. I have a contract drawn up — no permanent damage, no permanent marks unless you agree in writing, one year's service. We provide room and board, and you get a cool half a million at the end of the contract. All you have to do is exactly what we want for three hundred and sixty-five days."

Jason looked like he was going to pass out.

Rook put his arm around Jason's shoulders. "Drink your chai. Have a cookie."

Jason's fingers were actually shaking, but the man picked the mug up and drank deep. There was an electricity about this one, a spark.

Rook was beginning to believe.

"All your needs would be taken care of for a whole year. There's an amazing gym so you would still be able to work out, a pool in the backyard. And the house..." Rook smiled. It was his baby. "It's a beaut, if I do say so myself."

"But...I don't. I'm not gay. Don't you get it? I couldn't...perform."

Knight chuckled. "Wanna bet?"

Rook patted the thigh his hand still rested on. "It wouldn't be a condition of you taking the job. You don't need to come at all."

Bishop grinned, and even Rook had to admit it was a bit of an evil smile. "But you would."

"No. I don't..."

"Look, think about it. Sleep on it. Come over tomorrow and, if you don't get off, you'll know." Knight's voice was rich as velvet.

"We'll pay generously for your time, just to give it a try." Money wasn't an object. Rook had more than he knew what to do with.

Knight gently tossed a thumb drive across the table. "There's a contract on it. Take a look when you get home."

"I... You... But..."

Jesus, that was cute.

Rook leaned in to speak quietly near Jason's ear. "What does it hurt to look at it? You'll see it's more than fair, and then you'll come over and spend the afternoon as a trial run."

"How...how will I contact you?" He could smell Jason—the man smelt like heaven.

Rook grabbed a napkin and held his hand out to Knight, who gave him a charcoal pencil. He wrote down his cell phone number.

"I... You're serious? You're not like...axe murderers?"

"Do we look like axe murderers?" Bishop asked.

Rook giggled.

Bishop shot him a look. "Aside from him, that is."

Rook stuck his tongue out.

Knight held out a business card. "This is my lawyer, Hannah. Look her up. Call her. She drew up the papers. She'll vouch for us."

It was a positive thing that Jason took the card.

Rook offered him the cookie again. "Have something to eat, get your blood sugar up." He stroked Jason's thigh some more. Such a pretty boy.

He couldn't help but notice that Jason didn't pull away. Not queer? Bullshit. Not experienced, sure. Scared, absolutely…but so turned on.

He met Bishop's eyes, the look there telling him Bish saw it, too.

The pretty boy nibbled at his cookie and Knight picked up his cup, finishing his coffee and heading up for another. "Anyone else need a refill?"

They all declined, Rook laughing. "The stuff flows in the man's veins," he told Jason.

"He's very intense."

The kid had no idea.

"Yeah, you know…artistic temperament and all that. He's worth every quirk, though." Rook wouldn't trade Knight for anything.

Jason sighed and rubbed the back of his neck. "Artists can be something, I guess."

"I'm a sex-toy shop worker, if it makes you feel better." He also owned the place, but he didn't usually share that. Or the size of his inheritance. The size of his prick, on the other hand…

"No shit?" Jason grinned. "I don't suppose you'd put a word in with your manager, if this doesn't work out?"

"Trust me, honey, this pays way better. Has better perks, too."

"I just…" Jason blushed dark and Rook could suddenly see him, bound and bare, arched, begging to be fucked…filled. "Why me?"

Knight sat down, cup in hand. "You're pretty, innocent, and you have a great ass."

Ah, Mr Romance…

"We all like you—we agreed on you. That doesn't happen that often."

"You've hired someone before?"

"Oh, no. We have interviewed a man or two, though."

"No one said yes?"

"No one was a perfect fit. You, though…" He gave the man his best smile. It was a very good smile—sexy, earnest, come-hither. Knight told him all the time.

"I'm…"

Rook licked his lips and Jason blinked, eyes on his mouth. Shit yes. The man was totally interested, deny it as much as he liked. "You're perfect for each of us, for *all* of us."

"I should go." Jason licked his own lips, the pink tongue slipping out, mimicking Rook's motion.

"If you want. Or you could stay a little longer and tell us about yourself."

"I'm a personal trainer. I've been here in Toronto for about eighteen months. I'm beginning to understand why they said it was hard to find your way here."

Knight's head tilted. "Girlfriend?"

Jason shook his head.

Knight arched an eyebrow. "Why not?"

"I'm focused on my career." *Uh-huh.* Jason just didn't like girls. He wasn't queer, though, nope, not him.

Rook bit back his chuckle.

"It's an expensive place to live, especially if you're working for yourself."

"Yeah." That frown was back again, that worry.

"Hey, Jason. It's okay, yeah? This is a really good deal and we're good people. We can help you."

"If you were shitty people, you wouldn't tell me up front."

That made Knight laugh. "Absolutely true. That's why we're meeting you here, in public, in a place where people obviously know us."

"Yeah. We could leave so you could go talk to Rich and Les."

"In fact you *should* go talk to them," Bish added. "We're legit, which means we're not afraid to have you check us out."

Knight nodded. "We're honest—we're in the community. We just want someone to play with for a year. It's a fantasy life."

Jason looked a little stunned. "I'll look over the paperwork, think about it."

"Thanks, honey, that's all we're asking for." Rook bounced a little and pushed the napkin with his cell phone number at Jason. "And you call me if you have any questions, okay? Any questions at all."

Knight stood, stretched, went up on his toes. "Let's go, boys. It's getting late." Then those black, black eyes met Jason's. "Think about it. We'll blow your mind."

"And the rest of you." Rook added, winking.

He got up and went to stand with Knight—Bish joining them, putting an arm around both their shoulders.

They walked out, waving to the boys on the way. As the door shut behind them, Knight sighed. "Can somebody take me home now and fuck me?"

"Bish can. I want your cock down my throat." Rook's own cock was already pulling a major happy just at the thought.

"Bishop has evil in his eyes." Knight grinned. "You think the stud-boy will call?"

"I hope so. He'd be something else."

"Yeah. Come on, you two hooligans. Let's go."

"Yeah, we got a date with our naked bodies."

Knight's laugh echoed all the way down the street.

Chapter Two

No permanent marks without written permission of the above.

No refusals unless the contract is voided.

If the contract is voided at any time, payment will be prorated.

No images, video, etc. will be recorded.

All parties must be tested clean of communicable diseases. All parties agree to be exclusive among named parties for the duration of the contract.

All body parts of the above named will be accessible to the primaries, for whatever use they choose, barring previous exceptions.

Jason stared.

This was insane. Crazy.

But the money…

And a place to live for a year, to just train and get himself together.

He…

God.

What would they want to do to him? What did 'all parts' mean? He tried to imagine having another man touch his cock, his balls, his ass... His brain skittered away from the thought, his belly going tight. No.

No, he just couldn't, could he?

No. No way.

He picked up the phone and dialled the number they'd given him.

He was just going to say no. Sorry. Thanks. No.

"Hello!" A bright, cheery voice answered. "You've got Rook!"

"I... Hello. This is...this is Jason Myer, from the coffee shop?" *The guy you offered to make your sex kitten for a year?*

"Jason!" Rook laughed — the sound happy, really happy. "I'm so glad you called. I've been thinking about you a lot."

"I... I looked at the contract thing."

"That's great. You have any questions?"

"I just... I don't think... I don't think I can do it. It's a great offer, but I don't think I can let a guy touch me like that."

"Oh, honey. Why don't you come for that trial we offered? Just the afternoon. We'll share some lunch — we'll fool around a little. Then you can decide."

He sighed, leaned his head on his hand. He liked Rook, a lot. Of all of them, the man seemed the most approachable, the most real. "Can... Can you and I meet for a coffee, first?"

Somehow Rook was the...least intense of the three.

"Sure, whatever you need. Same place?" The agreement was ready, easy, like Rook didn't have anything to hide.

"Yeah. Yeah, thanks. When's good for you?"

"I can come now, if you want."

"Okay. I can be there in ten minutes." He swallowed hard. "Thanks, man. I'm just...this is a little wiggy."

"Of course. Anything you need to make you feel more comfortable, I mean it. Okay. Be there in ten. You're a non-fat chai, right?"

"Yeah." Dude, the man remembered.

"See you soon, honey."

The line went dead.

Jason looked at his cell. Well, that hadn't gone exactly like he'd planned. He went to find a clean pair of underwear and his good jeans and a sweatshirt. It was going to be cold soon and that eviction date was coming faster and faster.

He was at Z'va in slightly less than ten minutes, but Rook had beaten him there. The man was in a booth at the back, two drinks in front of him, along with three or four plates of baked goods—a cinnamon roll, two cookies, the biggest brownie ever and a muffin.

He breathed in deep—the place smelt like heaven. "Hey."

Rook was a good-looking guy—one of those people you expected to see on television or something. Blond and blue eyes with a perfect white smile—this was a face meant to inspire trust.

The man bounced up out of his seat to take Jason's hand, shook it, then laughed and gave him a hug. "Have a seat, have a seat. I wasn't sure what you were in the mood for or how hungry you were, so I got a variety. I love desserts."

"I do too. I try to avoid them, so I can stay lean, but...these look irresistible." He let Rook sit him down, lean against him.

"They are irresistible." Rook smiled warmly at him—right at him, like he was the only one in the place. "They aren't the only things at this table that are, either."

He blushed, chuckled. "I... That's flattering, but... Dude, I'm not into guys. I mean, I'm not really all that into sex."

He could be honest.

Rook's eyes widened. "You're not into sex? Honey, you just haven't had the right kind." Rook patted his leg and smiled. "I bet we'd make it good for you. I bet you'd like it with us. I think you should at least give it a try before you turn down the chance of a lifetime."

He picked up his tea, sipped it. "What...what kind of things are you into?"

"I love it all—sucking, fucking, watching, some kink, toys. You wouldn't believe some of the things I've seen at the store. I get all sorts of ideas."

Jason didn't get so many ideas. "What about the other two?"

"Bish's a bit of a top. He likes to dream up all these scenarios, likes to do all sorts of things. Knight likes to fuck and get fucked—everything else is just details." Rook laughed softly. "If you come home with me and you'll see for yourself."

"I'm just...not well suited to it. And they're a little unnerving."

"They can be a little intense, but they're awesome guys, I promise you."

Rook broke a bit off one of the cookies and pressed it against his lips. "Open up, honey."

His lips parted instinctively, tongue tasting the sugary goodness and Rook's skin at the same time.

Rook's finger slid along his lower lip. "Sweet, isn't it?"

"Yeah." He closed his lips, chewed.

"So are you," whispered Rook, eyes warm, admiring.

"I... Thank you." He couldn't look away.

"You're welcome." Rook held his gaze, blue eyes warm and steady.

"I don't know what to do, man." He was way out of his league.

"So come home with me for the afternoon." Rook grinned. "Or bring me home with you."

"With me? Just you?"

"Uh-huh." Rook's smile went all the way to his eyes.

"I... Your...friends won't be upset?" Was that cheating?

"They know I came — they knew I might be bringing you home or going home with you."

"Oh. I... Okay. Okay." One guy he could handle. He could try it, it wouldn't work, and then he'd figure something out.

"Shall we take our desserts to go?" Rook's hand glided up along his thigh.

He jerked and his belly went tight. "I... Okay?"

"Okay." Rook waved at the guys behind the counter and made a complicated hand signal, which brought one of them over with a box. Their food was packed up and the guy gave him a wink before heading back to the counter.

"I live right up the way. It's not far." Jason jammed his hands into his coat pockets, so stressed out he couldn't bear it.

"Okay." Rook grabbed the box of pastries and put a hand on his arm. "Lead the way."

He was so nervous that he babbled all the way to the apartment — about work and working out and things. Rook let him talk, smiling and nodding, looking at him like he was something.

They got into the elevator and suddenly all his words dried up as he pushed the 'four' button. Rook filled the space with small talk and then leaned against the wall as Jason pulled out his keys to open the door. He barely noticed the new eviction notice on his door as he led the man in. His place was tiny, simple — one room with a futon, weights and a laptop.

"Oh, honey, this is a place you're staying, not a home. We can give you a home." Rook put down the box and took his hand, squeezing it.

"I... What's your place like?" He couldn't do this.

"It's open and bright and there's lots of rooms." Rook shifted until they were face to face, bringing their lips close. "You'll have your own."

"I... I'm not any good at this."

Rook smelt good. How could the man smell good?

"I am." Rook smiled slowly, then ran his tongue along Jason's lower lip. He gasped and stepped back a half step. "Don't be shy. I'm not going to hurt you."

"This is crazy." He was going to kiss a guy.

"No, this is sex." Rook's lips pressed against his, soft and warm. He gasped again, lips opening instinctively. Rook's moan was quiet, tongue hot as it slipped between his lips and into his mouth. Oh, it was so good. He. He couldn't. He couldn't... *Oh, God.*

That tongue pushed in and out, twisted in his mouth. He moved his hands up Rook's arms, fingers dragging over the slick fabric of his jacket. Rook sort of nodded, deepening the kiss. Jason sucked in a wild breath, his tongue daring to touch Rook's. Rook moaned again, and stroked one hand up along Jason's arm. The touch was warm, firm, and his biceps tightened. Rook's hand slid up to his shoulder.

He stiffened, not sure what to do.

Long, capable fingers massaged his neck.

"Oh..." His eyes rolled and he melted a little. So much tension.

"I've got great hands."

"Uh-huh." He might die.

Then Rook's other hand came up too, worked his other shoulder. A deep moan tried to escape him as his head fell forward.

"Relax. We can have such a good time together."

"I'm trying. I'm trying. You have good hands."

"I told you."

Rook grinned at him and then he was being kissed again. It was insane—not at all like kissing a girl. This was firmer, stronger, and Rook's hands refused to let tension creep back in.

Rook didn't deepen the kiss at all, just kept at it, tongue gliding against his.

His cock jerked, began to fill and he leaned away.

"Mmm, you taste really good."

"I've never kissed a man before."

"You did a great job."

The words were unexpectedly welcome. "Thank you."

"You wanna sit with me?"

"Yeah." His knees were a little weak.

"Come on then, honey."

Rook drew him over to his own futon, tugging him down onto it.

"I hope it's comfortable enough." Their bodies were touching, all along the side.

"You're here with me, that's what matters."

Rook rubbed his hand along Jason's cheek, then wrapped it around the back of his head, drawing their mouths together again. His eyes widened, because this kiss was deep, stealing his breath away. Making him hard.

Oh, God.

Making him hard…

Like he knew, Rook worked gentle fingers over his prick.

Their eyes met and he had the sudden urge to ask Rook not to tell anyone. *Please.*

Rook's tongue teased his, those fingertips rubbing across the tip of his cock through his pants and underwear. His breath came faster, his heart slamming harder. *Oh, God. Oh, fuck.* He tensed, his body wanting to run.

"Shh. Shh. Just let it happen. So sweet and sexy."

"Please. I don't…"He didn't know what to do.

"Let me make you feel good."

Rook's hand slid, rubbed him. His thighs spread, his body beginning to rock.

"That's it, Jason. So pretty."

The kisses began again.

Slowly, Rook eased him back, leaning over him. That hand was driving him a little crazy, making him want to hump up. Rook shifted, the man's erection pressing against his thigh. His body shifted, rubbed against that hardness. Rook moaned, the sound needy as hell.

"Oh, honey. Yes. Please."

He moved again without thinking. Thinking wasn't helping.

Rook moved against him, pushing to rub them harder together. He moaned into the kiss, hips rolling up so his cock got more friction, more sensation. Rook matched him kiss for kiss, movement for movement— he wasn't alone in this, not for a second.

His cock ached, so full. Leaking. He missed Rook undoing his pants button, his zipper, but Rook must have, because suddenly his cock was pushing up into the man's hand.

"Oh. Oh, God." The world went white hot and electric, that touch perfect.

Rook's palm pushed against the head of his dick, and then it slipped along his cock, fingers closing around him.

"Please. I'm aching." He needed something to happen.

"I can help with that."

Rook held his gaze as the man shimmied down his body. The connection was only broken when Rook took Jason's cock into his hot mouth.

Jason stopped. The world stopped. Everything stopped.

All he knew was his cock and that wet, tight heat.

Rook took him in and in, swallowing him whole.

"Oh, fuck. Oh, fuck..." He fucked Rook's mouth, mindless with need.

Rook took it, working his hands beneath his ass and encouraging his movements. The man's mouth was like a hot vacuum, sucking hard.

"Fuck. Fuck, please." His balls drew up and his hips slammed forward, and the whole world went grey as he shot. Rook kept sucking—he could feel the man swallow around the head of his cock. His eyes rolled back in his head, the pleasure fucking increasing. He didn't even go soft.

Sounds tore out of him as he writhed on the futon, so excited and turned on he couldn't catch his breath. The sucking turned into licking, Rook's tongue finding and stimulating every single nerve in his prick. Jason couldn't think, couldn't breathe. It was huge. Then Rook made his way down to Jason's balls, mouth swallowing one up.

His eyes widened and he pushed up on his elbows to stare down.

Rook paused in his sucking and looked up, eyes shining at him. Then the man went back to business—sucking his ball, tongue lashing gently at it. His abs tightened, and he drew one knee up, the move instinctive, immediate. Rook groaned around his nut, fingers coming up to play with the other one.

"Oh, God…" His head fell back, his throat working.

Rook sucked a little longer and then his fingers drifted down, caressing behind his balls.

He should say no.

He should. He wasn't into this. Those fingers were making him crazy, rubbing his skin back there.

"I don't know what to do, Rook."

That mouth came off his ball with a 'pop'.

"Just lie back and let me make you feel good."

He groaned and eased himself back, moving his fingers down his sides.

"You wanna touch yourself, honey? You can. Pinch those little nipples or tug on your cock while I…" Rook's face disappeared between his legs, hot tongue wet on his skin.

"What…what are you…" His nipples? How did Rook know? He'd always been embarrassed at how much he touched them. Rook didn't answer his half-asked question—instead the man hummed and licked, his tongue feeling so unbelievably good, hair tickling Jason's inner thighs and balls. He found his nipples, pinched hard enough that he cried out, the zing perfect.

"Nice." The world was muffled, but Rook had definitely said it. "Do it again."

"Don't tell. Please. Don't tell anybody." This was his secret, his need.

"Just Knight and Bishop. It'll be a secret between us. A bond." Then Rook's tongue licked even further back.

He was going to scream. He pinched again and again, sobbing with a need that he couldn't begin to understand. Rook's tongue played across his hole, making his nerves dance and beg for more.

"You can't… Oh, God. Oh, God. Please." He twisted, unable to hold still.

It seemed that Rook could, lashing at him with that tongue over and over and then, unbelievably, pushing right into him. In. To. Him. His fingers clenched around his nipples again and his cock jerked, sending spunk splashing over his belly and chest, hot and thick and wet. Humming, Rook sent vibrations up through his insides, making him shake, the orgasm seeming to go on forever.

When it was over, he was boneless, empty, lost.

Rook rose up and lay half on top of him, fingers dancing on his skin, stroking gently. Shivers slid over his skin as his heart rate slowed.

"How was that?" Rook's words were soft, gently spoken.

"I..." He didn't have words. "Is...is it always like that?"

"You mean fan-fucking-tastic? It is if you're with people who give a damn about you getting off, yeah."

"Oh." He should care about Rook getting off. Even if he didn't take the job, it was only fair. "Do... Can I...help you?"

"You are the sweetest thing ever. Your hand would feel so good."

He nodded and worked on getting Rook's jeans open. He told himself this would be just like touching himself, that it wouldn't be too weird, and Rook had helped him out...twice. Rook's cock pushed out towards him as soon as he got Rook's pants undone. Shit, Rook was hung like a fucking horse. He wrapped his hand around the thick shaft, stroking up and down, rubbing along the way with his thumb.

"Oh, that's nice." Rook started rocking, pushing the hot cock through his hand. He was leaking, hot drops splashing on Jason's wrist, on his arm, slicking his fingers.

Rook nuzzled his neck. "You smell good, honey. Makes me want to eat you up." The man laughed. "Oops, I already did."

Jason felt his cheeks go red-hot. "Did you like it?"

"Loved it. You tasted wonderful." Rook's voice was husky, his hips pushing faster. "Want to taste you again."

Jason stroked his hand faster, taking his cues from Rook's body.

"You sure you've never done this before?"

"Only to myself."

Rook laughed again, the sound really happy. "Good. At least you've had that."

"I'm not a virgin, I just... It's not my thing." He kept touching, kept stroking, his arm sure and strong.

"What? Sex?" Rook blinked at him, body actually stilling at his words.

"Uh-huh." He slowed the motion of his hand, gentling his touch. "I..."

Rook shook his head and started pushing into his hand again.

"Tell me if I'm doing it wrong."

"You're touching me. There's no wrong there."

He blushed, smiled. The praise felt...so fucking welcome. He hadn't done anything right in a long time.

"Kiss me?" Rook asked softly, eyes taking on a shine.

He leant forward—nervous, unsure...reminding himself that this was the least he'd be asked for, and Rook seemed as though he wanted *him*, not just anyone. A soft moan left Rook's mouth as their lips met, those eyes getting brighter. Jason tasted tentatively, then with more confidence, tongue pushing in, pressing against Rook's.

Rook sucked on his tongue, hips thrusting faster as they kissed. He made sure his hand kept caressing, thumb working the tip the way he liked it himself.

Jerking against him, Rook cried out into his mouth and came. It wasn't gross, like he'd feared. It was good to know he'd done it.

"Mmm…oh, honey. Come home with me and this could be ours."

"I… I have to think. Would my bloodwork from my last physical showing I'm clean be okay? It was only three weeks ago."

"Yeah, that'll do. Me and the boys have paperwork, too. We're clean. We play safe."

"Okay. I'll… I'll call you tonight. I promise. I'll call with a decision." He found a smile for Rook. "I can't make a smart decision like this."

"No, that wouldn't be fair to you." Rook kissed him. "This could be yours, though. All you have to do is say yes."

He met those beautiful blue eyes. "You're something else."

"And here I was, just thinking the same thing about you."

"Right." His cheeks were burning.

"It's true." Rook took his hand and squeezed it. "I want you to come stay with us, honey. You're sexy and fit and sweet."

He was insane. Perfectly insane. "I'll call tonight."

"I'm looking forward to hearing from you."

Another kiss, a quick adjustment of clothing and Rook was gone.

He blinked.

That was…fast.

And, oddly enough, Jason thought he might miss the man.

Chapter Three

Knight glared at the TV.

He didn't want to go into the studio.

He didn't want to make lunch.

He didn't want to have a bath or anything.

He wanted to know what the hell had happened between Rook and Jason, damn it.

Knight hated being patient.

Finally, after what had to be fucking hours, the front door opened and closed. "Hellooo!"

He stood up, heading for the foyer. "Well?"

"Well what?" Rook grinned at him. The fucker'd got some. It was written all over his beautiful face.

"What did you do, ass-hat? Share!"

Rook laughed. "What? No kiss hello? No 'we missed you'? No 'come in and sit down'?"

Knight threw himself at Rook, trusting the man to catch him. "Now. Tell. Bish! He fucked our boy!"

"I did not!"

Bish came out of the den, frowning. "What's up?"

"He went to Jason. He's gotten off. I can tell!"

"I didn't fuck him." Rook gave him a smug look. "I blew him."

Knight grinned, the smile stretching his cheeks. "I *knew* it!"

Rook looped an arm around his neck. "Take me to bed and I'll tell you all about it." A look from under Rook's eyelashes included Bishop. "I think he's going to do it."

"Of course he will. I chose him." Thank Christ Rook had gone and done the charming boy thing. He had bragged and strutted about his choice.

"Well, to start with he called to say no."

"But you sucked him out of it." Knight grinned, feeling incredibly clever. "How was he? Tell us everything!"

"Well, I suggested he couldn't say no without knowing what he was turning down and invited him here, but he wanted to meet at the coffee shop instead. Just me. Apparently I'm less threatening than you two."

He shrugged, gave Rook a once over. "You look a little like a Ken doll..."

"Do you want to hear my story or do you want to continue to compare me to an anatomically-correct-if-you're-a-eunuch doll?"

"Ken doesn't have a dick, either." Knight held on as Bish carried him over to the sofa.

"That's what eunuch means, butthead." Rook sat, and Bish dropped to lounge next to them.

"Eunuchs don't have balls, dork."

"What? Are you sure?"

Bish started laughing.

Knight winked at his Bish, one hand held out to draw his lover closer. "So? Tell!"

Bish shifted close enough to press up against him, the three of them taking hardly any room at all on the couch.

"So I bought him pastries and a chai and we kind of wasted it all because it didn't take him that long to be convinced to give Rook the old college try. He took me back to his."

"Where's he live? And did you bring pastries home?" He was starving.

"He lives in this tiny little place, and I left the desserts with him." Rook grinned. "He said he wasn't into guys. Hell, he said he wasn't really into sex at all." He snorted. "I just want to know what idiots he's been having sex with because they've been clearly doing it all wrong."

Knight laughed. "That guy is sex on a stick. Did you fuck him?"

Knight was going to beat Rook if he'd done that before they all got to watch.

Rook smacked him on the ass. "I told you I didn't fuck him. I sucked him. I don't think anyone had ever even kissed him properly. It was almost sad, really."

"Almost." Knight's ass cheek tingled, and he bit his bottom lip.

"Well, it would have been sad if he hadn't had me to sex him up, teach him that kissing is good, getting sucked is better and that his hole is a sweet, sweet little bundle of pleasure."

"Oh, you horndog!" Knight chuckled and threw himself back against Bishop's arms. It was good— being in the arms of the man he loved, while the other man he loved smiled at him like he was something special. "He seduced the stud."

"The stud all but begged to be seduced."

Bishop grabbed his arms, stretched them up, so he was arched between his men. Rook leaned over him, hands stroking up his sides beneath his shirt. "He tasted like heaven."

"Did he fuck your mouth, baby?" Knight's throat felt a little tight, and Bish pulled him up higher.

"He did. Fuck, he was so hot. Came so fast. Poor boy's in big denial."

Bishop pulled him even harder, stretched him further, and Knight hummed. "You think he'll play with us?"

"I think so. I think he's desperate for the money, but he's even more desperate to be touched, to be loved."

Knight rolled his eyes, then stuck out his tongue. "Romantic."

Rook was the one with the soft, gooey centre. His love for his men was more…fierce. Rook leaned in and wrapped warm lips around his tongue. Knight moaned, imagining that he could taste Jason on their Rook's tongue. The kiss was long and deep, Rook pushing close as Bish held him tight.

Knight wrapped his legs around Rook's hips and held them together. Fuck, yeah. No one loved to kiss like Rook. No one. His lover fucked his mouth, tongue pushing deep before almost coming out. He tried to reach down, touch Rook, but Bish had him, held him. Bish's heavy cock pushed against his lower back.

"You just take what we have to give you." Bish's voice rumbled in his ear.

He groaned, spread out for his boys. They all loved Bish, loved how the toppy bastard worked.

Rook's fingers danced on his skin, traced him from hips to shoulders.

"Horny bastards," Knight moaned, arched into the touches.

Rook laughed. "Like you aren't begging for it."

"I never beg."

Bish growled. "Don't make me prove you wrong, Knight-man."

He grinned at Rook and winked. He loved this game. "I'd love to see you try."

"Oh-ho, it's like that, is it?" He could feel Bish all tensing up to move.

Rook pouted. "I worked my magic on the boy and got him this close to accepting the deal and now we're going to play make-Knight-beg before you guys even get me off?"

One of his eyebrows arched. "You're telling us he didn't help a guy out?"

That didn't seem very promising.

"Well...yeah, but it was only a handjob and then you demanded I relive the whole thing and now I'm horny as hell again!"

"How was he? Any talent?"

"He's got potential. He loved the way I smelled, and he kisses like a dream." Rook rubbed against him, making his ass press against Bish's crotch.

"Mmm. The things we're going to get to do..." He wanted someone to play with, so badly.

"You're going to blow his mind, lover. You and Bish. Fuck."

Bish nodded, grinned. "He'll fall in love with you, baby. Everyone does."

"Even you, Knight?" Rook batted his eyelashes, but he could see the need in those pretty blue eyes.

He reached up and touched those soft, swollen lips. "I was first, baby."

Moaning, Rook took his fingers in and sucked on them, tongue flicking at the tips. Bishop's hands dug into his hips, rocking him steadily. His cock was pressed tight between his and Rook's bodies, his lover's eyes holding his as that mouth and tongue made him crazy. He nodded, fucking Rook's lips with his fingers.

Rook made another noise that vibrated his fingers and rubbed against him.

"Let's slow this down a little," murmured Bish. "There needs to be a little more nakedness."

Knight smiled and winked up at Bish. "You just want to see if there's bruises from last night."

"There'd better be. I want to play connect the dots."

His body went tight and he nodded. "I want to play. Then tonight, when we get our boy home..."

They'd been looking for the right guy for so long.

"Once he's all ours, we're going to blow his mind. And our own."

Rook laughed at Bish's words and rubbed hard against him, their pricks bumping through far too many layers.

"Boys." He needed touching, loving. Sensation, damn it.

Bish growled at Rook, who laughed and backed off enough to start undressing Knight. Bishop's growl ranked up in Knight's top three hottest things of all time. Yummy. Not that he'd tell the arrogant bastard.

The arrogant bastard in question licked a line along Knight's neck, all the way from his collarbone to his jawline, as Rook's fingers bared him. It was the bite that left him shaken, though—gasping and painfully hard.

His erection was freed from his pants just then, Rook's mouth swallowing him down.

"Fuck! Rook! Baby!" Jesus, that mouth. It made him fucking stupid, he swore to God.

"Impatient," muttered Bish.

Rook himself might have said something, given the sudden vibrations around his prick.

Knight looked up at Bish, eyes rolling a little. "Hey."

Bish chuckled again and took his mouth, stealing his breath, and suddenly he was flooded with heat, his hips slamming up into Rook's willing lips. Rook took it, hands pushing beneath his ass and grabbing on, encouraging him to keep fucking Rook's mouth. He rocked hard, his abs screaming as he moved.

"Fucking sexy, Knight." Bish was still growling, the sound going along his spine.

"Bish. Bish, touch me, man."

"Now you're the one being impatient." Bish still didn't touch him, even as Rook's mouth really turned on the suction.

He snarled a little, his focus on the perfect pressure on his prick.

"Don't be a bitch." Bish pinched his right nipple. His temper flared, the fire in him burning against Bishop's eternal fucking calm. Bish growled and pinched his other nipple. "Careful or I'm going to make Rook stop."

He flipped Bish off. He wasn't the careful type.

"Rook. Stop."

Rook groaned around his prick, eyes flashing up, begging Bish not to make him do it.

"Baby..." He rolled his hips, loving on Rook's mouth.

"I fucking said stop."

Whimpering, Rook pulled slowly off his cock. "Bastard."

Knight looked at his lover, his sweet baby. "Come on, Rook."

"That's not nice, Knight." Bish slapped his hip.

"I'm not nice." That stung so good.

"You want to get sucked, though." Bish smacked him again.

"Fuck! Stop it!" *Or don't.*

Rook's tongue licked across the top of his cock and he could feel Bish's growl rumbling against his back. "Don't make me spank you both."

He smiled when Rook backed off. His Rook loved pleasure, but pain didn't get the man off. Pity.

Rook pouted mightily and stripped, cock hard and needy, pointing out from his body. "So mean, Bish."

"Knight was the one who made the choice."

"You're always blaming shit on me, Bish." Ever since he'd come to stay.

Bish just laughed, teeth working at his shoulder as those fingers found his nipples and pinched again.

Oh, fuck, that felt good. "You think he'll let us pierce him?"

Rook laughed, relaxing back and jacking himself. No fucking fair. "Not on the first day, no."

"No? You shouldn't be allowed to touch if I can't."

"Bish never said." Rook stuck out his tongue — brat.

"I could," Bish noted, his tongue doing naughty things to Knight's skin.

"One of these days, we're going to tie you to the big bed and beat your ass bloody." Knight knew it wasn't going to happen, but the threat was fun.

"The tying up part sounds fun." Rook was irrepressible.

"Not reddening his bubble butt?" He was pushing, he knew it, but the fact was, once the new boy came, he'd have to be much more controlled.

"Can I spank him? Please, Bish?" Rook turned those bright blue eyes on Bishop.

"Yeah. We'd better take this to the bedroom if we're going to full-on play with our naughty, naughty boy."

Bish stood and all but tossed him over one shoulder, much to Rook's delight.

"Naughty? Moi?"

Fuck, Knight loved how that word sounded in Bishop's voice.

"Fuck yes, you."

Rook slapped his ass as they went down the hall.

"Hey!" He kicked a little, made them work for it.

"Harder, Rookie."

The next slap he really felt.

"No slapping or I won't fuck you for a week!"

They chuckled at that—all three of them.

"Threats only work if you follow through, Knight." Bishop sounded positively cheerful.

"Blah, blah, blah." He gasped as another slap popped his ass.

"Harder, Rook." The way he was hanging over Bish's body, his lover's growling voice vibrated through his chest.

"Fuck... Baby."

"You want it, Knight—you know you do." Rook kissed his ass and then smacked it a few times.

Bishop got him into the bedroom, to the big bed. The thing was a mass of blankets and pillows, a tumbled mess of all of them—Bish's terribly expensive cream-coloured sheets, Knight's black and gold velvet comforters, Rook's fat, fluffy pillows...

Heaven.

He was dumped on his stomach, Bish moving and pushing, getting him just the way Bishop wanted him, which it seemed was ass up, legs slightly spread.

"Mmm. Yeah, that's right."

"He looks great, Bish."

His arms were spread out, the soft restraints slipped around his wrists, fitting him perfectly.

When the smack came, it wasn't Rook's hand that sounded against his ass, but Bishop's larger, hotter, surer one. His breath huffed out of him, his ass rolling up, rocking towards the touch.

"Such a bottom slut," Bish accused.

"Only for you." Knight didn't bottom for anyone but his boys.

"But you do it so well." Rook's fingers played with his crack.

"Don't make me kick your ass, baby."

"Bish wouldn't let you."

Bishop snorted. "I will if you're not careful."

He met Bishop's eyes—the look intense, serious, heated. "I'm ready, Bish. We won't get a chance to play hard for a long time, not together."

"Then hold on, babe, and get ready for the ride." Bish said something he couldn't hear to Rook, and the two of them started to spank him. Bish first, then Rook. Hard and then not so hard. Over and over, they worked his ass cheeks, his upper thighs.

He fought for breath, sucking air, his words all caught in his throat. *Fuck*. Fuck, that stung. So good. Bish began grunting with each smack, groaning so the sound went through him. It was Rook who began to talk, though. Dirty, filthy things that went straight to his cock. Rook promised pleasure, passion, forever, and Knight's eyes rolled. "Shit. Shit, you been reading how to talk dirty at the shop again?"

Rook's next slap was even harder. "Bitch, please. I know how to talk dirty. Learned from the best."

"Fuck!" He jerked forward, trying to get away.

"Enough," growled Bish. "Now we fuck him from both ends."

Knight whimpered, nodded. "Fuck. Fuck, yes. Please."

"You get his mouth warm, Rook. I'm going to slick him up."

He looked up at Rook and grinned. "Gonna fuck my mouth with that fat cock, baby?"

"I fucking am." Rook rubbed his fingers over his face, then that mouth covered his, swallowing his moan as Bish pushed two fingers into him.

Knight's eyes rolled back in his head as the kiss sent him to the moon. *Jesus.* Jesus, Rook kissed like there wasn't anything better to do, ever. Of course there was, though, and Rook proved it when his mouth disappeared and Rook's prick painted his lips.

"Mmm. Sweet baby." His tongue slipped out, brushing Rook's swollen, mushroom-shaped cockhead.

"Knight!" Rook's hips snapped, cock bumping against his mouth.

"Uh-huh." He licked again, teasing.

"Knight. Please."

He could hear the pleading in Rook's voice. He loved it. He let his tongue lick around the ridge, then pressed against the slit.

"Fucking tease."

Just then Bish pushed his fingers in hard, hitting Knight's gland. Lightning shot up his spine, his lips opening even more, and Rook took advantage with a groan and pushed right in. The man's cock was a work of art, spreading his lips, pushing deep. Long, thick, hard as diamonds... Knight was in lust as well as love.

Rook pushed in all the way, then rocked back, pulling the hard prick away. Knight surged forward, trying to keep Rook in. Growling, Bish tugged him back, one big hand on each of his hips.

"Fuck..."

Those fingers dug in—bruising, aching.

"He's fucking your mouth, Knight. You're not sucking him."

"Six of one, half dozen of the other, damn it!"

Bish's free hand landed on his ass. "No. It's very different and you know it."

"Shit. Shit, Bish, you prick." The sting made him shake, made him grimace.

"Yeah, that's me. A great, big prick."

"Our big prick." He winked at Rook.

Rook laughed and rewarded his words by pushing the fat prick back into his mouth. He groaned, sucking hard, giving Rook a reason to stay.

"Don't let him just suck, Rookie. Fuck his mouth."

Damn Bish and his fucking rules anyway.

Bish stroked his cheek — eyes warm, warning him — and he nodded. He was ready. Rook pulled out, cockhead rubbing against his lips as Bish's cock pressed against his hole, the fat head beginning to spread him. He groaned at the perfect, familiar burn.

"Together," murmured Bish.

"Yes, sir." He could hear the fucking grin in Rook's voice.

He grabbed hold of the straps, braced himself.

They both pushed slowly into him, spreading his lips and his ass like they were one. Knight groaned, shorting out for a second as the pressure inside him built. They sank inside him — Rook's cock going into his throat as Bish's hit his gland. He jerked, body tightening, swallowing hard as a zing of excitement and a hint of worry hit him.

"Out," growled Bish and Rook followed his lead.

He gulped in air, eyes rolling. Then they were pushing into him again, filling him up.

His body buzzed with it…stretched and filled…burning.

"Faster." Bish's voice was like a whip and Rook obeyed, hips pumping back and forth, just like Bish's did.

His bound hands scrabbled on the sheets as he tried to gain purchase, to hold himself up. Bishop and Rook didn't give him even a second to collect himself, though, their movements matched and growing quicker. There was a moment of panic when his arms gave out, but his men were right there—Bish's hands on his hips, Rook's on his shoulders.

"So fucking sweet, K." Rook's voice sang to him.

He moaned, trusting these two like he'd trust no one else.

"Nothing sweet about our Knight." Bishop's growl was the perfect counterpoint to Rook's voice and subsequent laughter.

He gripped Bishop's cock as hard as he could and squeezed his thighs together. *Fucker*. Bish's hand landed on his ass with a sharp slap. He cried out, bucked, mouth popping off Rook's prick.

"Hey!" Rook sounded affronted.

Laughing, Bishop began fucking him hard.

Wild cries pushed out of him—he was going crazy from the pressure, from the slap of their skin together.

"Jack off," growled Bishop and Rook took his cock in hand, began stroking off. "That's it. Come on his face."

"Yes, sir."

"Rook. Baby. So fucking pretty." Knight meant it with everything he was.

"Oh. Oh." Rook jerked, hips snapping as that pretty cock sprayed him full in the face.

Knight groaned, eyes closed, licking his lips. Without asking permission or anything, Rook ran his prick across Knight's face, rubbing in the cum with the silky heat of his cock. He lapped at it as it passed his lips.

Bish had slowed down, but now he picked the pace up again, his cock nailing Knight's gland as their flesh came together noisily.

"Bish..." *Hot. Hot.* That prick burned him bone deep. Rook bent and brought their mouths together, tongue-fucking him. Heat pushed into him from both ends, moans filling the air.

Bish's hand wrapped around his cock. "Come for us, babe." Bishop's lips brushed his shoulder, the gentle touch bringing him over the edge with a scream and a crash.

Rook was there to catch him, while Bishop's spunk filled Knight's ass, keeping him from being empty.

Knight groaned. "I swear, you two are something."

He wasn't sure what, exactly, but they were something.

Rook laughed and undid his hands, then pulled him into the centre of the bed, while Bish climbed in on the other side of him. "Nap a few minutes. You're going to need it."

"You too, lover. He's going to call and we're going to play." Knight kissed Rook, rubbing his foot on Bishop's calf.

"That's right. Because I talked him down from saying no." *Smug, beautiful bastard.*

"Bish, love. Kill Rook for me? It's naptime."

He felt so much better.

"Do your own dirty work." Bish sounded half asleep already.

"Lazy." He winked at Rook, then yawned.

Rook laughed, smiling at him like he was the king of the world, so he leaned and kissed the long, thin nose. Rook shifted so their lips met, the kiss slow and sweet.

Love you, baby. He didn't give the words voice, but he knew Rook had heard.

His sweet Rook smiled at him and cuddled in.

Good. Almost perfect.

Almost.

Chapter Four

Bishop napped for about half an hour and then climbed out of bed. He wasn't much into napping during the day, and a short bit of shut-eye after a good hard fuck was all he really needed. He stretched and went to the window, looking out into the backyard at the big tree moving with the wind. The backyard was surrounded by a high fence because of the pool, which also gave them a ton of privacy.

They were known to sunbathe in the nude. Rook didn't have any tan lines...in the summer at least. It was a great place. Jason could do worse. Hell, they were great guys and they'd bring the dear boy more pleasure than he knew what to do with. As long as he said yes. Bishop figured they just might have the right guy this time. Especially with Rook working his magic.

Knight came over, still mostly asleep, and rested against his back, heavy and warm.

"Hey, K." The man should still be passed out in bed, but Knight had given that up for Lent or something.

"Mmm." Knight kissed his shoulder.

"Why aren't you still curled up in bed with Rookie?"

"You know I can't sleep without you." Knight loved Rook, but needed Bish.

"I don't sleep during the day, you know that."

"I know." Knight didn't sleep, period.

"You ready to make room for a fourth person?"

"I am." That soft kiss came again. "I think Rook needs someone."

"Rook has us." The man wouldn't give them up for anything. He felt the same way. Their Rookie was pure love.

"I know." Knight's hands wrapped around his hips.

"Maybe I know what you mean, though. He needs someone just for him, huh?"

He felt the glide of Knight's cheek on his shoulder. "Somebody who needs him."

"We need him." He was their…their slice of normal.

"We do. I love him."

"Uh-huh." They both did. Truly. He bent and kissed the top of Knight's head. "So you think this'll really happen? That this guy is going to sign the papers?" Knight had been very sure. Hell, Rook was sure now, too.

"I think so. He needs money, Rook hooked him, and he's a sweet bottom. No question."

"Mmm…I do like me sweet bottoms." He could play and play.

"Mmm-hmm. You haven't had one in a long time."

That made him laugh. "Not a sweet one, no." Knight was the brattiest man in the history of men.

Knight swatted his butt playfully. "You hungry?"

"Yeah, I could eat. And you know Rook's gonna want to eat when he wakes up." Rook woke up starving after sex. Could eat them all under the table and never gained a damn ounce. Bitch.

"I'll order a pizza." Knight's relationship with the kitchen involved bananas, cold cereal, and peanut butter by the spoonful.

"I pulled a lasagne out of the freezer." He, on the other hand, made food in huge batches once every few months.

"Yeah?"

He noticed that Knight didn't move. "Uh-huh." He shifted, looping an arm around Knight, slowly leading them towards the kitchen. There was an island in the middle of it, just about the right height...

Knight followed, curled into him, hands stroking him restlessly.

"We'll get the lasagne in first." He didn't bother explaining what would come second — Knight knew him and should have a pretty good idea already.

"Mmm-hmm." Knight's tongue licked over his jaw.

"No distracting me. Rook will forgive us for not waking him, but only if there's food ready. We forget the lasagne, we're doomed to pouting."

"Pouting Rook is no fun."

No. A pouting Rook just meant an unhappy household.

He grabbed Knight and gave his lover a hard, quick kiss, then went to the counter to grab the pan he'd taken out of the freezer that morning. It didn't take him long to throw it in the oven...and get the damn thing turned on. Last time he'd tried to reheat food he'd neglected to turn it on. He even set the timer, just in case they got ambitious and lost track of time.

Done, he turned and found Knight. There was something extremely naughty about being naked in the kitchen...and naughty looked good on Knight. Really good. "I have plans for you."

"Do you, now?" Knight raised an eyebrow, challenging him. Just like always.

He loved that about Knight. "I do. Big plans for that ass."

"You're sure about that?" Knight licked his lips.

"Have you ever known me not to be sure?"

"No, beautiful." Knight's smile was brilliant.

"That's right." He snagged Knight's wrist, tugged the man in close, and took himself a kiss. Knight opened easily, tongue pushing into his lips, pushing him.

Bish wrapped his hands around the man's hips, shoving him back against the island that he would be taking Knight against, bent over. He wanted to bury himself in that tight ass again, slam into that red-hot hole. He put all that into his kiss—a warning...a promise...

Knight's thighs spread wide. So fucking easy. Maybe he'd been neglecting the man. He pushed his fingers into that swollen little hole. His. Hot and still a bit slick from earlier, it was going to be so good to push back in.

"Feel you. Want more."

He was fully aware of what Knight wanted. "You're going to get what I give you, babe. And you're going to like it."

"Am I now? Are you sure?" Challenging little fuck.

"I'm so fucking sure, I'm going to just turn you over and fucking do it."

Knight stuck the tip of that pink tongue out at him.

"Don't stick it out unless you plan to use it." Grabbing Knight's hips, he turned the man around and bent him over the island.

"This can't be hygienic." Knight spread...so pretty.

"You really worried about hygiene?" He pushed his thumb into Knight's ass.

"Bish!" Knight went up on tiptoe.

"Don't sound so surprised, you've been asking for this." He pushed his other thumb in with the first.

"Have not..." That tight ass rolled up, then took his thumbs in.

"Have, too." He pushed them deep, wriggled them around.

"N...not." Knight squeezed him tight.

"Have." He pulled his thumbs out and pushed them back in. Hard.

"Oh, fuck. Bish."

"Hard and fast, Knight. That's what you're going to get." He pegged Knight's gland with his thumbs.

Knight jerked forward, like he was going to let the bastard get away...ever. Laughing, Bish let his thumbs slide out and grabbed hold of Knight's hips, tugging the man back, right against his cock.

"Mouse. Love. Please."

He smiled, tickled. Knight had started calling him Mouse back in university, and he hadn't heard that in months, easy.

"You want this, Knight? Or you need it?" He rubbed, teasing that little hole.

"Fuck me, you asshole. Let me feel you."

Oh, fuck, he loved it when Knight got crazy from what he was doing. "You can't feel this?" he asked, still just rubbing.

"Motherfucker. Prick. Asshole."

"Oh, you want me to stop, do you?" He took a step backward.

Knight straightened up, foot stomping on the floor.

"Get back down there," he growled, pushing Knight back down over the island.

Knight's ass was just pink, so he swatted it a few more times, encouraging it back to that perfect red. His handprint looked good there...belonged there. "You are so impatient and pushy."

"You still keep me around."

"I can't imagine ever letting you go." Not ever. With those words, he pushed right into Knight's body. *Perfect.*

He stopped, sunk in fully, loving how Knight jerked and rippled around him.

"Fucking tight, Knight." Fucking good.

Knight nodded, dark head bobbing. "Full of you."

"Yeah. Fuck. 'S good."

He circled his hips, stroking his cock inside Knight's body and that tight ass fought him, tried to keep him in deep.

"So fucking pushy." He pulled out and shoved back in.

"You're pushing. Not me."

He snorted. "That's a matter of opinion."

Knight rolled that perfect ass, rubbing against him. "My opinion."

"But not mine." He punched back in again.

"Bish…" That soft moan rocked his world.

"Right fucking here, baby." He thrust a couple more times, pulling Knight back on to his cock to give it added oomph.

"Love how your cock feels. Going to miss it over the next year." Knight had some crazy idea that they were going to let him keep that little, tight hole away from them while Jason was here.

"You're going to feel it plenty, K." He could think of a thousand different scenarios with all four of them that included his cock and Knight's ass sharing the same space.

"Plenty…" Knight moaned as he slammed in deep.

"That's what I said. Plenty." He found a rhythm, pumping hard and fast. He was planning to stay right here for a while, really pound Knight's ass so he felt it for days. Knight braced himself on the island, pushed back into each thrust. "That's right. Just like that. Fucking slut." He slapped Knight's ass, loving every move the man made.

His fucking slut. This man was a motherfucking addiction. He pushed faster, harder, letting it all out.

"Harder. Oh, fuck. Bish. Pound me."

"Pushy fucking man." He gave Knight what he needed, though, filling him deep and hard and fast.

Knight nodded, head thrown back, throat working. Laughing from the sheer exhilaration of fucking Knight, Bish let everything else go and just did it.

He felt Knight's orgasm coming, rippling through that tight, tight ass.

"Fuck yes." He was right there, ready and eager to have Knight's climax pull out his own.

"Yes." Knight came—Bishop could smell it—rich and wild and male.

"Fuck. Fuck." He thrust four more times, short and sharp and perfect. Then he was coming, too...filling Knight up.

That tight ass gripped his cock, held him in, held him close, and he leaned over Knight, resting against his sweaty back.

"Good for me." Knight's heart was pounding for him.

"Yeah, me too." He patted one thigh.

"Miss this already."

Bish grinned. Silly man. He slapped Knight's thigh this time. "One—this was your idea and *you* found our man. Two—this is not going to end just become someone new is coming in. Three—my cock is still up your ass, and as soon as I've caught my breath, I'm going to fuck you all over again."

Knight's laughter rippled all around his fucking cock. "I'm not bottoming when he comes. I told you that."

"Not for him, you aren't." Knight couldn't last a week without rolling over and begging him to fill his tight little ass.

"Not for anyone." That was a lovely challenge.

He just laughed and smacked the pretty ass again. "If I believed it, I'd be pouting." Not that he pouted...that was Knight's job. And Rook's.

The tight sheath jerked around his cock, milking him for a second, making him cross-eyed. Horny fuck. He was already so sensitive it was almost sore. "Pushy, horny bastard."

"You know it." Knight wiggled, teasing him. "The lasagne smells good."

That had him laughing again. One hunger satisfied—another needing to be sated. Soon his lover would be heading downstairs to the studio. *That* hunger was huge, unbearable—Knight's art couldn't ever be denied.

"Let's take a plateful of lasagne into the bedroom and wake Rook." They could get some food into Knight before he disappeared into his art.

"He'd love that." Knight stood and Bish slipped free. "We have a good life, the three of us."

"We do. We have an amazing life." Who else had two men who loved him as hard as Knight and Rook did Bish? Nobody he knew. "It'll be interesting to see what happens when Jason comes."

"It will." Knight cleaned up quickly, letting him watch that lean body move. "It'll be hot."

"It's already hot and he isn't even here yet."

"No, but I think Rook's already a little in love."

"Just a little. We'll have to make sure Jason wants to stay long after his year is up."

"He will." Knight sounded absolutely sure.

"You really think you have a bead on this kid, huh?" He pulled down a large plate and got the lasagne out of the oven.

"I think that he's desperate, lonely, and closeted." Knight grabbed the Parmesan cheese.

"Then we're doing him a great favour."

Knight chuckled. "We're offering him a good deal."

"We are. It's a dream job, really."

"It is. You'll be a great boss." Now Knight was just being an ass.

He popped his lover's butt, watching his palm print come up in white on the rosy red bottom. "Grab a glass of milk, butthead."

Knight's laughter filled the air, made him smile. "Shit for brains."

"At least I have brains."

"Yeah, yeah, yeah." Knight stuck that talented tongue out at him. "Milk. Pasta. Go."

"I'm waiting on you." He grabbed the tray and headed back towards the bedroom, bumping hips with Knight.

Time to eat and get ready. If his men thought Jason was coming, then it would happen.

He was ready.

Chapter Five

Jason stood at the door of this huge fucking mansion thing, shifting from foot to foot.

This was a mistake.

A mistake.

Oh God.

He shouldn't do this.

Jason had called Rook, told the man yes, then spent the entire day freaking right the fuck out.

Still, there he was. Suitcases in his car, phone in his hand, about to agree to become a...

A...

A sex slave.

Jesus.

The door opened and Rook stood there, looking normal as anything, blond curls shining in the sunlight, blue eyes twinkling. "Jason! I'm so glad you're here!" The man bounced right over to him.

"I... Hey." He looked back towards his car.

"Is that your car? You can park it with ours in the garage." Rook pointed to the big double garage doors about halfway down the side of the building. "You brought the stuff you want with you, right?" Rook tried to look beyond him at the car.

"I did, yeah. I just packed my car up." He bit his bottom lip. "I just… I don't know about this, Rook."

"Oh, honey, now's not the time for cold feet." Rook's arm went around his shoulders, and he was given a bright smile. "This is going to be so much fun, I promise."

"I'm a little wigged." More than a little, really, but he let Rook steer him towards the garage.

"I can help with nerves." Rook grinned and waggled his brows.

Inside, the garage was filled with cars, trucks and motorcycles. It was insane. Rook led him through another smaller door and into a courtyard filled with flowers and plants. The house itself was the biggest place he'd ever seen—a two-storeyed monstrosity of brick. He stopped, stared, then stumbled as Rook urged him forward, and the big front door opened.

He blinked at Rook. "This place is huge."

"Yeah, well, we've got some money between us…"

"That we do. The studio's downstairs. There's an upstairs, too. Did you bring your things? You'll have a room with a private bathroom." That was the guy from the art class—Knight—who sounded intense.

"He brought his things. They're out in his car, which isn't parked in the garage yet. I thought I'd bring him in, show him around." Rook smiled at him. "Kiss on him a little."

"Did you bring your contracts, Jason?" This time Knight's voice was a touch gentler.

"Yeah, but…" He was going to fucking freak.

Rook turned him so he was facing the guy. "Come sit for a bit. I know you like my kisses and that'll remind you why you said yes."

"Just for a minute." He let those warm eyes woo him again as he was eased over to a soft, comfortable sofa. Rook sat next to him — cuddled up to him, really — and licked his lips, making them shine, making him notice them. "You're dangerous." Jason shifted, and that bumped their hips together.

"Naw, I'm just..." Rook wiggled and wrinkled his nose and then grinned. "Irresistible!"

Knight started laughing, and the sound was joined by another laugh.

Rook stuck his tongue out in the general direction of Knight and the other one — the tall one. "I am. And I dare either of you to say it ain't so."

"We resist all the time, Rookie." The voice belied the words, full of fondness, of...love.

That smile and blue gaze was turned back to him. "Looks like you've got my undivided attention, Jason."

"I don't know what to say to that." Those eyes were so focused.

"You don't have to say anything at all." Rook closed the distance between their lips, the press soft and warm.

He grabbed Rook's fingers, squeezed them carefully. Rook's hum filled his mouth as those fingers twined with his and held on.

"Oh, isn't that pretty..." He wasn't sure which voice he'd heard, but it made him squeeze Rook's fingers harder.

Rook hummed again, tongue pushing in between his lips and exploring him. He backed off, but Rook followed, his kiss distracting him.

"Be prettier without clothes."

Rook's hands slid to his cheeks at the words, cupping them, stroking.

"I don't know if I can do this." He whispered the words against Rook's lips.

"That's okay," Rook whispered back. "Because I know you can." Rook moved a hand down and barely cupped Jason's cock, which was getting hard again. "You're going to love every second of it. You're so hot and I'm hot and together we're really, really hot."

Warmth brushed his back. "Your body is begging to be adored, pleasured. Explored."

Jesus, Knight's voice was like sex.

Rook made a soft, sexy noise and nodded. "It so is."

He opened his mouth to tell them he wasn't gay, but Rook's mouth took his as soon as his lips parted. The man's tongue was magic, making him feel such amazing things.

"That's it, pretty boy. Open up. Welcome home." Lips were on his ear, tickling him.

He couldn't resist, couldn't protest…not with Rook's tongue down his throat. Someone's hand was on his cock, pressing down through his jeans and he tensed, his breath coming faster as he searched Rook's eyes. Rook smiled at him while teasing the roof of his mouth with the tip of his tongue.

"Should he have a welcome home orgasm, Rookie?"

"Uh-huh." The sounds vibrated inside his mouth.

"We're going to make you come, sweet, but I'll let you decide—jeans off or on?" Knight's voice was maddening.

Maddening. He moaned into Rook's lips.

Rook's lips slowly left his. "You might not get a lot of chances to make choices. Take this one."

"I don't have a lot of clothes."

Knight chuckled. "You won't need a lot. Take them off."

His hands were shaking so bad he couldn't get the zipper down.

A huge, warm pair of hands landed on top of his — gentle, but big and sure. They guided his fingers and helped pull down the zipper. "We're going to blow your mind, Jason. It'll be wonderful."

Knight's tongue was wet on his ear. "Just breathe, huh? Trust in Rook. He knows."

"That's right," murmured the other man. "Rook won't lead you wrong."

He could see the faint blush on Rook's face. The man looked pleased. "It'll be so good, honey."

He lifted his hips to let the jeans and his briefs be pulled down. Four hands were there to help him tug them off, while Rook pushed his fingers through his hair. *Oh, God.* All three of them were touching him, welcoming him. Someone tugged his runners off; someone else was unbuttoning his shirt. The whole time Rook was kissing him, fucking his lips with that tongue. It was smooth and easy, but it didn't feel practiced or fake — it just... it just was.

It was hard to be bare with everyone else dressed, but then a hand wrapped around his cock and it didn't matter anymore. Rook's tongue imitated the hand on his cock, thrusting in and out in time.

"You're going to come for us, then we're all going to sign our contract, then we're going to play." Knight's words slipped into his ear, into his head. "We're going to change your life."

"We already have," murmured Rook, beaming at him before stealing his breath again.

His balls were cupped, rolled, pressed up towards his body. Fingers found his nipples and tugged on them, pinched them lightly. He bucked, pushed up towards the touch.

"You're so sexy," Rook told him, lips licking along his face.

"I'm not..."

The pinch came again, sharper, and he gasped.

"That means 'are too'." Rook smiled, rubbed their noses together.

He actually smiled back, Rook easing his nerves a little bit. The drugging, magical kisses started again — it felt like he was the centre of Rook's attention. The hand on his cock started moving, the pressure slow and steady, rubbing him base to tip. Meanwhile, the fingers at his nipples played them like they were the best toy ever. They started to ache, burn, and it made him so hot.

"Wanna suck him," Rook murmured against his lips.

"Later, Rookie. He's close now."

He felt Rook's pout, but the man dived back into kissing him like it was the only thing on earth worth doing.

Jason cried out, balls drawn up tight as he shot. Rook moaned into his mouth, eyes going heavy-lidded.

"Mmm. Better." Knight licked his ear and Jason shivered, trying not to freak out.

"Fuck, you're gorgeous, Jason." Rook had his arm around his shoulders again, cuddling him.

"All right, boys. Business first, then we can keep playing." The tall one gave him a smile that seemed more predatory than reassuring. "You remember Rook's name, I'm sure. I'm Bishop, that's Knight."

He nodded. "Jason."

Rook giggled softly as Bishop rolled his eyes a little. "Yeah, we know."

"Well, it seemed like the best response. I really need my jeans back."

"No, what we need is for all of us to be naked. Then you won't be the only one." Rook matched actions to words, pulling off his pants. "Come on, Bish, Knight."

"We need to sign the contracts, guys." Knight handed him a pen. "It's important."

Rook nodded. "It is. It protects you, signing. It means you know what's not going to happen, that we aren't going to hurt or damage you."

"It protects all of us." Knight looked so serious, looked completely sure.

Rook opened the contract to the right page and pointed out where Jason was supposed to sign.

"You first."

His hand was shaking too badly to sign.

Rook took the pen and signed before passing it over to Knight. Then Rook took his hand and squeezed it. His signature was the last one, his hand shaking violently.

Rook clapped once it was all done. "Welcome home, honey!"

"Th...thank you." God. What had he done?

Rook cuddled right up to him, his hands all over his skin.

"We should show you your room, help you bring your stuff in." Bishop gave him another smile, this one feeling less predatory.

"I'd definitely need my pants then."

"I don't know. Wandering around naked is definitely allowed, if not downright encouraged." Rook pushed the hair off his face.

"My car is on the street." He was never going to stop blushing.

"Well, I guess we'll have to get dressed after all, then." Rook pouted.

Bishop laughed. "Jesus Christ, you're a slut, Rookie."

Jason pinked even more, then Knight nudged his arm. "Give me your car keys. I'll park you inside where it's safe.

Rook beamed at Knight. "You do love me." Rook cuddled back up against him. "Now we can stay naked.

"Here in the living room?" He handed Knight his keys.

"Anywhere we want. It's not like we have neighbours who're gonna take a peep."

"No. No, it's very different." He had posed naked a lot—he could do this.

"We have a celebratory meal planned. You hungry?"

"Really?" That was...unexpected. "I am. Thank you."

"Cool. Come into the kitchen." Rook bounced up and grabbed his hand.

He looked back towards his clothes, but Rook drew him away from them.

"You're so gorgeous, I think you're going to be naked a lot." Rook was naked too, and both Knight and Bishop had disappeared. Rook kept him close and the house was pleasantly warm—completely comfortable.

The kitchen was large and airy, smelt delicious, but was a complete disaster.

"I'm cooking," Rook confided with a grin.

"Wow. It smells great. Shouldn't we put pants on?"

Rook handed him an apron that said 'Kiss the Cook' on it. The one Rook put on had a picture of a naked man, from chest to knees.

"This is the strangest thing I've ever done..." At least the apron was soft.

"I bet it's the most fun, though, too." Rook poked around on the counter, coming up with a cookbook.

Fun. Well, it was different... "What are you cooking?"

"It's a roast beef with potatoes and onions and mushrooms and carrots right in the pot. There's a lemon meringue for dessert." Rook laughed. "Don't worry, I didn't even try to make that—it's from the store."

"I like lemons."

"Yeah?" Rook looked hard at the recipe and then opened the oven door. "Hey, that looks about right."

It looked a little overdone, actually.

"Let's get it out, then." He wasn't going to bitch.

"It's not burnt!" Rook looked so damn pleased with himself.

"No, shit? We have to mark this down on the calendar." Bishop came in, grinning widely.

"It looks good." Pretty good. Mostly.

"We can always order Chinese if it tastes like shit."

"Gee, thanks for the vote of support, Bish."

The man held out his hands. "Hey, sorry, Rookie, I've just eaten at your table before. Once burned, twice shy and all that. Only in this case it's more like twentiethice."

Jason couldn't let them tease Rook, not after all the man had done for him. "I've eaten way worse. Trust me. My mom went to cooking school when I was a kid. She experimented on us."

Rook laughed, the sound warm. "I promise not to experiment on you...with food."

"Thanks."

Knight's voice sounded. "I make no such promises, though."

"Oh fuck, no. Knight's likely to do all sorts of weird things in the name of art or sex." Rook bumped their hips together. "You get used to it."

"I hope so." He was fiercely glad for the apron covering his cock.

Rook put the roast on the counter. "Who's gonna carve?"

"You know I will," Bishop murmured.

"I know." Rook rubbed up against Bishop as the man came closer.

"Bathroom?" He needed a minute.

"There's one just down the hall over there. First door on your right." Rook pointed at a door on the opposite side of the kitchen from where they'd come in.

"Thank you." He headed for the bathroom, almost at a run. He shut himself in, then washed his face at the sink.

He'd been in there a while when there was a good, solid knock on the door.

"Yeah?" His hands were shaking so bad.

"It's Bishop. You okay in there?"

"Y...yeah. Just...washing my face."

"It must be very clean by now. You can't spend the next year in the washroom. Besides, it's going to get easier the longer you know us."

He nodded, knowing Bishop couldn't see him. His hands were gripping the sides of the sink, holding on tight.

"I'm coming in." The handle turned and the door opened, admitting Bishop.

"I..." He couldn't move.

Bishop gave him a smile. "It's weird, huh?"

"Yeah. I'm fucking freaked." And frozen, somehow.

"It will get easier, I promise. And we're good guys. And we're going to make you feel things you never even dreamed of." Bishop went behind him, big hands landing on his shoulders, massaging. He let his head fall forward at the strong, sure touch that was forcing his muscles to relax. "Rook's the sweetest man you'll ever meet."

He let go of the sink. "He's amazing. What about you and Knight?"

"Sweet isn't the word I'd use for either of us."

"No?" He actually chuckled. "I don't know what to do next."

"Come and eat. Have a glass of wine," Knight suggested.

"K's right. We'll…um…enjoy Rook's dinner and get to know each other a bit better and you'll start to feel more normal."

"Okay." He nodded and headed out, able to walk now. Knight handed him and Rook a light robe each. "Oh, thank you."

"No burning important bits."

"That would suck," Rook agreed.

The small table was set for four, candles in the middle, meat cut and saved by the gravy on top of it.

"Go sit next to Rook, Jason. He's excited."

He nodded and headed over to Rook, to the open arm that waited for him.

"Don't let them fool you, honey. They're excited, too." Rook's arm was warm and comforting around his shoulders.

"If we didn't all want this, we wouldn't be here right now." Bishop passed him the bowl of potatoes.

He dug in, suddenly starving. "It all looks so good."

"Oh, we're definitely keeping you." Rook beamed at him and kissed his cheek, then they were all eating.

It *was* good—simple, real food—even if it was a little overdone. He felt better at the end of the meal, like he could almost breathe. The guys talked about easy things, teasing each other, including him in the conversation a little, but not making him the focus.

"Who wants coffee with dessert?" Rook asked, getting up to start clearing the table.

"I'll help." He wasn't helpless. He liked doing things.

"Cool." Rook bumped their hips and they made quick work of clearing the table and resetting it for dessert.

Bishop and Knight watched them, murmuring quietly together.

He washed up while Rook made coffee. Every so often Rook would touch him, the caress simple, relaxing. Easy. Rook sliced the pie, then ran a finger along the knife, collecting the excess lemon and meringue, before holding that finger out to him.

He looked at Rook, then leant forward and licked the meringue from Rook's finger.

Rook hummed softly, eyes lighting up. Jason's cheeks heated and his cock started to fill.

Crazy.

"Is it good?" Rook asked.

"Sweet." It was luscious.

"Sweet is good. Especially for dessert."

"It is." His eyes felt like they were burning.

Rook leaned in and licked at his bottom lip. "Mmm, it is sweet."

"Please." He met Rook's eyes. "You're making me hard."

"And that's a problem, why?"

"It's just...different." He hadn't been so hard so much since he was a teenager.

Rook tilted his head. "I gotta warn you, man. I'm a horndog. Bishop is a horndog. Knight takes horndog to a whole new level. It's not gonna be different for long."

"That's almost comforting." He liked routine.

"Mmm, comfort sex rules."

Bishop snorted. "Somehow, I don't think that's what he meant, Rookie."

Rook stuck his tongue out at Bishop. "Make four coffees? Knight likes cream, no sugar. Bish likes it black. I want it light and sweet."

"We want you here for more than just your coffee-making skills," Bishop assured him with a wink.

That made him laugh, really laugh. When he stopped, they were all looking at him.

"What?"

"I told you he was fucking stunning, boys." That was Knight.

"He so is." Rook beamed at him. "You should do that more often, Jason. It lights you up like, whoa."

"Let me pour coffee." He grinned, pleased. He worked hard to look good.

"I bet it tastes better because you poured it." Rook didn't look like he was teasing at all...more like he meant it.

He fixed four mugs, then they all took a piece of pie and headed for the huge sofa again. He had Bishop on one side and Rook on the other, with Knight pressed up against Bishop's other shoulder.

It was cosy somehow.

The coffee was strong and rich, the pie sweet and tart, and Jason let himself relax again. The situation was so unusual, he couldn't quite believe it. Rook snuggled up against him, finding his neck with his lips. Jason shivered, the coffee cup clattering on the edge of the dessert plate. Someone took them out of his hands as Rook's kisses turned into sucking. There was going to be a mark.

"Open your robe, Jason." Knight's voice was soft, sibilant.

Rook's groan vibrated along his skin. "Yes, please."

He hesitated, and Knight rumbled, "Now, pretty boy. Open."

He worked the tie open.

"That's it, honey. You're so, so pretty.'

Jason closed his eyes, his prick swelling, growing. "Thank you."

There were hands on him, not just Rook's but Knight's and Bishop's too.

"I don't know what to do."

Knight's chuckle was almost evil. "We'll tell you."

"You can just do what feels good, too. Touch if you want to, don't if you don't." Rook's mouth went back to sucking and licking at his neck and shoulders.

"He's like a big, muscled jungle gym." Someone needed to gag Knight. Really.

There was a smack and Knight went "Ow!"

Rook giggled.

Jason reached for Rook, wrapping a hand around the man's shoulder. Rook pulled him up against his warm body, hands wandering along his chest. Someone eased the robe off his shoulders and down his back, baring him.

"Soon you'll know us by the touch of our hands or lips," Rook murmured, eyes looking into his.

Someone's finger caressed his ass and he scooted forward.

"That was Knight. He wants inside you."

"I…" He was going to scream.

"It's going to be so good, Jason. I swear. You're going to love getting fucked."

He shook his head, then his breath caught as a finger rubbed over his hole.

"Just relax. Enjoy it." Rook took his mouth, this kiss with a little heat behind it.

The touch never settled—sometimes rubbing, sometimes disappearing. Another set of fingers found his nipples and played them, worked on them. His eyes widened, and Rook murmured into his lips, the sound somehow comforting.

"You're beautiful, Jason. So sexy. Made us all want you so badly." Rook's tongue traced his lips.

Something hot and wet and slick slipped down his spine.

"Fuck, that's pretty," murmured Bishop.

"Are you going to take him, Bish? Make him ours?" The words slid down his spine along with Knight's wicked tongue.

"I am."

Rook moaned at Bishop's words.

"Don't hurt me..."

Knight's teeth scraped the small of his back. "Only if you beg for it."

"Bishop's gonna blow your mind," Rook whispered.

"I haven't ever..." He hadn't even fingered himself, not really.

"Don't you worry," Bishop murmured. "We're going to make it good."

"We should take him to the big bed, Rookie. Make sure he's comfortable." That tongue licked lower, and he bucked, cock driving against Rook.

"Okay. Though I think he's pretty comfortable right now."

His eyes rolled back as heat circled his hole. Rook grabbed one of his legs, helping him spread wider.

"Ever felt anything like that, honey?"

Jason couldn't breathe, couldn't think. It felt so slick, so hot. So perfect.

As Knight's tongue worked its way towards his hole, Rook moved down his body and began to lap at his prick.

"Oh, God. Oh, God." His hands were fisted against the arm of the couch.

Rook's tongue felt so good...and Knight's felt even better.

"Feel them, Jason. Let them take you there." Bishop's voice was like a golden touch across his skin.

Knight's tongue pressed into his body and he stilled, unsure whether he should press forward into Rook's mouth or back against Knight. Bishop's hands landed on his hips, rocking him back and then forward, encouraging him to rock. His body followed the touch, pumping in and out, his body driving onto the hot, slick tongue. Bish moved one of the hands at his hips, gliding up towards his nipples.

His stomach tightened, balls drawing up tight. All he needed was a simple touch or a pinch and he'd shoot.

Bishop didn't do that, though. Instead those fingers stroked around his nipples, the touch never quite in the right spot, never exactly what he needed. He groaned, then shuddered, his focus suddenly on his chest, on the teasing touch there. Bishop's fingers came closer and closer, then—finally—skated across his nipples.

"Fuck!" The word tore out of his mouth and he humped, fucking Rook's mouth a few times before he shot. Rook's throat closed over the head of his cock as Rook swallowed his cum, making him shudder and squeeze tight around Knight's tongue.

Sounds pushed out of his throat, his entire body on overload.

"Bed now," murmured Rook, nuzzling his belly. "Bishop?"

"Yeah, I've got him." Knight and Rook moved away, and suddenly he was lifted into Bishop's arms, being carried.

Jason blinked, looked at Bishop. "Tell me you work out."

He loved training gym bunnies.

Bishop laughed. "I do. We have a gym built in here, too."

Rook's voice piped up, sounding proud. "He's run Ironmans and everything."

"Cool." He wasn't little, but Bishop wasn't struggling at all.

"Don't worry, I won't be dropping you. I pump way more than you weigh on a regular basis. I like being able to carry my lovers around."

It was a little weird, really...being carried. A little unnerving.

It wasn't long before he was carried into a bedroom with the biggest bed he'd ever seen taking up a good portion of the room. Bishop put him down on the bed, and Rook immediately bounced on next to him.

"Where did you get this bed?"

Knight chuckled. "Had it made."

"Before we had it, we kept all disappearing into our own rooms after making love. That really puts a kink in the whole afterglow." Rook snuggled up close to him.

"You have your own room—we all do. This is the main room." Knight settled on the edge of the bed, watching.

"Someone get me the lube so I can get him ready for Bish." Rook kept touching him, keeping his skin sensitised.

He didn't look to see who moved, if anyone. He focused on Rook, on the touches.

"You're so fucking pretty. I can't believe you're ours."

"I can't believe any of this."

Knight chuckled as a cold tube rolled over his back towards Rook's hand. "And this is just the beginning."

"It's going to be so much fun, Jason. I promise."

"I'll trust you." That was it. He trusted Rook, those eyes.

"I won't lead you wrong." Rook sealed the words with a kiss.

He pushed into the kiss, the connection of their mouths safer than the idea of what Bishop wanted. He was moved, though, as Rook kissed him—that amazing mouth following his as four hands rolled him onto his stomach, then placed a pillow beneath his hips.

He tensed—he couldn't help it.

Rook cuddled up to his side, and nuzzled against him, fingers gliding through his hair. "Shh. You liked Knight's tongue inside you, right?"

"I. Yeah. God." What did that mean? Was he queer? Was he crazy?

"This will be good, too. I promise." Rook pressed kisses over his face.

"Keep him nice and relaxed, Rookie." Bishop's fingers rubbed along his crack.

"Just think of all the things we're going to learn together, Jason." Knight sounded like a...devil or something.

He could feel Rook's grin against his skin. "Like we're in school or something. If school had been like this when I went..."

That made him chuckle, actually helped him relax, and he heard Bishop hum. "Good job, Rookie."

Rook's tongue licked along the shell of his ear. Jason shivered and buried his face in the pillows as cool lube dripped over his hole. The soft kisses and tongue touches continued, accompanied by Rook's hand rubbing over his shoulders and down along his spine.

"Spread your legs, pretty boy. Let Bishop in."

Rook's hand moved down his spine to his ass, then to his thighs, encouraging and helping him to do it.

Jason thought he was going to scream, run, but he didn't.

He spread.

"That's my pretty boy." Bishop's fingers stroked along his crack, rubbing in the slick.

"Have you done this?" His fingers twined with Rook's.

"Oh fuck, yes, honey. So many times. Bishop has the most magnificent cock and it feels so good inside me."

More slick was added, then the touch started circling his hole, pressing in just barely.

Rook kept trying to distract him with his tongue, warm and wet and so good on him. Another set of hands started caressing along his skin, stroking him.

He couldn't miss it, though, even with all the wonderful distractions, when Bishop's finger breached him. He tensed, ass muscles squeezing, trying to push the intruder out.

"Relax, pretty boy. I'm not going to hurt you. I'm not." Bishop's voice seemed deep, rich. Fascinating.

That finger pushed in deeper, spreading him open.

"Good boy. Just think how you'll feel, full of Bish." Knight always sounded like he was laughing.

"It's exquisite." Rook's fingers danced along his spine as Bishop's pushed even deeper inside him.

The touch was maddening—too big, yet not big enough…not enough.

"Need more, pretty boy?"

He nodded, whimpering softly, his nerves on overload.

He thought he heard a voice whisper, "Sweet slut."

Rook encouraged him to turn his head, then took his mouth as the pressure at his hole got stronger, bigger. There were hands touching him all over—sliding and stroking and caressing. It felt overwhelming, huge.

Even bigger were the two fingers opening him up, stretching him.

He rocked forward, but his hips were caught, cradled in the pillows.

"Relax into it, pretty boy." Bishop's voice was like an extra touch, like drinking expensive whisky.

"He's a natural, Bish, so hungry for it."

"He is. And all ours." Another finger pushed in with the first two, the stretch unbelievably large.

Jason cried out, his body jerking and shuddering.

"You can take him," Rook assured, nuzzling his face.

"Full. I won't stretch."

"You will, Jay, just you wait and see."

"You'll do fine, pretty boy." Teeth bit the curve of his ass and he jerked.

"Just go with every sensation. Every one." Rook went back to kissing him as Bishop's fingers disappeared.

His lips opened, the kiss deep, stealing his breath. Rook's eyes held his as the kiss went on and on. It wasn't distracting enough to keep him from noticing when the thick, blunt heat of Bishop's cock pressed against him. He gasped, and Rook squeezed his fingers.

As Bishop kept nudging, pushing at his hole, Rook's tongue played with his, danced inside his mouth. Jason felt his hole stretch, felt a burn as Bishop kept pushing in. Rook's fingers stroked through his hair and over his shoulders, digging into his skin when he tensed.

"Press back against him, Jason. It'll make it easier." Knight's hand wriggled under him, working his nipple.

The thick cock just kept pushing, stretching him.

Rook nodded and Jason took a deep breath, tried to push back, but his body tensed, refusing to do it.

"Shh. Shh. It's okay, honey. You're going to be just fine." Rook's hands caressed his arms and Knight pinched his nipples.

"I don't think I can do this."

More lube cooled the heat around him, eased the pressure a bit and Bishop slipped in, the head piercing him. "Oh, God."

"No, that's Bishop." Rook gave him a wink.

"It's big." His ass clenched.

"He is. But he's good. He knows how to make you feel so good."

The pressure made him groan and he thought he would just scream, then Knight pinched his nipple hard and he jerked backward, taking more of Bishop in.

"There you go. So good. He's going to take such good care of you."

His muscles trembled, the sweat springing up on his skin. The ache eased into a pressure deep inside him.

"Tell him when you need him to move," whispered Rook.

"Please. Please, I need."

"It's okay. Let Bishop give you what you need." Rook nodded, and Bishop suddenly started stroking inside him. That heavy cock rubbed over something and he gasped, the zing unexpected.

Rook moaned. "Yeah, right there, Bishop. Just look at his face as you hit it."

"Please." He didn't know what he needed.

"Bishop's got you. It's going to be so, so good." As Rook spoke, Bishop's movements got bigger and Jason could feel the thick cock sliding away, then pushing back and nudging that place inside him again.

"Yes…" He rocked back, trying to get that again.

Bishop obliged, cock never quite leaving his body, but rubbing all up inside and making him zing every time.

"There you go. He's learned something, Bish. You've got him." Knight sounded like a big cat, purring.

"I know." The movements got bigger, better.

He let his head drop, focusing on the pressure and heat in his hole, how it felt. Rook moaned like he was the one being fucked, the man's hands caressing his skin in random patterns now, sort of making the sensations in his ass spread out.

Knight's lips brushed his ear. "There's no one better. He's going to make you come so hard."

Again, Rook sounded like he was the one being fucked, the noise he made so sexy.

"Keep talking, Knight." Bishop pushed in hard, jabbing that spot.

"We're going to teach you so much. Stretch you. Plugs and dildos. You'll take Rook's hand one day, deep inside you."

He whimpered, hips jerking violently.

"Fuck! Knight!" Rook moaned again, then kissed him hard.

Bishop's thrusts got harder, faster.

"That's right, pretty boy. We'll make your ass glow, make you come just using those tender nipples. Watch you ride our cocks…"

Jason's eyes rolled and he cried out, fucking himself on Bishop's cock, needing to come more than he needed to breathe.

"Fuck! Knight!" Rook whimpered.

Bishop's hands tightened on his ass, pulling him back into each thrust. "Come on, Jason. Give it up."

His balls drew up, his cock jerked, and he shot so hard that the room greyed out. Bishop was still buried inside him when the world slowly came back into focus. Rook was kissing him, Knight touching him. It was all gentle and fuzzy.

"Shh. You're safe. You're home. Just rest." The words were surprisingly soft and comforting and he wasn't sure who said them, so Jason just nodded.

They all cuddled in around him, keeping him cosy and warm.

"This is okay?"

Rook nodded, kissed his temple.

He was so worn out. So fucking tired.

He'd just let them love on him a little as he rested…

Chapter Six

Rook woke up and snuggled with Bish and Jason for a while, but he was horny and awake and they were both still asleep. So he climbed out of bed and padded off in search of Knight. The man never slept anymore. Of course, he wasn't constantly stoned out of his gourd anymore, either, so it was a trade up, really. He grabbed his silk robe from the floor by the couch, slipping it on as he made his way towards the studio. The music was blaring. He heard it as soon as the heavy metal door creaked open. The sounds were hard, driving, wild. It boded well, really. Quiet meant Knight would yell at him and classical music meant deep in the peace of the work...this meant fucking and passion and that Knight needed.

He bounded over, making sure to not come up right behind Knight, but sort of sideways front, so Knight saw his movement, saw him. Knight had an unlit cigarette in his lips, a huge piece of paper taped on to one of the big windows, paint splashed across it.

"Hey," he said softly, attention torn between the painting and Knight himself.

"Hey, Rookie." Naked and sheened with sweat, Knight was pure heat.

"You about ready for a break?" He didn't see any reason to beat around the bush.

"Uh-huh. Was waiting for you." The cigarette was placed on the window, along with the lighter. Knight hadn't lit one in two years, Rook guessed.

His cock jumped at Knight's words. He did love being needed. He pushed into Knight's space and wrapped his arms around his lover's neck. "Hope I didn't keep you waiting."

"Not too long, babe." Knight leaned down, lips on his like the man was starving and he was the only thing on earth that would sate him. Rook sank right into the kiss. Knight was intense in a way that Bish, and now Jason, weren't. He loved how each of his lovers brought something different to the table. Knight's tongue pressed into his lips, the pressure immediate and sure.

He'd been mostly hard already, but now he was all the way hard, his prick poking through the silk of his robe to rub on the heat of Knight's belly. Knight's hand landed on his hip, shifting him, helping him rock into the lean heat.

"Oh, fuck. Love you." He did. He loved Knight so much. His crazy, intense, passionate artist.

"Love. Love, babe. It was hot—the baby stud and Bish, huh?"

He groaned and nodded. "So hot. Bed was on fire."

"Mmm-hmm." Knight took his hand, brought it to that long, thin cock. "Touch me."

"Fuck, you feel good." He wrapped his fingers around Knight's length and began stroking.

"Babe, need you." Knight framed his face with his hands, and one kiss became two, three…

"Got me, got me." Knight so had him. "Want you to fuck me, Knight."

"Mmm-hmm." The next kiss was a little wilder. "Mattress."

"Yeah, that works for me." He pushed into another kiss, rubbing all up against Knight.

Knight walked them across to the mattress, cock kissing his belly on the way.

"Wanna taste you first." Rook pushed Knight down onto the mattress, climbing up after his lover.

"Babe..." That long body rocked up towards him, arching. He didn't say anything, just took Knight's cock in. "Fuck. Fuck, Rook. Babe...your fucking mouth. So hot!"

He hummed happily. It was his thing—blowing his men's minds. He loved the taste, the way their cocks felt in his mouth. He took more in, working his tongue. Knight cried out for him, bucked up and fucked his lips, so he just put on the suction and let Knight take his mouth. One of those amazingly talented hands found the back of his head and tangled in his hair.

He loved it when Knight held him in place and took him. He hummed around the hot, hard cock in his mouth.

"Gonna shoot. Gonna come down your fucking throat, babe." He sucked harder. Rook wanted that, he wanted Knight's spunk in his belly. Knight's feet thrummed on the mattress, then cum was splashing on his tongue. "Fuck!"

He swallowed and then swallowed again, pulling it all in. Fuck, Knight tasted good.

"Babe... Oh, fuck. Your mouth." The motions slowed, became lazy, undulating.

Rook kept working Knight's prick, keeping it hard. He knew that Knight would be able to fuck him until he was sore now, enough to make him scream, so he gave that sweet head one last swipe, then let it pop out of his mouth.

"Ride me. Let me feel that tight ass around my cock."

He took it back in for a second, making sure it was good and slick, then he knelt up over Knight and slowly took his lover in.

"You're so fine, babe." Knight looked debauched, lazy...happy.

It was like a touch, those words from his lover.

He licked his lips and sank down farther until his ass rubbed against the hair on Knight's thighs. Knight started stroking his fingers up Rook's legs, tracing circles around his hip bones. Groaning, Rook began to rock, moving up and sinking back down again.

"So pretty." Knight's eyes were like a second touch.

"You still think so?" He loved how Knight saw him.

"Every day. Every day, babe." Knight's chin pointed to a canvas by the window — his face there...lovely.

He beamed down at Knight and rode faster, his hands resting against Knight's chest. Knight hummed for him, eyelids heavy.

He could feel the sensations building, the pleasure spreading out through his body.

"Love how you feel around my cock, babe."

"Good from this end, too." He managed to flick one of Knight's nipples with his finger. The dark, tight flesh jerked for him, and Knight moaned. "Touch my cock, K. Please."

"Anything, babe." That slender, firm hand wrapped around his prick, held him tight and stroked him, base to tip.

"Fuck, yes!" He kept riding, up into Knight's hand and back down onto his cock.

"There. There, babe. Look at you..."

"Yeah. Yeah." He was on fucking fire.

"Fucking hot, baby." Knight never looked away from him.

"Oh, fuck! Knight!" He pinched his own nipples and his vision exploded into fireworks, colours dancing behind his lids as he came.

Knight groaned, fingers dancing over his thighs and up to his belly, avoiding his sensitive cock.

Rook licked his lips and moaned softly. "Gimme a minute and I'll help you out." He was just all melted.

"I'm good. Come here." Knight eased him down, still buried deep inside him.

He slid his hands along skin, his mouth reaching Knight's, caressing.

"Comfy?" Knight murmured against his lips.

"Yeah." He kissed him softly. "You feel so good inside me."

"Mmm... Babe. I love filling you, feeling you around me." The words were soft, gentle, and Rook knew that this part of Knight was all his.

"Anytime you want me, I'm yours."

Soft kisses bruised his lips and made them swell. Fuck, he loved Knight. So much. And it was so good.

"Stay for a little while?" Knight didn't ask him often.

"Yeah, I can do that." He smiled against Knight's lips.

"Good." Knight's tongue tickled his mouth.

He laughed, happy down to his bones.

It was a very good day.

Chapter Seven

Bish woke up sometime in the middle of the night…well, it was still dark out at any rate.

It was just him and Jason in bed and he had to grin, because that meant that Rook was giving their Knight some late-night loving that had lasted into the snuggling phase, which was going to leave them both in a good mood come morning. Gave him a little time to bond with Jason, too. He had a hunch that, just maybe, despite the welcome fuck, Jason was a little shy of him. So he examined their new addition.

Fuck, but Knight could pick them. Jason really was gorgeous.

Muscled and tanned, with blond hair and sharp cheekbones, Jason looked a little like a Greek god. He reached out and traced one of the ridges of Jason's abdomen. The skin was smooth, almost silky, and warm. He watched as Jason moaned and then arched lazily. Oh, yeah. Not into sex? This man needed touching more than anyone he'd ever met, besides his Knight.

He leaned in and whispered into Jason's ear. "We're going to take care of you, make sure you're never starved for touch, long as you're with us."

Jason's eyebrows lowered, then the man scooted closer. Bishop grinned. Oh yeah. This man was theirs as long as they wanted him, and he had a hunch that would be for a very long time. Knight had called it right—their boy Rook was halfway in love already.

He curled his arm around Jason, fingers finding the lovely ass, testing its bounce, watching as Jason's hips rolled back, then pulled away, like he wasn't sure what to do.

"Shh, just go with what you want." He knew what Jason wanted. He let a finger slip along the man's crack. Hot, swollen—the little hole had to be beautifully sensitive. He stroked it gently, hummed happily.

Jason's breath caught, then evened out again.

"Sweet, pretty man." He kissed Jason's temple.

"Is it morning?" Jason moaned, hummed softly.

"Not quite yet." He suddenly wanted Jason's mouth around his cock, wanted to feel that inexperienced innocence around him.

"Mmm." Jason blinked slowly, waking up.

"Hey, pretty."

"Hey." Those beautiful blue eyes made him hard. So innocent, so interesting.

"How are you feeling?" He stroked Jason's ass.

"I... Tender, a little bit. Not hurting, but...weird."

"Weird because you liked it, huh?" He ran his finger back down along Jason's hole.

"Weird because it was... Oh. You're. I." Jason's lips parted and his cock would fit, so perfectly.

"You're something else, Jason." He leaned in and licked at those Jason's lips.

"Is that good?"

"That's very good." He licked his way to Jason's ear. "Very, very good."

Oh ho. Sweet spot.

Jason shivered, rocking into him.

"I like how needy you are." He'd like to see Jason deny it—that was a very interested cock poking at his belly.

"It doesn't make any sense. I haven't ever before…"

"You didn't know." It was as simple as that.

"How stupid do you have to be, man? Not to know?" Jason asked.

Oh, no. It was way too early in the morning for thinking. He covered Jason's mouth with his own, putting a stop to the flow of words. Jason's gasp left the soft lips parted, the man's cheeks and chest smooth under his touch.

"I want your mouth." He whispered the words against Jason's lips.

Jason groaned. "I'm not very good at it."

"How do you know that?" From what Rook had said, Jason hadn't done this before.

"I tried going down on my girlfriend. She hated it."

Bishop bit his cheek to keep from laughing. "It's not the same thing at all, trust me. Besides, the worst blowjob in the world is still a blowjob. And yours is not going to be the worst blowjob in the world."

Jason blushed but laughed too. "You promise?"

"I swear, you get your lips anywhere near my prick and it'll make me a very happy man." He meant it, too.

"Okay. I'll try."

Bishop didn't point out that trying was what Jason had signed on for—one year of trying anything they suggested. Instead, he encouraged the man, stroking his cheek, running fingers through his lovely hair.

Jason shivered for him before carefully scooting down.

"You liked it when Rook did you, yeah? Just do what he did, what felt good. Trust your instincts." He kept his voice low, soothing. Jason was going to be doing this a lot—he didn't want the man's first experience to be unpleasant. Jason nodded, chin bumping the tip of his cock, nudging it firmly. He groaned and reached down to touch Jason's lips. "Your mouth, Jason. Please."

When the soft lips brushed his cock, Bishop almost went up in flames.

He managed somehow not to pump his hips and push himself into Jason's mouth, but fuck...it took all his control. "That's good," he managed to get out, his throat tight.

Jason explored his cock slowly, carefully. The touch was almost unbearably light.

He took it as long as he could before murmuring, "It won't break, I swear."

"No?" He got another of those tentative smiles, then Jason sucked around the tip of his cock.

"Oh fuck! No. No, I won't. Fuck." His hands stroked through Jason's hair, a low moan coming from him.

Jason was going to be good at this. The boy needed encouragement and attention, but that mouth was made for fucking.

"That's it. Suck me. Touch me with your tongue." He felt Jason's hands on his thighs, fingers tightening. "You're good, honey," he murmured, picking up Rook's nickname for Jason.

The suction got stronger, Jason's head beginning to bob to take him about halfway in.

"Fuck, yes." There really wasn't a bad blowjob unless you got bitten. And, despite his lack of experience and supposedly disinterest in sex with guys, Jason was enthusiastic.

He watched his cock disappear into the swollen lips. Fuck, that made his balls ache. So fucking pretty. Jason kept sucking, started humming around him.

Oh, yes. A fucking natural, that's what Jason was.

His hips started rocking—he couldn't stop himself. He needed.

He didn't hold Jason's head in place, though. He let his hands drop to Jason's shoulders instead, holding on there. Jason's hand wrapped around the shaft of his cock, his lips meeting his fingers.

"Good. Yeah. That's good. Uh-huh. Don't stop." He wasn't paying any attention to what he was saying, he was just trying to encourage more of the touches, the sucking. Jason was a quick learner, sucking him in, hands working at the base. "Touch my balls, Jay."

Those pretty blue eyes looked up, then his sac was palmed in a gentle, gentle touch.

"Yes! Fuck!" He nodded, squeezing Jason's shoulders tight.

He wanted to fuck those swollen lips so badly. He rocked gently, testing the waters. Jason groaned but took him. Such a good boy. He kept rocking, making sure to not go deep—which was almost as hard as trying not to rock at all had been earlier—but he kept reminding himself he wanted this to be good for Jason.

"Won't be long," he warned. He really got off on being sucked. That Jason didn't pull back, pull away, said something about their new, sweet little bottom.

Anticipation, the sensations around his cock and the look on Jason's face as he sucked all worked together and Bishop moaned loudly as he came, pouring spunk into Jason's mouth. Jason choked a little bit but managed to swallow most of it, only a few drops running down his chin. Bishop wiped them away, bringing his fingers to his own mouth. Jason moaned softly, eyes on him.

Smiling, he rubbed his thumb along Jason's swollen bottom lip. "That was *not* the worst blowjob in the world."

"No?" Look at those cheeks go pink.

"No, it was pretty damn good. Especially for your first." His smile turned into a grin. "Did you enjoy it?"

Jason's blush went almost purple.

"I'd say that was a huge yes." And fuck, that was sexy. He dragged Jason up, knowing that the pretty boy's cock would be hard, aching. "What have we here?" He wrapped his hand around Jason's prick, squeezing it.

Jason groaned, cock swelling in his fingers. "I… I'm sorry. I just… Biological."

"You're sorry? For enjoying sucking my cock." He let go of Jason's cock and tapped it. "This is a good thing, not something to apologise for."

Jason grunted, but that pretty cock got harder.

"You want something? Need something?" He knew Jason did.

Jason nodded but didn't answer.

"You want to tell me what you need?" He kept holding on, but he didn't try to jack the hard cock at all.

"I… I need to… You know." Jason motioned to his cock.

"No, you need me to." He leaned in and licked at Jason's lips. Jason gasped, but there was a nod. "If Rook was here, I'd make you beg him to suck you."

He started slowly moving his hand. Jason's lips parted, his eyes wide and shocked. Christ, this was fun. He plundered the open mouth, letting Jason taste his passion even as his hand continued its slow dance on Jason's cock.

Knight was going to make this sweet boy scream.

He was willing to bet it wouldn't take long for the touch-starved prick to give it up to him. He speeded up his strokes a little. Jason's hips began to roll, to rock up towards his touch. So needy. He knew it—it just surprised him again and again how starved Jason was for it. Sweet baby. Sweet hungry boy.

"You can come," he whispered against Jason's lips, thumb flicking across the head.

"Oh, God..." Heat sprayed over his fingers, wet and rich.

He gave Jason's cock another jerk or two, then brought his fingers to his mouth, tasting their new lover's cum. Jason's eyelids got heavy, the moan lazy and soft, and Bishop rubbed his fingers along Jason's lips. "Taste."

That flush came back, dark, but Jason's lips parted.

"This isn't the first time you've tasted yourself, is it?"

"No. No. Doesn't everybody?"

"Yeah. I just wasn't sure you had." Jason seemed so damn innocent.

"It didn't taste so good. Not like..." The soft words trailed off.

He raised an eyebrow. "Not like mine?"

Jason's teeth sank into his bottom lip, but the boy nodded.

"It's yours. Any time you get a hankering for the taste, just let me know." He settled Jason down. The kid had had a long day yesterday. It was time to rest. "Naptime," he murmured.

"Mmm-hmm." Jason was tense for about two heartbeats, then he melted.

Bishop grinned. Fuck, it was going to be a fun year.

Chapter Eight

Knight left Rook sleeping and worked until dawn, then headed down to create coffee, shower, and ponder going for a run. Maybe something long and lazy, down by the river. It wasn't too cold yet.

"Oh." The soft sound had him turning from the coffee pot to find Jason standing there in just a pair of jeans. "I didn't realise anyone was up."

"I don't sleep. You okay?"

Jason nodded. "I get up early. Work out. Usually."

"There's a gym set up in the basement. I'll show you. Your bags are in your room. I'll show you that, too."

Kid looked dazed, confused. Bish must have torn him up again last night.

Rook came in, looking like he was still half asleep. "Fuck, why is everyone awake?"

"Because it's the morning, butthead." He grabbed four mugs. "I'm going to run here in a minute. I just needed some Joe."

"Oh, a run." Rook blinked a few times, and gave Jason a soft smile. "Don't tell me you're a morning person, too."

"I used to have to train people at five a.m. I don't have any clients now, though." Jason stepped towards Rook.

Knight chuckled. "Take Rookie back to bed, blow him, and you both have another nap."

"That's a great idea." Bishop came in, already wearing his running clothes. "Jason's not half bad at blowjobs, actually."

That woke Rook up. "You got a blowjob?"

Bishop just looked smug.

"It wasn't a suggestion, pretty baby. Go blow him, and you can sleep." This was kind of fun.

Jason's eyes went wide, but Rook chuckled and slid his hand into Jason's. "Did you really give Bishop a blowjob?" Rook asked as they disappeared down the hall.

Bishop laughed.

Knight grinned over. "Rookie's jealous."

"Yep. Wanted that mouth for himself. I got Jason warmed up for him, though." Bish stopped next to him, bumped their hips. "You and Rook had a little quality time, huh?"

"Mmm-hmm. He was restless. He slept, after."

"With you." Bish smiled and drew him close. "You kept him. You still feeling that mellow?"

"I'm okay." He rested against Bish's body. He loved this man. He'd known that wouldn't change when Jason got here, but still. It was good to feel it was still true. He had enough love to go around...they all did.

"Did you sleep at all?" Bish asked, fingers moving slowly on him.

He shook his head, his body shifting helplessly against that touch.

"Do you want to?" Those fingers knew just where to touch him to get him all hot and bothered.

"Do I want to what?"

"Sleep? I can make you nap, you know." Bish tickled him. "I'm the magic make-Knight-sleep man."

"Are you?" He chuckled as he leaned in. "I made us coffee." He'd rather have Bish's attention, though.

"Coffee isn't going to help you sleep." Bish grabbed his lower lip and tugged on it, Bish's tongue tickling him.

"Mmm..." They swayed together and he found himself blinking slowly.

The tugging turned into kissing, Bish keeping it slow, sensuous. Knight's mind couldn't focus and he couldn't quite remember what he was doing. Had been doing. Whatever.

They rocked and Bish hummed softly and it all kind of swirled around in his head. His eyes closed, his hands slipping over Bishop's shoulders.

"Mmm... I could do anything I wanted to you, couldn't I?"

"Hmm?" He was easy.

"I want to fist you, and I want Jason and Rookie to be there, to watch...to help."

"What?" He blinked over, frowned. "Wait. What?"

Bishop laughed softly. "Not paying attention?"

"I told you, I'm not bottoming while Jason is here, Bish."

"Fisting isn't about bottoming."

His head tilted so fast his neck cracked. "What?"

"It's about intimacy and love." Bishop rubbed his lips. "It's about love."

"That's cheating, Bish." He hated when Bish cheated.

"What? How am I cheating?"

"I need to rest or run or something."

"Then come to bed, babe, and let me put you to sleep. We'll save the fisting, but it's going to happen."

"It won't. Not for a year." His fingers twined with Bishop's.

"You'll see. You know I'm right, deep down." Bishop brought his hand up and kissed the back of it.

"Not happening." They wandered down the hallway.

"Sure it is." They stopped at the big bedroom, peeking in on Jason and Rook. Rook was curled around Jason, both of them moaning and moving slowly as they touched each other. "Oh, now, that's a pretty sight, eh, K?"

"Mmm-hmm. Take me to bed." He needed Bishop more than he needed the pretty right now.

"You got it." Bishop brought him to his room at the far end of the hallway. The place was dark and leather, and totally Bish—masculine, quiet, strong...perfect. Bish led him to the bed, then sat on it, pulling him in between his spread legs. His lips were taken moments later.

He hummed, crawling into Bish's lap, happy as a clam as he settled. The slow, drugging kisses started up again, Bish honing his focus until nothing else existed. Knight was melting, moaning and relaxed...lazy against him.

Bish knew how to do it to him—how to derail him and leave him spread out and relaxed. Of course, not all of him was relaxed just yet.

Bish's hand caressed his spine, then spread him out over the mattress as the kisses faded and worked their way down over his neck, his chest.

"Mmm...Bish. Love..." His legs felt so heavy...

"Right here, giving it to you."

He nodded, floating...soaring.

Bish worshipped him with his hands, caressing his skin like it was something holy. Deep sounds started bubbling from him, pouring from him.

Hot lips wrapped around his right nipple, a tongue flicking across it, and Knight moaned, whispering to his lover about his art, his night, his need. Bish translated his words into sensations, playing him like an instrument.

He wasn't even sure if he was hard, if he was aroused. He simply needed.

Bish touched him everywhere, kissed him everywhere. That tongue touched every inch of his skin. Knight moaned, shivering, legs spread, world spinning. Pushing his legs up and out, Bish speared his ass with the hottest fucking tongue on earth — the sudden move surprising him, shocking him.

"Bishop." His head and shoulders left the mattress. He could feel Bish's smile pressed against his ass as that tongue delved into him. "Oh, fuck. Please. So good…"

Strong fingers held his cheeks apart, Bish's tongue not stopping for a second. Knight rubbed his hand down his belly, wrapped it around his cock and started stroking.

That's when Bish stopped, rising up over his body. "Ready, baby?"

"Love…" He nodded. He was ready for anything. The head of Bish's prick pushed against his hole, spread him open. Knight hummed, bearing down, his entire focus on where they connected, and Bish pushed in and in, stretching him wider every second.

"Yes…" He moaned, hips rolling a little bit faster.

"Such a sexy bottom slut." Bishop murmured the words against his lips, cock pushing into him over and over. Knight grumbled softly, but the pressure was so good, the pleasure so big, that he let the words go. Bishop rubbed hot lips along his cheek and jaw to his earlobe and then bit it. "You're mine." The words whispered through him.

One strong hand dragged along his side, burning through him. Then Bish's mouth covered his again, tongue pushing in, thrusting just like that cock.

Knight squeezed tight, came hard, shuddering. His. His Bish.

Love.

Once he came, Bish speeded up, hips humping hard for about twenty seconds. And then Bish came, filling him with amazing heat.

"Bishop." He groaned, almost sobbing.

"I've got you, baby." Bish stayed buried inside him, the kisses on his face feeling soft and necessary.

"Ought to go for a run..." His head was so heavy.

"You ought to close your eyes and sleep. It's okay, I've got you."

"Stay with me?" *At least for a little while?*

"Yeah. I'm already doing my plans for this morning."

"Mmm." He cuddled in. "Mine."

Sleep took him easily, grabbing him and sinking him into dreams.

Chapter Nine

Jason woke up — for the third time — and headed into the bathroom. His ass hurt, his balls hurt, and he thought he was going to just die.

Someone had said there were weights. Maybe after his shower a workout would help.

"Mmm. You don't mind if I shower with you, do you, honey?" Rook didn't wait for an answer, coming into the bathroom all sleepy smiles.

Jason shook his head. How could he mind? Rook had been...exceptionally good to him.

Rook got the water turned on, hot spray coming into the enormous shower stall out of a half-dozen nozzles at various heights and angles. "After you."

"Wow..." He blinked, more than a little stunned.

Rook grinned. "What can I say? We're hedonists."

"It's stunning." He stepped in, moaning softly. God. Hot water. Hot water with massage heads.

Of course some of the massaging was Rook, the man's hands working magic on his shoulders and back.

"It's hugely decadent and I love it to death."

"Uh-huh." He let his head hang down, tried to make his muscles relax.

"You're tight."

"Sore." Things he didn't know could be sore were sore.

"We worked you hard, huh?" Soft kisses landed on his shoulders. "Don't worry. I plan to pamper you today."

His cheeks heated. Rook was so good to him. The massage continued, Rook working one stubborn knot after another.

"Thank you." His knees were actually a little weak. "You're very good at that."

"I've had lots of practice. Not that you aren't special, I didn't mean that at all."

"No. No, of course not." But he knew better. He was hired help. Not a partner. Just…theirs.

Rook's lips wrapped around his skin, sucking gently where his neck met his shoulder.

"I… Oh." He could feel the blood rising to the surface of his skin. The hum that answered him vibrated all along his skin. That was going to leave a bruise.

A bruise.

When Rook was done, he pressed a soft kiss to the spot. "There. Now you belong to me."

Oh. Oh, God. His knees went a bit weak.

Rook's hands glided around to rub at his abs. They shifted and moved under the touch—he knew Rook had to feel them. "So sexy, so sweet. So glad you're here, honey."

"Thank you." He leant back, his cheek against Rook's.

"Mmm. You're welcome." Rook rubbed their cheeks together.

It was strangely intimate, standing in the steam naked together.

"You want to work out today? Just relax? Watch some movies and cuddle?"

"What kind of movies do you like?"

"I'll watch anything, but I like ones with hot guys the best." Rook laughed softly in his ear. "Yes, I know I'm shallow."

He chuckled. "I like Jason Statham."

"Oh, he's a great actor. We've got *Crank* and the *Transporter* movies for sure."

"I like *The Transporter*."

Rook's arms wrapped around him. "We can watch that. We can do anything you want."

"I'm a little overwhelmed. I could spend the day with you. Maybe napping some."

"Oh, I was hoping you'd say you wanted to spend it with me." Rook licked some water from his collarbone, then tugged him closer.

"Who wouldn't want your attention?"

Rook was so nice, so attentive, it made him feel amazing.

The man beamed at him. "You're good for my ego, honey."

"What do you do? I mean, for a living? Are you an artist, too?"

"Fuck, no. I'm, uh... I work at Bitten Apple. Well, I own it actually. I got some money from my grandma."

"Yeah? That's kind of neat, huh? Do you get to pick what you sell?"

"It works better if I leave that kind of stuff to the manager. But if I see something I like or want to try, I get to order it for the store."

"I..." What kind of things would Rook want to try?

"You should see the catalogues." Rook laughed. "In fact you can — but maybe not today."

"Maybe not. Do you like eggs?" He was starving.

"Sure, doesn't everyone? Are you going to make me breakfast?"

"I am, if you can help me find my pants." He was starving. *Starving.*

"You have a thing about being dressed."

"Most people do, Rook."

Rook pouted. "We're in private."

He started chuckling, then was surprised by the urge to lean in and lick Rook's lips.

Like Rook could read it in his face, the man leaned his face a little closer and whispered, "Do it."

"How do you know?" His body leaned in.

"How do I know you want to kiss me? I can read it in your eyes, in the lines of your body."

"Oh." He had, mostly, decided that Rook was magical. That was the only answer.

"So are you going to?" Rook had moved in, all but closing the distance between their lips.

"Yes." He thought it was probably insane, but he was. He let their mouths touch, then traced the soft lips with his tongue. Rook groaned, eyelids drooping partway closed as he slipped his tongue out to touch his.

Jason found himself stepping closer and Rook's fingers caressed his skin, heading down towards his ass. The little worried sound that left him was instinctive. That was sore. Stretched.

"Shh. Shh. I've got you." Rook massaged his ass, fingers not straying towards his crack at all.

His head landed on Rook's shoulder, eyes dropping closed. Oh, God, that was good. He could feel the heat of Rook's prick as it slowly firmed, pressing against his hip, his belly.

"Do you need me to...do something for you?" He really just wanted to stay like this, safe.

"No, let's just rub off right here under the hot spray like this." Rook's words tickled his lips. "It's perfect like this. Like there's nothing in the world but you and me and a long, slow rubbing off under the water."

"I don't know if I'll get hard."

That pout was back. "Aren't I sexy?"

"Yes, but...I came four times yesterday. I think it's broken."

Rook giggled softly. "It isn't broken, honey. Trust me." One of the hands on his ass pushed its way between their bodies to rub along his prick. He groaned and tensed, but the touch was gentle, slick and easy. "We're not looking for anything earth-shattering here. Just enjoy yourself."

"Everything feels earth-shattering today."

"Aw, I've got you, I do. You don't have to think about anything, okay?"

"I'm sorry, Rook. I just... There's all these emotions."

"That's okay. You're allowed to feel! Hell, I bet you're confused as hell by how much you like doing it with guys." The hand on his ass and the one on his cock touched him gently, both soothed and aroused at the same time.

He nodded, breath hitching a bit. *Yes.*

Rook licked at his earlobe and then whispered. "Just go with it. You can worry about what it all means later."

That tiny touch made him shiver and he put his hand on Rook's hip.

"Mmm. You feel good." Rook got their pricks together then let the friction of their bodies move them. Jason's eyes closed and he let himself rub, let himself touch Rook.

"Nice. Yes. Please." Rook had lovely skin, smooth and soft against his hands, and he found himself fascinated by all the lines and textures and shapes. Rook kept their hips pushing, cocks gliding and bumping between them, and his prick began to fill, to swell, the steam making the air heavy and magical. All the while soft sounds came from Rook, fed into his mouth one after the other.

It was a heady thing, to know he was making Rook feel so good.

"Oh, don't stop, honey."

So he didn't. And it was easy to just touch and touch.

Rook slowly increased the speed, rubbing harder and harder against him as he started to rub back, groaning softly. "Mmm. Yeah. I have you, and you have me. Just feel it."

"Mmm-hmm. Feel." *Want.*

"Oh, Jason. Soon." He could hear the need in Rook's voice.

He nodded. He wasn't close, but he was happy. Rook's eyes widened, pleasure darkening them.

"Pretty." Rook was.

"Not as pretty as you," Rook gasped, body slumping against him. Jason held Rook up, supporting the man easily. "You're so strong."

"Hours in the gym."

Rook giggled and hugged him, rubbing them together so his prick was squeezed and caressed. "We have a gym here."

"Good. I love using my body." *Wait...* That had come out much huskier than he'd anticipated.

"Mmm...me too. Me too."

His cheeks felt like they were going to set flame.

"Let me finish you off." Rook went down onto his knees.

"I. You. Oh." He was already sure he loved Rook's mouth.

Chuckling, Rook kissed his belly, then licked at the tip of his cock.

He stepped backwards, shocked. "Sensitive."

"Yeah? I'll be gentle."

"Thank you. I'm sorry." He'd never come so hard.

"For what? You gotta stop apologising. I like you just the way you are." That tongue licked across the head of his cock again.

"Mmm..." God, they had a fabulous water heater here.

Rook pulled him in, suction gentle, and his hips began to pump, rolling so slowly. Rook took it, took him, allowing his movements, seeming to revel in them. His focus was completely on keeping his feet, keeping his brain from spinning, and all of a sudden Jason could feel his orgasm coming, creeping up on him.

"Rook..." He thought it was only fair to warn Rook. Rook sucked harder, fingers gliding up to cup his balls. "I—Oh... Oh, I..."

The ache was so good. So good...

Rook swallowed it all when he came, taking every bit of him down.

His knees did buckle then, and he fell down the tile wall while Rook pressed soft kisses over his face, his hands touching him randomly. "You taste so good."

Jason cuddled into Rook's arms, overwhelmed.

"I've got you, honey."

He kissed Rook's jaw, the only thanks he could manage.

Rook smiled and patted his back. "I'm so glad you're here."

He nodded. He thought, maybe, he was too.

Chapter Ten

Rook snuggled with Jason under the quilt on the couch, only half paying attention to the movie. He'd seen it before and, frankly, he was far more interested in the hottie in his arms. Poor Jason was a little shell-shocked after his first day. He'd been blown, fucked, blown again, had given a blowjob and come more times than he probably had in the last year, if he had been telling the truth about his apparent lack of interest in sex. He thought they were well on their way to proving to Jason that that just wasn't true at all.

Something on the TV blew up and Rook chuckled, cuddled in closer. "Lots and lots of explosions. Stand-ins for orgasms, or so I'm told."

"Then these guys have sore testicles."

He'd discovered that Jason had a dry, fabulous sense of humour. Not only that, but the man could cook. Like…food. That tasted like food.

"Are yours still sore, honey?" He stroked Jason's cheek.

"A little. My... I'm tender...inside." Jason leaned into his touch.

"I have some gel that'll make things feel good. And I'll enjoy applying it." He waggled his eyebrows. That blush was beautiful.

"Are you teasing the baby again?" Knight came out of Bishop's room, looking rumpled and well rested.

"No, I'm offering to help him!" He shifted over, holding up the cover invitingly.

"Mmm." Knight hesitated, but then cuddled in. "Where's Bish?"

"He wasn't in with you?"

"Nope. Was for a long time. His jeans are gone, though."

"Bet he went out for food or something." It was yummy, being snuggled between Jason and Knight.

"That sounds like him." Knight kissed his temple. "You two have a good day?"

"Uh-huh. We're watching 'splody movies."

"Cool. Our baby boy doing good?"

Rook nudged Jason. "Knight wants to know how you're doing."

Jason looked at Knight, eyes unsure. "You have a fabulous shower here, and Rook's been wonderful to me. I made him breakfast. Are you hungry?"

The man was adorable.

Knight shook his head. "No. I'll just sit for a minute. Bish will bring something."

"I'm a lucky, lucky man. Knight doesn't always just sit for a minute. Not as much as I'd like, anyway." Rook beamed at both of his lovers. He could get used to always having someone to rub up against.

"No, he seems busy." Jason smiled at Knight, whose eyes were already closed again. Bish must have fucked him into oblivion.

"He's an 'artist'." He put air quotes around the word, teasing Knight. He knew how fucking good an artist Knight was.

Knight's dark eyebrows arched. "Don't make me beat you, Rookie."

He giggled. "What if I want you to beat me?" he asked, batting his eyelashes.

Knight swatted him playfully, even as Jason gasped.

Laughing, he gave Jason a quick squeeze. "We're just playing. And every now and then, I like it a little rough."

"You'll learn to like it. I have faith." Knight's voice was like silk.

"Don't worry," he reassured Jason. "We're not anywhere near there yet." He didn't want to scare Jason, not when he was doing so well. Jason's fingers twined with his, and Knight chuckled evilly. Rook leaned his head on Jason's shoulder and put his feet in Knight's lap. "The only thing missing now is our Bishop."

"He'll be home soon." Knight closed his eyes again.

"You think he'll want to do stuff?" Bishop always had the best ideas. The best wicked ideas.

"He will. He liked the baby."

"I'm not a baby."

"You're just at the beginning, though, right?" Rook nuzzled against Jason's shoulder. "That's all he meant by it."

"Still…"

Knight laughed. "No worries, I'm not into children. It's just a word."

"It's affectionate. Hell, he's still calling me Rookie, and I'm hardly that. Don't know if I ever was."

Knight's chuckle was fond, warm. "Maybe a bit."

"Maybe a long time ago." He turned to Jason and smiled. "Unlike you, I knew I liked sex and men right away."

"I just... I like to work out."

"So does Bish—you'll get along there just great. And I love sex, and you're discovering you love sex. And you and Knight...well, he's an artist and you're a model. See how well you fit in, honey?"

Knight was cracking up. He popped him on the arm.

"Mean little turd." Knight spun around and pounced on him, tickling him hard.

Rook shouted and started laughing, pushing back against Jason.

Jason's arms wrapped around him, protecting him. "Now, now. No name calling."

Oh, now, that was more than just adorable. Rook's laughter died and he smiled up at Jason. "My hero," he said softly. He wasn't teasing or being facetious, either.

Jason's cheeks flared, those eyes on him, warm and gentle.

Knight snorted. "The sweetness is unbearable."

"Hush, K. Watch the movie explosions a minute." He reached up and cupped Jason's right cheek, bringing him down for a long, slow kiss. Rook moaned as Jason loved on him. There was an electricity between them, something deep that made it hard to breathe.

He was breathless and just a little stunned when their lips parted, his eyes locked with Jason's. Jason didn't look away from him, but stared into him. *Oh, fuck.* Rook stared back, still not able to catch his breath.

One hand cupped his cheek, thumb rubbing his cheekbone.

"What's going on?" Bish leaned against the doorframe.

"They're being gooey." Knight groaned.

Rook stole himself another quick kiss before laughing. "God forbid there should be some sweetness in this house." He winked over at Bish.

"Ick." Bish winked back. "Come on and help me unpack the bags, Sleeping Beauty. I bought you liquorice."

Knight stood up and headed for Bish, unashamedly nude.

Rook watched him all the way over to Bish. "Want us to come help, too?" If Jason was going to be their main cook, maybe he needed to be involved with the shopping.

Knight was already digging for the candy as Bish stood there, holding the bags. The man was weird with food.

He and Jason joined Bish and Knight in the doorway. "Hey Bish, Jason can cook. I had an amazing breakfast."

Bishop smiled and looked at Jason. "Yeah? I do casserole-type shit to freeze and eat as needed. You do more than breakfasts?"

Jason nodded. "Nothing fancy, though. I'm not a chef or anything."

Knight was halfway into one of the other bags. "Oh. Almonds."

"Well, what kind of food do you cook?" Bish grabbed Knight's arm and tugged. "That's not exactly helping."

"I'm looking."

Jason chuckled. "Steaks. Chicken. Mashed potatoes. Tacos. Eggs. Shrimp. Just basic food."

"Oh, that's good food!" Rook threw his arms around Jason. "You're awesome!" Jason chuckled, arms wrapped around him. "I like him, Bish. We're keeping him, right?"

"For at least a year, yeah."

Jason ducked his head, hid in the curve of his shoulder.

Rook whispered into Jason's ear. "I want you for longer than a year, Jason."

He could feel Jason shiver against him. "You just met me."

"I know. But I like what I see in your eyes."

Bish rubbed a hand over his shoulder. "No scaring the new boy, Rookie."

He looked up into his oldest friend's eyes and saw a gentle understanding there...a caring. He wrapped one arm around Bish's neck and gave him a kiss.

Fuck, he was a lucky, lucky man.

Bish gave Jason a kiss, too—not pushing, just casually touching—and Rook couldn't help but make a little noise. It was beautiful to watch them together. Bish stood, smiled over like he was going to beckon to Knight, but the bags and the artist had gone. Poof.

Rook pouted. "You think he was inspired?"

"I think he was hungry. I smell coffee, liquorice and...olives?"

Rook shuddered. "We'll have to make him brush his teeth before there's any more kisses."

Jason nodded. "Please. Wow."

Laughing, Rook hugged Jason tight. "How about you make dinner, and I cheer from the sidelines?"

"I can do that, or try to."

"I'll be your sous chef," Bishop offered. "Just tell me what you need me to do."

Rook beamed at them both, feeling obscenely content. All they were missing was Knight actually in the same room with them for it to be perfect. "Kitchen?" he suggested.

Bishop hauled him up. "Before Knight eats all the snacks and won't have supper."

He grabbed Jason and the three of them headed for the kitchen. "We're coming for you, Knight!"

Knight was sitting on the counter in a pair of shorts, cross-legged, eating grapes. There was a half-eaten jar of olives, an open liquorice box and someone had been into a can of chocolate frosting.

"Your stomach is a scary place, K." Rook looped his arms around Knight's shoulders and kissed him. Knight smiled at him, his long, dark hair curtaining them as Knight took his mouth. Fuck, Knight's kisses made his toes curl. He pushed close and felt Knight's low hum, the man shifting so that the bare legs wrapped around his waist.

Rook opened right up, inviting Knight in deeper, and someone moaned behind him. He glanced back, smiling into Knight's mouth as he saw Bish kissing Jason, holding their lover. Knight nipped his bottom lip—just the barest sting, but it ached so well. He pushed his hips towards Knight, tried to rub off on the man a little bit.

Knight chuckled and rubbed their noses together. "Horndog."

"Hey, you started it." Which probably wasn't exactly true, unless you counted looking sexy as starting it.

"I was just having dinner."

"That's not dinner. Jason is going to make us dinner. Bish is going to help. You and I can be entertainment."

"I like almonds for dinner." Knight was licking his lips again.

"I'm not sure that's hygienic in the kitchen."

Rook giggled. Should he tell Jason that they fucked on the dining room table on a regular basis?

Knight winked at him. "Don't be prissy, now. We bathe."

Jason giggled. "Be nice."

"I am. Sometimes."

"You are a lot more than you like to admit." Rook rubbed his hips against Knight's, listening as Jason and Bish started getting stuff out for making supper.

"Shh. Don't tell my secrets." Knight drew him in again, the drugging kisses making him sway.

"I can't think when you kiss me like that." There, he'd shared one of his secrets, too. They were even now. Or they would be if he had half the effect on Knight as Knight had on him.

Knight's eyes watched him like he was fascinating, addictive. Art. It felt so good, to be looked at like that, to be kissed like Knight was kissing him.

Rook lost himself in it, moaning and rubbing. He drew Knight closer until the man was almost off the counter.

"More." He muttered the word into Knight's mouth.

"Horndog. Don't you ever get enough?"

He shook his head, laugher spilling from him. "Never! It's my gift."

"Gifted fucker."

"Yes. That's me." Still chuckling, he turned and rubbed his naked ass against Knight's crotch, mourning the fact that his lover was wearing shorts. Knight's fingers started tickling again, digging into his ribs, and Rook shrieked, not caring how he sounded, wriggling and pushing and laughing.

He could hear Bish and Jason laughing with them, and it felt amazing.

The second day and it was amazing.

He was the luckiest dude on earth and he knew it.

Chapter Eleven

Bish set the table as Jason put the finishing touches to his supper. It looked and smelt amazing. He was going to have to start working out extra if they were going to eat like this. Of course, that was something he could do with Jason, so that worked, would give him an in with the kid. He imagined Jason and Knight were going to have the hardest time finding common ground, but Jason was Knight's choice, so he was sure they'd figure it.

Besides, if Knight got out of hand, he'd deal with it. Bishop had a PhD in Knight.

"Supper's on," he called.

"It smells good, baby boy." Knight had managed not to disappear into the studio. Bish was impressed.

"It does!" Rook bounced over to one of the chairs around the dining room table, looking happy.

"It's just simple food." Jason had a touch for it, though. The food appeared as good as any restaurant meal. "Made with love." Rook gave Jason a besotted smile, and Bish had to chuckle even as Knight rolled his eyes. "Eat, before the sugar level in here makes me explode."

Rook giggled and started filling up his plate. "Maybe I was talking about Bish."

"Oh, no. I was just the helper."

Knight grinned. "Maybe I should get them both frilly aprons."

"Oh, that would be great. You'd both look lovely."

Bishop flipped Rookie off. Jason's cheeks were bright red and his broad shoulders tightened.

"We're only teasing, Jason," Rook said softly. "You'll have to get used to that kind of thing."

"I'm cool."

Knight arched one eyebrow. "You must be an only child."

Jason stared. "How do you know?"

"No siblings to toughen you up, baby boy."

"It would have been more fun if you'd made him think it was magic," Rook pointed out.

"I don't believe in magic, Rookie. Only art."

"Your art is magic, Knight." The thing was, Rook believed it. He believed in the best of all of them. Knight's cheeks went dark as he took Rook's hand and squeezed it without a word. Rook squeezed back, looking happy as a clam.

"Okay, let's eat before it goes cold." Bish pointed at their plates, currently filled but the food untouched.

They started eating, all four of them quiet as they devoured the food.

Jason seemed to be settling in okay—still a little nervous, but he thought the kid would even out—would flourish, really—under Rook's tender care. Once they all relaxed, then they could really play. Bish thought it was Knight, though, who was going to have to learn to breathe. His lover was going to have to accept that he didn't have to be a tough asshole to keep his place here…that it was his just because he was Knight.

"I bought some of that honey cake for dessert."

Knight moaned around a bite of meat. His Knight was addicted to the treat.

"Maybe we should tie you down and take turns feeding you." He met Knight's eyes.

"Ha ha." Knight arched an eyebrow, challenging him.

"No, it wasn't a joke, and I think we'll go ahead and do it." He turned to Jason and smiled. "Our Knight's a slut for a little bit of kinky play." A little bit? A lot, actually, but Jason would learn that in time.

"Bishop, we discussed this."

Jason looked between them. Rook shifted and took Jason's hand, giving the new boy a smile.

"You said you wouldn't bottom and there you were this morning, with my cock so far up your ass I'm sure you could taste it."

"Fuck off, Bish. Thanks for dinner, baby boy. I have work to do."

And there Knight went, that temper flaring.

"Give me a half hour, boys. And then come into the main bedroom with the honey cakes."

He gave them a wink and headed off to tame his Knight.

* * * *

Knight stormed into the studio, heading immediately for his stereo. Driving music filled the air as he stripped off his shirt and grabbed a brush.

Fucker.

He.

That.

They.

Fucker!

All of a sudden, Bish grabbed him, spun him and pushed him with his back up against the wall. "You don't get to run away from me."

"I get to do whatever the fuck I want to! You're not fucking allowed in here!" His fucking cock jerked, and he tried to reach it, thump it.

Bish's hands were wrapped tight around his arms, though, keeping him pinned in place. "Sure you do. But running away from me is a direct challenge, K. It's you telling me you need a good ass-whipping."

He didn't get a chance to tell Bish to fuck off because his lover's mouth landed on his, the kiss hard, their teeth knocking together. He pushed into the kiss, fighting back, making Bish growl and work for it. Bish brought his whole body to bear, pressing him against the wall.

He tore his mouth from Bishop's. "Working, asshole. Fuck."

"No. We didn't get dessert yet. You can work after. If you still want to." Bishop's eyes bore into his.

"Fuck you." He was so fucking hard.

"No. I think I'll be fucking you." Bishop broke his stare and leaned in to bite at his earlobe. "After we eat dessert off your hot little body."

"Not going to happen." His hips belonged to somebody else — they were moving on their own.

"Sure it is."

"It is not. I'm not doing this in front of Jason, damn it."

"Doing what? Having great sexual experiences? Making me and Rook and yourself happy?"

"Stop it." He didn't want to be...vulnerable in front of Jason.

"You going to tell me what the problem is?"

"No." He was pretty damn sure he didn't want to talk about it at all.

"Then come on. I promised the boys dessert." Bish kissed him again, then grabbed his hand and headed to the big bedroom.

"I said no!" Jesus, no one was listening to him these days.

Bish pulled him up against his strong body. "You know you want it. Stop fighting it so hard."

He flipped Bish off. "Make me, asshole."

"If that's how you want it." Bishop bent, lifted him up and put him up over one shoulder.

So shocked that he didn't even scream, Knight just went stiff and still. Bish carried him into the bedroom and put him in the middle of the big bed.

"I…" He wasn't going to do this. No fucking way.

"You're beautiful and you make the best dessert table."

"I'm not doing this…"

Bishop cuffed one hand, chaining him to one bedpost.

"You are, though." Bishop restrained his other hand.

"No." His cock was aching, and he pulled against the bonds, fighting harder as a blindfold covered his eyes.

"Yes, my Knight."

Bish's lips circled his cock, the kiss wet, hot. His ankles were stroked and petted as he felt bonds wrapping around them.

"Jason and Rook are coming. They've got cake."

He shook his head and Bishop's fingers touched his lips. "Don't make me gag you."

He shook, tugging at the bonds again, groaning low.

"Oh, look how pretty he is." Rook was there now.

Knight opened his mouth to scream and Bishop's fingers pushed into his lips, giving him something to suck.

"Come on, Jason. It's okay to come closer."

"I… Is he okay?"

"Uh-huh." Rook sounded close, and a gentle finger stroked along Knight's prick. "See how hard he is? He loves it when Bish gets all toppy on him. I love that they let me be a part of it."

Rook's lips rubbed across his. "I love you, Knight."

He whimpered. "Let me go, Rookie."

"Shh. You're beautiful. Besides, it's not me in charge here." Rook gave him another kiss, Bish's low chuckle sounding in the background.

"Who wants a bit of salt to go with their dessert? Knight's leaking and we wouldn't want to waste any."

Rook was the one who took the bait. Knight knew it, because he heard the happy cry before the man's lips dropped over his cock. Rook sucked like the man was starving for it, tongue playing as the tight lips pulled up and down along the shaft.

"Don't let him come, Rookie. He needs to wait."

Fucker. Bish was a motherfucker.

He felt Rook's whimper all around his prick, but the suction decreased a little and Rook's bobbing slowed.

"Hate you, Bish."

"I hate you too, babe." He could hear the damn smile in Bish's voice.

"What do you want me to do?" Jason sounded so nervous…unnerved. See? He'd told Bish this was a bad idea.

Rook popped off his prick. "Wanna help me, honey?"

"I don't know."

"You can just watch. Or kiss him. Or feed him some cake—he loves that stuff."

"Oh. I can do that. With the frosting?"

"Yeah, that'd be perfect."

"Open up, huh? I have a bite."

"Jason's going to feed you, Knight. Let him." Bish's fingers glided across his lips. He frowned, but his fucking lips opened. "Easy. Just little bites since he's on his back."

The tiniest bite of sweet brushed his lip and he opened wider.

"Yeah, just like that. It's so good, isn't it, Knight?"

"Let me up."

Jason fed him another bite.

"Don't listen to him, boys. I'm the one in charge here."

"Yes, Bish." He could almost hear Rook's eyelashes batting at Bishop.

"He's an asshole. A mean asshole." Another bite of cake shut him up.

"You love it," Rook accused, tongue slapping across his cock. Knight's eyes widened behind the blindfold. *Rookie!* Rook's tongue poked at his slit next, pushing against it.

He arched, his feet fighting the bonds. Bish rubbed his strong hands along his legs, the touch solid and there and Knight panted softly, focusing on that touch. It continued, Bish's hands stroking back up his legs along the inside this time.

Rook hummed softly. "See how Bish relaxes him? It's like magic."

Bish chuckled, his hands still dancing on him. "I thought Knight's art was the magic."

"It is! You've got magic of your own, though."

"Do you want another bite, Knight?"

No. He wanted up. He wanted... Knight's lips parted for the treat.

"That's right, Jason. Feed him as much as he wants, he's being so good." Bish's hands cupped his hips.

Rook hummed, kissing the tip of his cock again.

"I want up." His hips rolled, trying to get more of Rook's mouth.

Rook bobbed, taking more of him in and then pulling off again, the sound of it slurpy and ending on a pop.

"You're good where you are," murmured Bishop.

"Fuck."

The touches started up again, settling him, easing him.

"Jason, feed him a couple more pieces and then touch him."

Another bite pushed into his lips. "What if he doesn't want me to?"

"I've told you to. That means he wants it."

Knight heard Jason gasp, fingers pushing another bite in between his lips.

"It's okay, sweet thing. He loves this—look at his cock."

"Come here, honey. Suck him with me." Rook's words were whispered around his prick. Soon there were two mouths on his cock, two sets of lips, two tongues bathing him.

"Bish…" He pulled at the cuffs, heart pounding hard.

"You want me too?" Another set of lips landed on his balls. Bish. His sac drew up tight, his hips rocking hard.

"No coming," Bish growled, just before his hot mouth took in one of Knight's balls. His toes curled and he fought the urge to scream, the sensations perfect. The three of them worked his cock and his balls, their mouths like brands on his skin.

"Going to come."

"Everyone back off." Bish's words flew out. The mouths on his cock disappeared immediately.

"Bastards... Rookie, please." He knew it wouldn't work on Bish.

"Bish..." Rook pleaded with their lover. He could just picture the big eyes.

Bish only snorted. "He doesn't come yet."

"Fucker."

He heard Jason's gasp.

"Jason, are you ready to watch a spanking yet? Because, if you're not, you and Rookie should go and watch another movie or something." Bish sounded like he was ready to really dish out the spanking he was threatening.

Knight growled, pulled harder. "No way. No fucking way."

"Rook, get me Knight's gag."

The words made him screech, and Bish's hand landed over his mouth, dulling the sound.

He felt Bish's lips against his ear. "I know you need this, babe. I'm going to beat your ass, then fill your ass, and then make you come and come. Then I'm going to hold you the rest of the night."

The words made him whimper, made his eyes water.

He heard two sets of footsteps pad back in.

"Here's the gag, Bish. You want me and Jason to stay?"

Bishop's fingers kept caressing his face, stroking his cheeks. "You up to watching this, Jason? If you're not ready, I won't be pissed."

"I don't... I don't think so. Rook? Please?"

"Take him out and make love to him, Rookie." There was a noisy sounding kiss, and then another. "Knight needs this, Jason, and one day you'll be able to watch, to participate, and you'll understand."

"Come on. I'll make it better." Rook's voice was gentle, leaving the room as the gag pressed against Knight's lips.

"Open up, Knight. You're in for the ride of your life." He groaned and shook his head. Fuck, he was losing his mind. *So good.*

"I said, open up." The gag pressed harder and pushed past his lips, his teeth, and his eyes opened behind the blindfold.

"There you go, baby. Now you can scream as loudly as you need to." He felt Bish kiss him around the gag.

He did, too. He screamed and kicked and fought.

A ring of jingle bells were pressed into his hand, and he knew if he dropped them this would stop. He held on.

"Good boy." One of his legs was undone, Bish pushing his leg across his body. He was stretched, a bit twisted, but the position exposed his ass to Bish's hand. He could feel the air on his skin as Bish waited.

Time stopped. Everything stopped for a long minute.

"Love you." The words were quiet, and they were immediately followed by the first hit of Bish's hand landing on his ass...hard. The blow was so hard that the burn didn't catch him for a second, then his body flushed with heat and he screamed, the sound muffled in his head. It was followed up by a second, and then a third and fourth in quick succession.

He tried to twist back, but Bish was solid against him, holding him down, keeping him where the big man wanted him. The burning smacks covered his ass — side to side, up and down — getting full coverage.

Stop. Stop. Oh, fuck. More...

He was going out of his fucking mind. The backs of his thighs got hit, too. His lower back just above his crack took slaps from two or three of Bish's fingers. His entire backside was soon burning.

He found himself sobbing, grunting out his stress and worry into the gag, and Bish kept going, kept pushing him, and then all of a sudden, when he didn't think he could take it for another second, it stopped. His hands were unfastened, his wrists freed, and Knight reached out for his lover, completely undone.

"I have you, baby. You're all mine." He felt Bishop unfasten the other cuffs, then Bishop drew him close, fingers already touching his hole. "Gonna fuck you. Gonna fill you. Leave you plugged all fucking night long."

And hold him. Bishop had promised.

Bishop's fingers came back, slick with lube, pushing into him, and Knight groaned, the coolness feeling so good. "You're a sexy beast, Knight. My sexy beast."

Two fingers went deep, hit his gland.

He groaned, squeezed Bish's fingers tight.

"Yeah, baby. Very nice." Bish's knee pushed against his cock.

He arched—rode Bishop's hand, rode that touch. He needed. It was so good. Another finger pushed in, Bishop spreading him open.

Bishop.

Bishop.

Love.

He rubbed his face against his arms, spreading wide, opening.

"So fucking sexy." Bishop pushed his legs up against his chest, pressing his cock against his hole now.

Knight moaned around the gag, needing that pressure so badly. Then he got it, Bishop's cock going in deep in one long push.

His grunt was audible through the gag, all his focus on his aching ass.

"Nice." Bishop started thrusting, fast and hard, giving his abused backside no quarter.

Knight didn't care. All he cared about in that moment was the pleasure, the pain, all intermingling together. Bishop leaned into him, his cock going deeper as his mouth closed over Knight's, hot around the gag. *Fuck, yes.* He wanted the gag off, wanted the kisses, but he still needed the hard, forceful plugging more. Bishop's tongue wet the gag, his mouth staying with his as the thrusts continued unabated. Bishop's grunts vibrated against his lips.

Love. He loved. Needed. Wanted. Please.

The sounds became words. Single syllables that meant 'love' and 'mine' and 'always'.

He nodded furiously.

Yes.

Yes.

Over and over, Bishop punched into him, and the need built inside him, growing, his cock and balls screaming for release.

"I want you to come around my cock." The words were sweet, necessary.

Oh, Christ.

Yes.

Yes, please.

Please, Bish. He begged with everything inside him.

A few more punches landed against his gland before Bish bit at his lower lip. "Okay, baby. Give it to me."

He didn't even have the breath to scream as he shot, his body gripping Bishop's cock tight. Jerking against him, Bishop's spunk filled him, hot inside him. He managed to hold on, barely, clinging to Bish.

"Got a plug here for you, baby."

He nodded, his body keeping Bish in.

"Which means I've got to come out."

He nodded again, but he held on.

Bish licked his ear next. "Gag and blindfold stay on until you're plugged up, Knight. Just so you know."

He groaned, one hand holding on to Bishop's nape.

"I can stay here all night, just like this." Bish jerked his hips, pushing the tiniest bit deeper and nudging across his gland again.

He groaned, whimpered, held on.

"Beautiful, needy asshole." Bish bit at his earlobe and jerked inward again. Knight nodded and moaned, his muscles starting to tremble. "My, beautiful needy asshole."

Yes.

Bishop's.

Please.

He could feel Bish slowly slipping out of him, the thick cock dragging along the inside of his body, and he gasped for air, his body squeezing Bishop's cock.

"Gotta let me go sometime, baby."

His body did, even if his heart didn't.

Bishop slipped out, a slick dildo getting pushed in the minute the wonderful heat was gone. "There." Strong fingers petted him, Bishop's touch everywhere.

The gag came out and he groaned, then Bishop pulled him close and held him.

Bishop took off the blindfold next, but Knight kept his eyes closed as soft kisses pressed along his face.

"Bish…"

"Shh."

The blankets covered them.

"I've got you, baby. That's all that matters."

He nodded. *Yeah.*

Yeah.

Chapter Twelve

Rook grabbed the rest of the honey cake in one hand and Jason's arm in the other and led him out of the big room back towards the living room. They could watch another movie, snuggle together on the couch and hopefully he could convince Jason that Knight really was okay and actually wanted what Bish was dishing out.

He detoured them through the kitchen to grab a couple of cans of Coke.

"You're awfully quiet, honey," he pointed out.

"I..." Jason looked at him, eyes huge.

"You're a little freaked out, huh?" He stopped and gave Jason a quick kiss. "Come on. We'll sit and eat honey cake and drink Coke and talk. Or watch a mindless movie or whatever floats our boats, 'kay?"

He led Jason back to the living room and the couch, which was still covered with their blanket from earlier.

"A little, yeah. That was...intense."

"It was, but Knight loves it. Hell, he needs it." He set their stuff on the coffee table and pulled Jason down onto the couch with him. They cuddled up together under the blanket. "Knight used to take all sorts of drugs and he doesn't anymore. Me and Bish—he does us instead of the drugs."

"Still, he said he didn't want it."

Jason's hands reached for him, drew him close.

"Oh, no, that's a part of the game. He has a safeword—that's a word that if he says it, everything stops. So if he really didn't want it he could make it stop so easy. And I don't know, maybe he doesn't *want* to want it, to need it. But he does. Look at his eyes sometimes, when he's looking at Bish without realising he's being watched. It's like there's this black hole in him and he knows Bish can fill it."

"It's like working out, pushing yourself too hard?"

"I guess." He actually blushed a little. "I don't exactly push myself too hard when I'm working out." He left that kind of thing to Bish.

"It's not for everyone. Hell, lots of times it's not for me." Jason brushed his cheek with one hand.

He tilted his head, nuzzling against Jason's palm. Then he turned his head and kissed it. "No, neither is what Knight and Bish have together. It keeps Knight sane, though, without drugs or medication. He just needs the painting, plenty of caffeine and Bish. I like to think he needs me, too." And Knight did, he knew that…just in a different way.

"What do you need?" The question was gentle, quiet. How could Jason make him feel so…warm with just a few words?

"I…" He shrugged. "I don't feel left out, even when Bish and Knight are doing their thing. We love each other."

"I don't know if that was an answer, really."

He tilted his head. "I guess I don't know what you're asking. I'm not like Knight. I don't need to lose myself like that." He shrugged and laughed. "I do need hot and cold running sex, and I get that. I get loved on whenever I need it." He stopped and reached out to stroke Jason's cheek. "I think I could get to need you." Only he was pretty sure maybe he already did.

"I'm not very sexual, but I like you. Really." Sweet, gentle boy. And not very sexual? Rook was hard pressed to think of very many people, outside of Bishop and Knight and himself, who were more sexual than Jason.

"I like you too, Jason." He grinned and waggled his eyebrows. "Shall we show each other just how much we like each other?"

"You can't want to! Your balls will fall off."

"Nah, it's like a superpower—or the Energizer bunny, only instead of banging on a drum, I'm just banging." He laughed, rubbing his nose against Jason's. And he did want to. He'd had a flash of them sixty-nineing and suddenly he was hard as a rock.

"It can't be healthy." Jason was laughing, though. Laughing with him.

"Best exercise in the world." He pressed their mouths together, capturing Jason's laughter between their lips.

Jason was getting better at kissing after just over a day, Rook couldn't imagine how wonderful Jason's mouth was going to be in a week, a month…a year…

He wouldn't think about that, though. Jason was just starting with them.

This was just the beginning.

He leaned into the solid, warm body, sinking into Jason with his body and mouth. It felt so good as Jason stroked his hair and petted him. He pulled back just far enough to smile into Jason's eyes. "Wanna sixty-nine?"

"I… Yeah?"

"That's where we suck each other. It's really good for everybody involved."

Jason chuckled. "I know what it is. I haven't done it, but I know."

That made him laugh, and he hugged Jason tight. "Okay. Good. It's even better when it's a three-way sixty-nine, so I'm betting four-way will rock. But for now..." He pulled Jason down onto the couch and then headed under the blanket, wriggling around so by the time his mouth was in line with Jason's cock, his was up by Jason's lips. Jason wasn't hard yet, but he was getting there — the quiet prick still a good size.

Rook pressed kisses over it, breathing in the scent of Jason that lived there. It made him moan, his own cock responding happily to the tastes and smells. The heat.

He felt soft caresses against his cock, Jason's cheek, the hint of warm lips, and Rook moaned happily and wrapped his lips around the head of Jason's prick, sucking softly.

Jason's moan was so soft and low that he almost missed it. He flicked his tongue back and forth across the head, teasing, and the pretty prick started to swell, even as Jason repeated the caress.

He moaned in encouragement, knowing even that would send vibrations around Jason's prick. It was dark, private, quiet in here. He wanted to explore. He let go of the tip and mouthed his way along the side, tongue tracing one of the many veins there. Jason smelt so good, so he kept moaning, licking while he buried his nose right into Jason's pubes, breathing deeply as his tongue tasted around the base of Jason's cock.

Jason was focusing on the tip of his prick, touching and sucking so carefully. It sent gentle waves of pleasure rolling through him. It was nice, actually —

not enough to distract him from what he was doing, but enough to make him feel good. Not overwhelming, not painful. Just perfect.

He hummed again, nosing Jason's balls, then taking one into his mouth, slapping it gently with his tongue.

Jason's mouth left his cock. "Rook?"

He lifted his head. "Yeah?"

"That... Sorry. That startled me."

"Felt good, though, didn't it?"

"I don't know." Jason's soft laughter was embarrassed.

"Oh, honey, I better do it again, then, so you do know." He went back to loving on Jason's balls.

Jason's moans started vibrating against his legs. He was going to take that as feeling good. Rook continued, fingers gliding on Jason's inner thighs and his cock. Jason's kisses became more steady, more sure, even as Jason spread.

He flicked a finger across Jason's ass and then took the tip of the now fully erect cock into his mouth. He felt that sweet hole tighten and jerk, but it didn't matter because Jason was sucking on him, pulling on his cock.

Groaning, he took more of Jason in, head beginning to bob, and Jason wrapped his hands around Rook's hips to hold him. Rook pulled Jason's finger into his mouth with Jason's cock, rubbing it across the tip before pulling it out again and touching the little puckered hole once more. Swollen, that pretty hole tightened under his touch. His wet finger skated over and around it, no doubt shooting sensation through Jason's body.

Every touch made Jason's mouth tighter.

Rook pulled hard on Jason's cock, fingers continuing to play with his hole as he rolled the sensitive balls with his other hand. He could feel the needy little cries around his prick.

He loved that, loved how wonderfully sensual and needy Jason really was.

Knight was a genius when it came to seeing things that most people missed.

His tongue licked around the head of Jason's cock as his finger circled the little hole. *Come on, honey, give me your pleasure.*

Jason's mouth popped off his cock, his hoarse cry muffled by the blanket, so Rook bobbed his head harder, increasing suction for only a minute before spunk splashed on his tongue, salty and hot. He swallowed it down, moaning happily around Jason's cock.

Jason panted against his shaft, breath hot and heavy. He kept licking and nibbling, cleaning Jason's prick. Slowly, Jason started working on his prick again.

"Oh fuck, so good." He encouraged Jason to keep going. Jason hummed in response, his lips wrapped around his cock, tugging with a steady, slow intensity.

He nuzzled Jason's crotch, loving the smell, the soft, velvety skin. An addiction. Living here, loving these men — it was the best addiction. Rook tried to keep from thrusting into Jason's mouth, but, as he got more lost in his pleasure, it wasn't easy to hold back and his hips slipped, rocking his cock deeper into Jason's mouth.

Jason did well, only backing off a few times.

"So good. Feels amazing." He reached down, fingers tangling in the heavy hair, the strands like raw silk. "Yeah, don't stop. Fuck." A shudder went through him — he was getting close.

He felt the gentle, soft touch to his balls, Jason tugging.

"Honey!" He gasped, spunk pouring out of his cock at the unexpected touch. Jason rode out the orgasm with him, cheek on his thigh.

He lay resting against Jason as he caught his breath before he wriggled back around until he was face to face with him once again. "Thank you — that was wonderful."

Jason offered him a smile. "You're welcome."

He licked at Jason's top lip. "You liked it too, right?"

"I do. Did. You're amazing. Thank you."

He grinned. He would have bounced if he hadn't been lying down on the couch. "You're pretty amazing yourself." Rook snuggled in. "You feeling better? More settled?"

"I. Yeah. Yeah, I think so. I mean, I have questions."

"So ask, honey."

"Where am I supposed to sleep at night?"

"We never showed you your room, did we? I'm sorry. You have a room of your own, and you can sleep there if you want. But I...well, I hope you'll sleep with me. Either in my room or in the big bedroom. Knight doesn't sleep, but I bet if Bish is in his bed he'll let you sleep with him, too. I usually curl up with him. We both could." He grinned, feeling sheepish. "You can sleep where you're comfortable sleeping."

"I just didn't know. The last day has been...a whirlwind."

"I know I can be pushy." He hadn't bulldozed Jason, had he? "I'm just so happy you're here and you're so sexy..."

"You're not pushy. You're like magic." Jason drew closer. "I feel...silly, somehow. I just got here. I'm not your lover. You're paying me, but...I feel things for you."

"We don't have to pay you..." Rook winked and hugged Jason tight. "I'm feeling things for you too, Jason. I never expected it, but I do."

He felt Jason's nod, heard his soft sigh. "Can I sleep with you tonight?"

"Oh, yes, please." He wriggled up and held out his hand. "Come on. I want to show you my room."

Jason reached for him and let him haul his muscled body up.

He rubbed against Jason when they were both standing, enjoying the closeness and all those warm, solid muscles.

"Are Knight and Bishop okay?"

Sweet boy.

He cocked an ear — all was quiet. "They are. Come, I'll show you."

Holding on to Jason's hand, he quietly made his way down the hall to the big bedroom. They peeked in.

Knight was curled up in Bishop's arms, sound asleep, his cheeks still wet with tears. Bishop was holding on tight, sleeping too, but rocking their lover.

Rook sighed, leaning against Jason. "Aren't they beautiful?"

Jason nodded, eyes wide.

Bishop's hand slid down Knight's back, stroking him.

"See? Knight never sleeps. Except when Bish makes him." He patted Jason's ass.

"Never? That's unhealthy."

They left, heading down the hall.

"Uh-huh. That's why he needs Bish to make him." He brought Jason into his room. It was homey and warm, with quilts and comforters on the bed along with a hundred or so pillows. "I hope you like it."

"It's amazing. Like a fairy tale or something." Jason looked embarrassed, head down.

"Oh. Honey, you are so sweet. Thank you." He drew Jason onto the bed. "You can be my Prince Charming."

"I'll be whatever you need, Rook."

"Because we're paying you?"

Jason looked at him, shook his head. "I...I know it's silly. I know it is, but...no."

Warmth filled him and he pushed into a kiss. "Thank you."

"You're the reason I'm here. Thank you."

"It was Knight who found you." He cuddled in close, pulling the quilts up over them.

"It was you who seduced me." Jason's hands wrapped around him, held him.

"Yeah, I did. I'm going to keep doing it, too. I hope that's okay."

"I do, too."

MIDDLE GAME

Dedication

For my readers.

Chapter One

Jason had been watching the snow falling for hours, mounding up around the window sill, white and fluffy. The studio wasn't cold, not at all, but a part of him felt a little chilled just from watching the ice crystals build.

Jason shivered, making sure the motion was tiny, not moving on the lounge chair in the least.

"Be still, Jase. I'm almost done." Knight was painting furiously.

"I am." He was naked, except for a soft, silken drape over his thighs.

The front door opened and closed, Rook's voice singing out, reaching them even here in the studio, "Hello, honeys, I'm home!"

Jason smiled. The sound of Rook's voice made him happy every time he heard it.

"Don't move!" Knight spoke loudly enough that Rook no doubt heard it from the front of the house because it was followed by the sound of his laughter and he appeared at the door.

"Look at this! Two of my favourite people in the whole world, both together." Rook draped himself over Knight and kissed Knight's cheek.

"Working, Rookie." Knight did smile, though, which Jason had learned over the past month was rare.

"I know." Rook's eyes wandered over the canvas, and he licked his lips. "God, you're a talented asshole, aren't you?" Rook gave Knight another kiss, then backed off, blowing a kiss at Jason. "So how long before we can puppy pile?"

"Ten minutes, tops." Knight growled the words, eyes dragging over Jason's body.

"Does he need fluffing or anything?" Rook asked, voice hopeful.

"No touching. You'll destroy my view."

Rook pouted and sighed loudly. "I've been working all day long."

"You've been playing with dildos, Rookie." Knight sighed, then set his brushes down. "Go on, Jase. I'm done."

He pushed himself off the chair towards Rook. The man fascinated him, so pretty with his blond hair, his bright blue eyes. So different from Knight's slender darkness.

Rook stuck his tongue out at Knight but gave the man a proper kiss even as he held out his arm to Jason. Jason went to them, moving carefully, suddenly painfully aware of the plug inside him.

Rook's hand slid over his skin as soon as he was close enough and the kiss with Knight ended noisily. Then Rook's mouth covered his, tongue pushing in. A sweet hum sounded, Rook's blue eyes staring into his own like he was the most fascinating thing ever.

It was Knight's hand, though, that slid down his back, moving to jostle the plug. He jerked away, cheeks burning. Knight shook his head. "Still so shy?"

Rook's eyes widened, his lips pulling up into a grin. "A plug? Knight, you naughty, naughty man." Rook slid a hand down his back just like Knight had done, heading right for his ass.

"I wanted to make sure he stayed awake."

Jason groaned. He'd stayed awake.

Rook laughed, the sound happy and sweet. "Can we play on your couch, Knight? Or should we find a bed?" Rook found the base of the plug and began to tap it.

"Let's go upstairs. Bish will be back soon."

Rook bounced happily and grabbed Jason's and Knight's hands, leading the way like a naughty Pied Piper.

"I need to clean up, Rookie!" Knight was laughing, though. Rook was the only one who made the man laugh.

"We'll help. *After*." Rook shook his ass, making it very clear what came before the after. Jason was given a sweet smile. "I think someone needs some help with that plug up his ass…"

"Rook…" His cheeks heated, but his cock jerked, filling.

Rook grinned and squeezed his hand, moving faster.

"Horndog. I love the way Jase walks when he's full." Knight's voice had a sexy, husky note to it.

"And you call *me* a horndog?" Rook laughed and took a half step behind him. "Knight is right, though, honey, you move like magic with that plug."

His cheeks were burning and he ducked his head then shook it.

"You should have seen him take it in for me." Knight's fingers slipped over his skin.

Oh. Oh, God. He… He still wasn't used to being a…plaything for these three men.

Rook moaned and rubbed against Knight. "I wish I'd seen that."

"I'm sure we can revisit after we play…with a bigger plug."

Rook beamed. "That would be perfect." Rook wrapped his arms around Knight, giving the man another one of those kisses. And then Rook's attention focused on him, mouth latching on.

There was nothing on earth—nothing—like Rook's kisses. Slow, lazy, drugging. They made him dizzy. He almost didn't feel the hands that slid down to his ass. It wasn't until two held his cheeks open and more fingers played with the plug that he realised there were in fact four hands touching him.

He whimpered into the kiss. God, that was so perverse, so hot.

Rook teased him with his tongue as the fingers on the plug twisted it, tugged it partway out before pushing it back in again.

He shook his head, and Knight chuckled. "Sweet baby. Our hot little size queen."

Size queen? Him?

Rook moaned. "God, yes. I need to start bringing home some of the merchandise."

"You know it. Big ones. Metal ones. Tiered ones. Vibrating ones." Knight sounded evil.

Rook jerked against him. "Oh, yes. I'll do it. Tomorrow, I swear."

"Bring me one of the shower nozzles, too. What do you think, Jase? A long weekend of assplay?"

How did he answer that?

"Bring two, Rookie." Bish's voice was deep and sure. "Knight needs in on the fun, too."

"Bish!" The outrage in Knight's voice made Jason feel good.

Rook laughed and pushed the plug back into his body. "Pileup in the big bedroom!" With that Rook turned and ran.

A sharp slap stung his ass. "Catch him, Jase. He's waiting on you."

There was a more solid slap to his other ass cheek and Bish chuckled. "Damn right."

Jason headed for his dear, loving Rook and those dazing kisses.

Rook was lying on the bed, face down, ass up, wiggling enticingly.

Jason chuckled. "So glad you're home."

"Me too, honey." Rook turned to look at him and smiled. "Come and get me."

"We're all going to come and get you, Rookie." Bish had his arm slung around Knight's shoulders. "We'll make a lovely beast with four backs."

Jason got there first, cuddling into Rook's arms, seeking the comfort he found there. Knight excited him and Bish was his buddy, but Rook was... Yeah.

Rook kissed him, shifting to wrap around him. So warm, exciting.

"They're so pretty together." Knight hummed. "We should turn a hose on them."

"Fuck off," muttered Jason around their kiss.

Bish laughed. "That was the idea."

Knight's hands landed on his ass, fingers spreading his cheeks.

Rook gasped. "Oh, God, Knight, I can feel what you're doing to him."

His entire body was shivering, his body fighting to tighten up. A big, warm hand landed on his hip—Bish—massaging even as Rook's kisses got more intense. The end of the plug was tapped and twisted, tugged.

Rook moaned, pushed against him.

"Our Jase was a very good model today, Rookie. An excellent boy." Knight's words made his cheeks heat.

"You deserve a reward," Rook told him then began to wriggle downward.

Jason gasped, eyes going wide. *Oh, please.* Rook kissed his skin the entire way down.

Bishop appeared in front of him, smiling. "Hey, kid."

"H-hey."

Rook was taking his time, loving on every inch of his abs with that magical tongue.

Bish leaned in and took his mouth. Bishop's kisses were like being stormed by a bunch of Marines—the pressure strong, fierce, a little wild. Jason was still reeling and breathless under the onslaught when Rook's mouth closed over his prick. He cried out into the kiss, then his breath stopped when Knight yanked the plug free, that long, hard cock slamming into him instead.

The three of them worked together like a well-oiled machine—Bish tongue-fucking his mouth and playing his nipples, Rook sucking hard on his prick, and Knight fucking him fast and furious. Need flooded him and he couldn't breathe, couldn't move. He met Bish's eyes, panicking.

Bish leaned their foreheads together. "Breathe into it, baby boy. Let the pleasure have you."

"So big." It was too big.

"That's my boys," murmured Bish, cupping his cheek, thumb rubbing his lower lip.

He opened at the touch, sucking that thumb, the act relaxing him, easing him.

Bish held his gaze. "Fuck, you're an amazing cocksucker, Jase."

His cheeks heated, but he sucked harder, his entire body tightening.

"You want my cock instead of my thumb? Want to make it a triple play? All your holes filled, Rook sucking on you..." Bishop was moving, not even waiting for his answer.

The thick cock painted his lips with pre-cum. He opened, his heart beating like a huge drum in his chest. Bish's prick slid in, stretching his lips. He began to suck, using Rook's rhythm.

"Pretty cocksucker. You've got amazing lips, Jase." Knight's voice was right by his ear.

Rook whimpered around his prick and sucked harder, the pleasure not letting up for a second. Bish's hum only made it that much better. Then Bish's hand cupped his jaw, tilted his head, and he pushed deeper. Sounds began to fill the air—moans and groans and the wet sound of flesh on flesh.

Knight slammed into his body, filling his ass. It pushed his prick deeper into Rook's mouth and Rook swallowed around him. He groaned low, pulling harder, hungry for the flesh in his mouth.

Bish began thrusting, matching the rhythm Knight filled his ass with. Both thick cocks took him, as did Rook's mouth around his own cock. They humped wildly, sliding together on the huge bed.

Rook's tongue did something wicked to his slit, just as Knight's hand came up to cup his balls. Jason swallowed hard, spunk pouring out of him, waves of pleasure crashing into him.

"Oh, fuck," muttered Bish and flooded his mouth with cum. Jase groaned, sucking and swallowing hard.

"Come on, Knight," growled Bish. "Give it to him."

That made Rook moan around his cock.

"Mmm. Get a fat plug, Rookie," Bish murmured.

"Gonna plug him up with your spunk still inside him?" Rook's lips were swollen from sucking him. And red.

"You are. I want him full."

Rook whimpered.

Bish chuckled and licked at Jason's mouth, distracting him with a warm, lazy kiss.

"Oh… Look how hard Rookie is. He didn't shoot." Knight actually sounded almost sorry.

Bish ended the kiss and they turned their cheeks together. Rook was coming back to the bed, dildo in one hand, hard cock leading the way. Jason moaned, the combination of need and desire and fondness huge.

"We should give Rook a chance to fuck him before he puts in that dildo." Bish smiled at him. "You'd like that, wouldn't you, Jason?"

Oh, God. He… He met Rook's eyes, moaning.

Knight slapped his ass. "Little slut."

"Our little slut," added Bish.

Rook nodded, eyes on Jason's as he climbed back up on the bed. "Mine. Fuck, honey, I want you."

Jason couldn't refuse that need — he just couldn't.

"Face to face," Rook said, climbing onto the bed.

Knight slid out of him, tugged him over onto his back. Bishop grabbed his legs, spread him wide, and Rook groaned.

"God, you're perfect, Jase." Rook lined up, cockhead teasing his aching hole. He held Jason's gaze as the thick cock slowly speared his ass.

He moaned, and Knight eased him upward to bring his mouth closer to Rook's. Rook licked his lips.

"Rook." He leaned in, straining for that sweet kiss.

Rook gave it to him, lips pressing against his, tongue sliding into his mouth, just like that hard cock pushed into his ass. Oh. Oh, Rook.

Tongue and cock synced up, Rook fucking him eagerly. Knight helped him wrap around Rook, his lean body surprisingly strong behind him. Groans filled his mouth, one after the other, Rook making it clear he was loving this. He moaned back, his cock trying to recover, to fill. Rook stared into his eyes — it was mesmerising.

A soft keening sound left him, his ass clenching. Rook moaned again, started moving faster, pushing harder. Knight pushed him up and suddenly he was riding Rook, bouncing on his prick, supported by three men.

"Yes!" Rook shouted, pushed in hard and nailed his gland.

Jason gasped, his nails digging into Rook's arms. "Please…"

Bish's hand wrapped around his cock, pulling hard. He was hard…hard again…still hard. His eyes went wide.

"So good," muttered Rook. "Live for this, for you, honey."

He arched, balls drawing up tight.

"Right there, honey. Right there." Rook had found his gland and was pegging it over and over again.

"Want to pierce his nips, Rookie. Maybe his cock." Knight was groaning, growling in his ear.

"Fuck!" Rook's thrusts got even harder, the man almost wild now.

Bishop's pressed his thumb into the slit of Jason's cock, and spunk sprayed from him.

"Oh, fuck! I feel you. I feel you." Rook thrust a few more times then came, heat spilling inside him.

Jason slumped forward, dizzy, stunned. Rook's arms slid around him, held him close even as Bish and Knight cuddled in from behind him. He let Rook hold him, cock deep inside him. Rook stole another kiss, this one long and lazy. Then the man leaned his head back and Bish and Knight each kissed him and Rook.

Knight pushed the plug into Rook's hand. "For when you come out."

Rook nodded at Knight and then looked into Jason's eyes. "You're going to hold me in you all evening."

"All evening." His ass was going to ache.

"You can help with supper," suggested Bish. "You're going to be moving very gracefully."

He hid his face in Rook's shoulder.

Rook kissed the side of his head. "Bish is right. I love watching you move when you've been filled."

"Rook." God, that was so weird, how much he wanted to please them.

"Mmm." He got another one of those drugging kisses he loved so much. "Time for me to come out, yeah?"

"Squeeze around Rook, now. Keep the spunk in."

The three of them moved so well together, working to get Rook out and the plug in him without losing any of Rook's spunk. By the time the plug was seated, he was trembling, sweat popping out across his shoulders. Rook kept kissing him, rubbing against him, giving him something else to focus on and think about.

"Shower. All of us. Now." Knight was so demanding. Thank God the master bedroom shower was enormous.

Rook giggled and pulled slowly away, leaving kisses and touches on him.

Bishop grabbed Knight in his arms, carrying the artist into the bathroom, laughing and kicking.

"Come on. We don't want to miss the shower." Rook waggled his eyebrows outrageously.

He moved slowly, the plug huge, filling him. Rook slid a hand to his ass and squeezed lightly, making the plug move. Jason's steps stuttered and he stumbled forward.

Rook caught him. "Careful, honey."

"Sorry."

Rook's hands were so warm.

"Wouldn't want to hurt anything important."

"No. No." He leaned in, begged one more kiss.

Rook gave it to him—Rook always did—stopping to press him up against the wall and rubbing against him as their mouths slid together. He moaned, stupid with need, with hunger. It had to be the plug—it was making him wild.

"Poor honey. Knight making you need all day." Rook's words made him moan.

Rook rubbed up against him. "I'll make it up to you all night long, I swear."

"Tomorrow is my day with you, at the store." Rook and Knight took turns having him with them while they worked.

"Oh, good. I have some new toys I want to show you."

New toys. *Oh, God.*

Rook kissed him again, then dragged him into the bathroom where Bish and Knight had already started the shower. Knight was wrapped around Bish's muscled body, the huge man pushing him up against the wall.

Rook moaned, tugging him into the huge stall, under the spray where they could hear Bish's and Knight's moans. The heat poured around them, the steam making things a little dizzying.

Rook leant back against the tile close to Bish and Knight and drew him in, arms wrapping around him. "Aren't they gorgeous together?"

"Mmm." They were like fire and ice.

Rook's mouth landed on his shoulder, pressing little, sucking kisses on him. Jason leaned, eyes closing. How had this become a familiar place, so quickly?

Chapter Two

To say he worked at the Bitten Apple would be generous. Rook did own the place, and he did his best to show up and put in half a dozen hours most weekdays, but there was a reason why he'd hired a really good manager, who worked full-time and was in charge of the details.

Rook's job was to schmooze the customers, talk to the suppliers and test out the products — which, granted, he mostly did at home.

Mostly.

Today he had Jason at work with him, which was always fun. He loved showing Jase all the different toys, especially when they shocked his lover.

Jason looked lovely in jeans and a sweater, all bundled up for winter. Everyone flirted with him and it was so charming to see Jason flush and flutter.

A shipment arrived and Rook all but bounced once the boxes had been stacked in the back room. "I'll check it," he told Darby, his best hire ever. "Jase, honey? Come to the back with me." He couldn't wait to see what had been delivered, to see if he and Jason could play.

"Sure, Rook." Jason followed him immediately, easily...hell, eagerly.

Rook locked the door to the stockroom and gave Jason his best grin.

"Rook?" Jason looked at the door.

"Yes, Jase?" He moved to Jason and slid his fingers over Jason's shoulders. God, he loved all the sweet muscles.

Jason moaned softly at his touch. "I just... The door's locked."

"I did that for you. I didn't think you'd want anyone to walk in on us. If I was wrong, I can open it again..."

"No. No, please."

His Jason opened up to him, to all three of them, really, but that was it. And Rook wouldn't have it any other way. "That's why I locked it."

Jason nodded, stepped closer. "How can I help?"

"Let's start with a kiss to get warmed up, hmm?"

Jason chuckled softly, cheeks pink. "You have amazing kisses." So said his not-queer lover.

"And you have an amazing mouth." He leant back in and took another kiss.

"Uhn..." Jason arched into the kiss, his tongue caressing Rook's.

Every response was eager and it made Rook need, made him want to lay Jason over the nearest flat surface and fuck him blind. Of course, having help with the toys was going to lead to that, no question...

"Come on. Let's see what came in." He grabbed Jason's hand and tugged him over to the boxes.

"You're so excited." Jason chuckled happily.

"You're here with me and there's new toys—of course I'm excited!"

Jason grinned. "What am I supposed to do? Count them?"

"We have to do that, yeah, but we might need to test some of the stuff, too." He grabbed a knife and cut open the first box. *Mmm.* Oh, the fun steel cock rings. Man, they were heavy. He took one out of the package and hefted it, offered it over.

"Wow." Jason's eyes were wide. "That's for a huge cock."

Rook chuckled softly. *Right.* They cupped the whole package in steel. "Wanna see how it works, honey?" He could just imagine Jason, all wrapped up.

"Huh? Rook, I'm not that big…"

"You wanna see how it works?" Clearly a demonstration was in order.

"Do I?"

He grinned and nodded. "I know I do."

"Okay." Jason reached for him. He reached for Jason's pants.

Jason was already half-hard for him.

"Mmm, nice." Rook smiled. God, he was more than halfway in love.

"I…" Jason shivered. "This is still hard."

"Yes, yes, it is." He stroked Jason's prick, waggled his eyebrows.

The truth was that Jason had come so far. His sweet, scared lover was now a sweet, tentative lover who submitted reluctantly, but beautifully.

He kept tugging on the lovely cock until it was hard in his hands. "No coming now."

"No. No, I won't."

"I know, because we're going to put the cock ring on." He grabbed it running it along Jason's cock to warm it up.

"My cock's too small."

Uh-huh. Too small.

"You, honey, have a lovely, *big* cock. And this doesn't go around just it."

He loved Jason's confusion.

"Don't worry, I'll show you." He slid the steel ring to the base of Jason's cock and then very carefully worked one of Jason's balls in through the ring. Fuck, it was obscene and beautiful. He would have to bring one of these home because Bish and Knight just had to see.

Jason was already panting, and by the time he eased the second testicle through, his lover was flushed.

"Still think it's too big?"

"Uh-uh. No. No, Rook."

"You look sexy as hell. I might have to take you home like this." He touched the tip of Jason's cock. The sweet, swollen flesh was hot, damp. Moaning, he bent and licked, needing to have the flavour of his lover on his tongue.

"Rook." Jason groaned, hips bumping against the door.

He grinned, took more of Jason in and got himself a good suck. That earned him a soft moan, Jason shifting against him. He let his head bob twice, and slowly, reluctantly, pulled off. They did have half a dozen boxes to go through, though, and he'd hate to blow their load in the first five minutes.

So to speak.

The thought had him giggling and he gave Jason a kiss. Jason tucked himself in and zipped up.

"You didn't have to do that." It wasn't like Jason wouldn't be naked soon enough.

"But we're at your work..."

"The door is locked, honey."

"No one has a key?"

"Only the manager and he knows better than to disturb me if the door is locked." Rook came in here for his 'breaks' and to 'test' the merchandise.

Jason relaxed for him. "Wh-what's next?"

"Well, we need to put the rest of these steel cock rings on the stock shelf. There should be six in the box." He dug through the box, being very good and ignoring the other goodies as he counted while handing them to Jason. "One, two, three, four…five… I can't find six. Oh, that's right—it's here!" He fondled Jason through his jeans.

"I…" Jason arched, pushed into his hands.

"Feels good, hmm? I'm hoping we find some plugs or dildos too."

"Do you sell a lot of them?"

"They're probably our best seller. They're good for singles and couples, you know? Not to mention for either girls or guys."

"Yeah. I never used one before you guys."

"Now you know what you were missing." He grinned and reached in for the next item. "Oh, flavoured lube."

"Ew." That wrinkled nose was definite.

Rook happened to agree, but he laughed anyway. "And have you ever tasted it?"

"Yeah. It's…chemically."

"It tastes like shit," he corrected. Then he grinned and gave Jason a quick peck. "So you and the ladies tried that, huh?" Jason had believed he wasn't gay. Hell, the guy had told them he wasn't really interested in sex at all. It was amusing how wrong a man could be about himself.

"Yeah. I… I didn't like going down on a girl."

Look at those burning cheeks.

"Oh, honey, the lube would have only made things worse." He gave Jason a kiss. "And you're home now." Because Jason was a world-class cocksucker, and that pretty ass... *Fuck.*

Rook tossed the lube on the shelves and gave a cheer as he came upon a bunch of fancy dildos with bumps and veins on them. They ranged from fairly small to quite large.

Jason came to him, obviously curious. "What did you find?"

"Jackpot!" He grinned and showed Jason a few of the dildos.

"Good lord." Jason's finger traced one of the dildos through the packaging.

Rook took out one of each of the half-dozen styles and displayed them. "So, which one do you like best?"

"They're all surprisingly pretty."

Grinning, Rook nodded. "They are. Think about how they'll look going in and out of your ass." He gave Jason a wicked little smile. "Or mine."

Jason groaned, fingers shaking. "Which one would you choose?"

"Oh, no." He shook his head. "This one is all you."

"I... What should I look for? Size? The...bumps?"

He opened them all and pushed one into Jason's hand. "Explore them all."

Jason refused the little light plastic one right away. The thicker dildos were explored, the bumpy ones given wide eyes. Rook couldn't wait until they uncovered the plugs. He was pretty sure there should be some in the shipment.

He ran his own fingers over Jason's. "So what do you think?"

"I don't know. Is it... Am I a slut if I like the bigger ones?"

"No, honey, I'm a slut because I like it *all*. You're just a sweetheart."

Jason reached out, squeezed his fingers. "Thank you. I like the glass one." Big and heavy, but smooth, the one Jason had chosen was lovely.

"Oh, I can picture this sliding in and out of your ass." He moaned happily at the thought.

"It's heavy." Jason's hand was jacking it, up and out, the motion unconscious.

Groaning, Rook looked on the shelves for some good, old-fashioned K-Y.

"Should I put them back in their boxes?" Jason's voice was husky.

"No. Let's play with the one you chose."

He grabbed a bottle of K-Y and one of the novelty blankets with penises on it that they'd overstocked — he should bring a couple of these home — and headed for a clear patch of floor.

"P-play?"

"Oh, yes. We need to test it, right?"

"We do?" Jason stepped closer.

He laughed softly. "It might be more accurate to say I *want* to. You do, too." He put his hand on Jason's crotch again, feeling the heat of Jason's hard cock even through the layer of denim.

Jason rolled, rubbing against his palm.

"See? Just imagine how this is going to feel inside you." He squeezed Jason's package a few more times, massaging it.

"It'll be big." Jason groaned. "I shouldn't...but I want to."

"Why shouldn't you, Jase? You want to, I want to." He grinned. "And you know we'll take it home and Bish and Knight will want a re-enactment followed by some time with it and your ass themselves." It was endearing, really, how, even after nearly two months, Jason could still be shy about things.

In fact, if Knight was here, he'd already have Jason bent over, spreading his hole, exposing everything.

Rook had the blanket on the floor, though, and was going to have Jason lie on his back. That way Rook could see his face and the sweet prick, as well as watch the dildo going in and out of Jason's hot little hole.

"Strip for me. Let me see your beautiful body."

Jason nodded—pinked but started pulling off his sweater.

Rook took his own clothes off, not the least bit shy. His prick was hard, a drop of liquid at the tip as it curved up towards his belly. God, he wanted Jase. So much. It was always like this when it came to Jason.

Jason shocked him by sliding one finger through the drop of pre-cum, then sucking the liquid away.

Moaning, he reached for Jason. "Kiss me," he demanded.

Jason pushed into his arms, the kiss-hungry, happy, sweet man. He could taste himself there, just the barest hint from the taste Jason had taken. God, he was addicted. Entirely, wholly, wantonly.

"Now lie down. I'm going to make you fly with this pretty little thing." Or not so little, as it happened.

"On the blanket?"

"Uh-huh." He took another kiss, ending it reluctantly.

Jason stared at him, eyes on his lips like the man was stunned. He smiled and helped Jason lie down, his fingers sliding on the lovely skin.

"So hot, honey. I want to just eat you up." Rook bent, closing his mouth over the skin of Jason's inner thigh and sucking hard. That was going to leave a mark. He loved that—leaving their marks on their lover. Knight actually left the most, playing hard with Jason.

Rook bit lightly and swiped his tongue along the smooth skin behind Jason's balls.

"Oh, God."

Fuck, he loved the smell of Jason—rich and male. He spread the lovely legs wider, licking at Jason's sweet little hole. He was going to fill this.

"Rook. Oh... Oh, my Rook." *His Rook.*

Yes. He was Jason's. And Jason was his. He hummed, tongue pushing into Jason's body. The tiny ring of muscles tightened around his tongue, gripping him. Groaning, he tongue-fucked Jason's hole.

"Please. Oh, God..." Jason's hips bucked and rolled, ass bouncing off the floor.

Jason wrapped his hand around Jason's prick, giving him more stimulation. The steel ring around his cock was hot from Jason's skin.

"I. I. Fuck. Oh, fuck..." Pretty, needy boy.

Rook pulled away and smiled at Jason. "You're going to look so pretty with that dildo sliding in and out of you."

Jason's answer was a low moan.

He took the dildo and offered it to Jason, wanting to see Jason's lips wrapped around it.

Jason took the dildo in shaking hands. "Rook?"

"Suck on it. Wrap those sexy lips of yours around it and suck."

"Oh, God..." Jason's hand shook.

Rook wrapped his hands around Jason's and guided the dildo to those lovely lips. "It's okay, Jase. Open for me." Those lips parted, just a bit. "Yeah, just like that. Fuck, you're sexy, Jason. I've never been so turned on as I am by you." And he knew from turned on.

"Never? With them at home?"

"I know! But you're even hotter, honey."

Jason's cheeks were almost purple.

"It's true." He pressed the dildo back to Jason's lips.

Those sweet lips took the dildo in, spreading wide, stretching for the cock. Rook groaned at the sight and pushed it in deeper. His own cock ached, wanting in Jason's body.

He was going to open Jason up with the dildo first, though. Bish would be so proud of him—delaying his own gratification to do this first. Besides, he wanted to watch, wanted to see.

He fucked Jason's mouth with the dildo, watching the pretty glass disappear over and over again. Fuck, that was the hottest thing ever. Rook moaned, his hips humping the air. Jason's eyes were on his face, his lover's moans muffled.

"You're fucking stunning, Jason." The prettiest thing he'd ever seen.

"Mmm." One of Jason's hands reached for him.

"You ready for me to fuck you with it, honey?"

This time he got a soft whine.

"Mmm, that's a yes." He took Jason's hand and wrapped it around the dildo so he could let go and get his fingers slicked up. "It's gonna look so hot, stretching your hole."

He slid a finger into Jason's hole, then another, stretching him slowly. Jason was so soft inside, silky. It was like magic, the inside of a man. The inside of Jason. He kissed Jason's prick and spread his fingers wide.

Jason moaned low, legs opening. "Rook."

He grinned. "Gonna fuck you with that dildo, and then with the real thing, see what you like best."

"You. I'll like you."

"Mmm. I knew there was a reason I liked you so much."

"You knew from the beginning."

"I did. You're special, honey. I could tell that from the start."

"Thank you." Jason reached for him.

"Let's do the dildo thing first." He got it lubed up.

Jason's gaze was clinging to him, watching every move he made.

"You looking forward to this, honey?"

"I don't know. I think so? It looks bigger in your hand."

"You had it in your mouth—you tell me if it was any bigger than me or Knight or Bish."

"It's bigger than Knight."

"But not Bish." Rook grinned at him. "Mmm...Bish's cock..." Bishop was legendary.

Jason actually grinned, beamed at him. He grinned back and then nudged Jason's thigh. "Hold your legs back for me. I want to be able to see."

"Oh, God." Jason looked like he'd swallowed a frog, but grabbed his thighs.

Rook petted the lovely cock, the pretty balls. Then he touched that little hole, the skin shining with lube. Oh, damn. That was so hot. So hot.

He moaned and set the head of the dildo against Jason's hole and began to press in. Look at that tiny ring of muscles spread, stretch for him. He pressed harder, pushing it in deeper.

"Rook."

The glass pressed deeper. "Yeah, Jase?" He kept pushing the dildo in.

"It's full."

"Then I should pull it out, hmm?" He tugged the plug almost all the way out.

"Oh..." Jason's body followed the dildo.

"You want it in again?" He slowly pushed the dildo back in.

"Y...yes. Please." Pretty baby.

"You look amazing, Jason. Spread open by this pretty glass cock."

Those bright blue eyes went wide. "Rook."

"Honey, you should see yourself. You're stunning." He pushed the cock in deeper, knowing it was stretching his lover wide. Then he slid it halfway out and pushed it back in again. Then again. Fuck, it made him want.

Jason groaned, pushing up on his forearms to bear down. Size queen. Beautiful, sexy, stunning, lovely size queen.

Bending, he kissed Jason's prick again, admiring the hard colour, the steel around the base and Jason's balls.

"So full, Rook. I need."

He knew. "I'm not going to leave you hanging." That didn't mean he wasn't going to keep playing for a while first.

He settled into a rhythm with the dildo. Jason's moans filled the air, his tiny hole spreading.

Rook wanted to fuck that hole, jack off, something. He was good, though—he just kept fucking that sweet hole with the dildo. It was fascinating—to see his lover move, hump up into the dildo. Jason was so sexy, had taken to being theirs like a fish to water. It was like they were all made for each other.

He let his fingers nudge Jason's hole as he pushed in, imagining Jason with all his holes filled—a needy cock in his mouth, a sound in his cock, his hole plugged. Oh, he had to talk to Bish and make plans.

Groaning, he tugged the dildo out and tore open his jeans.

"Want you. Please, Rook." Jason begged better than anyone.

"Yeah, me too." He got the jeans off and settled between Jason's legs. As soon as the dildo was out, he was in, sinking into the most perfect heat.

Jason lifted, arms wrapping around his shoulders. "Yes!"

He nodded. "Yes, Jase." He started fucking Jason with long, eager strokes. Jason fed him one happy cry after another, clinging to him. It felt so fucking good, so right. Rook didn't think he'd ever get tired of doing this. Jason's hole pulled at his cock, trying to keep him inside.

He met Jason's eyes. "So good."

Jason nodded, hole clenching around him. He felt the pleasure all through him as he continued to fuck Jason, to fill his lover over and over.

"Harder."

Oh, God. Was that…? His sweet boy needing more?

"Like this?" he asked, putting more strength behind his thrust.

"Rook. Rook, yes. Please."

He sped up as well, really letting Jason have it. The tight muscles gripped his cock, ass squeezing his shaft on each thrust. "Gonna make me come."

"Good." Jason squeezed tighter.

He laughed, the sound breathless and needy, just like he was. His knees were beginning to ache, but his hips couldn't help moving, pushing in, over and over.

"So fucking beautiful." He was so close.

Jason arched under him, riding him harder. He pounded in, searching for his climax, for that last little push. His thighs slapped against Jason's ass.

His mouth opened as his orgasm began to crash over him. "Lo—"

Jason bit out his name as his body convulsed around him. Rook jerked in a few more times as he came and came, filling Jason with his spunk.

Now he could plug that sweet ass, keep his spunk inside Jason. Leaning down, he brought their lips together, his tongue sliding into Jason's mouth. Jason held on, moaning into his lips.

"Gonna plug you up, keep my spunk inside you until we get home to Bish and Knight." He felt the effect his words had on Jason, all around his prick.

He licked Jason's nose and grabbed the dildo. It would do until he could go grab a new plug off the shelves. Something big enough to make Jason move carefully all afternoon. Groaning at the thought, he slowly pulled out of Jason's tight, needy body.

He kept his finger on Jason's hole. "Keep it in. For me."

"For you."

"That's right."

He grabbed the dildo and slid it over Jason's hole, pressing the head of the glass prick in. Jason moaned — the sound pure sex.

"Oh, Jase. God…" Rook thought maybe he was in deep, desperate love with this man.

Jason nodded, rubbing their noses together.

"Gonna find you a pretty plug. Something nice and big for you to wear."

Jason whimpered, fingers clenching into fists.

"Yeah, I'd say that was a perfect idea." He sauntered over to the racks, bent over to look on the bottom ones.

"So pretty." Jason's voice sounded raw.

He looked back, smiled. "Takes one to know one."

"Flatterer." Jason tried to smile back.

"Oh, no, honey. You're the prettiest of us all."

He loved how Jason flexed for him. He watched a moment longer before going back to his search. There, right there was the perfect plug. It was heavy, but shaped to stay inside even if the wearer was fairly active.

Jason's pretty blue eyes were wide. Rook carried the plug over to Jason, slowly taking it out of its packaging.

"Rook. That's..."

"Stunning? Beautiful? Obscene...?" He gave Jason a wink.

"Big. I'm going with big. And shiny."

He laughed. "Those work, too."

"Love your laugh."

Oh. He smiled at Jason. "Thank you, honey."

Jason's response was a soft smile.

"Now let's get you plugged!"

He laughed again, moving between Jason's legs.

It was going to be an amazing afternoon.

Chapter Three

Bish curled around Knight, kissing a line across his shoulders. "You think Rook is blowing our boy's mind?"

"Mmm-hmm. He had plans. Inventory plans."

"I hope he filmed it."

Knight chuckled, stretched out against him. "Perv."

"You know it—the best kind of perv."

"My kind." Knight sighed. "I should get some work done."

"No, you should stay in bed with me until our boys come home." Bish moved those amazing hands over his skin.

"Fuck, you're warm." That wasn't a *no* from his stubborn lover.

"All the better to keep you in bed." Bish cupped Knight's balls and his legs opened like magic. He chuckled. Fuck, he loved this man. This complex, brilliant, sexy, amazing, subby-but-fighting-it man.

He let his thumb wander back along the warm, smooth patch of skin behind Knight's balls. There should be a ring there. Why had they never seriously thought of piercing before? Knight had mentioned it yesterday and he was right—Jason would look perfect with a matching ring in the same spot, and Rook's nipples called out for a pair to tug and twist.

They could have someone in, make it a party.

"You look wicked." Knight hummed softly.

"That's because I am." He bit at Knight's earlobe. "I think we need a piercing party. Maybe this weekend."

"Piercing party? Is that a euphemism?"

"A euphemism for what? No. I meant we bring someone in, get a little jewellery on all my men."

"You want to pierce Jason and Rookie?"

"Among others, yes." He waited for the penny to drop.

Knight's eyebrow lifted. "Uh-uh."

He slid his hand behind Knight's balls and pressed that spot again. "Right here, babe. With a matching ring on Jase."

"No way." Knight's hips rolled up into his touch.

"Yes, way. Can you imagine how good it'll feel?" He pinched Knight's skin.

"I want Jason's cockhead pierced."

"Oh-ho, you do, do you?" He moved his fingers to pinch Knight's. "Yours, too?"

"No. No fucking way." Knight's eyes rolled back.

"I think you'll love it." He kept playing with the tip of Knight's foreskin.

"Not going to." Knight was right there, with him.

"I think you will." He chuckled, slid his thumb across Knight's slit.

"Not a chance."

Before he could reply the front door opened, Rook calling out, "Honeys, I'm ho-ome!"

"In here, Rookie."

Knight snuggled in, cuddled into his arms.

Rook and Jase came in, Rook looking pleased as punch while Jase looked just a tad stunned.

"Someone's been naughty!" Knight sounded happy about it.

"Yeah, it was Jase!" Rook sounded the same.

"Jason? My baby boy?" Knight snorted. "I don't believe it."

Jason had gone about four shades of red, and ducked his head.

"Wear it proudly," Bish advised.

Jason's big blue eyes met his.

"He's wearing his plug very proudly." Rook patted Jason's ass.

Jason's lips quivered and Knight moaned. "Come here, baby boy. You need a hug."

How did the word *hug* sound so raunchy in Knight's voice? Jason headed for him, though, with Rook right behind, pulling Jason's clothes off.

"Did you spank him, Rookie?" Knight gathered Jason close.

"Nope. We played with an amazing glass dildo and he's wearing a wicked steel ring." Rookie grinned wickedly. "And my spunk's inside him thanks to this lovely plug."

"Mmm. Bish wants to pierce his cock, too."

"Oh, God! What a wonderful idea!" Rook laughed and kissed him hard.

Bish grinned. "Actually, I wanted a guiche on him. And Knight's getting a guiche as well, while you get nipple rings. We're going to make a party of it."

"I am not." Knight sounded so shocked. Jason just hid his face.

Bish laughed. "You are, too. Matching guiches, my dark-haired and blond beauties. And a bonus penis piercing for you."

Rook pouted. "If they're dark and blond beauties, what does that make me?"

"You, my dear Rookie, are one of a kind." Bish dragged Rook in and took their lover's mouth with an eager, hungry kiss. Rook melted against him, opened to him, giving himself up wholeheartedly.

Knight was kissing Jason, keeping the kid close and involved. Bish reached out, found the kid's ass and squeezed. He loved how Jason jerked, snuggled in, pushed against him. He hummed happily and squeezed that ass again.

Rook was happily kissing everyone, rubbing and humming and making a slut of himself.

"Did you not get him off, kid?" Knight bit one of Rook's nipples hard enough that their Rookie gasped.

"Of course I did. I wouldn't leave him hanging!" Jason looked indignant.

Bish chuckled. "I don't think you *could* leave our Rookie hanging."

Knight snorted. "At least he's well-hung."

Rook broke off the kisses long enough to grin and say, "You know it, baby."

Bish grabbed Knight's ass, squeezed. God, there was nothing like having a bed full of lovers. He was a lucky fucking man. They all rolled together—one moaning, one laughing, another biting.

"So you guys down for a piercing party on Saturday?" Bish asked.

Rookie's answer was a soft, happy laugh.

"I'm not getting pierced."

"Sure you are, Knight. If Bish says so, you'll do it." Rookie knew how they all worked.

"Am not." Knight swatted Rook.

Rook laughed and wriggled his ass back towards Knight. "Are too!"

"Not." The next slap was firm, well-placed, and Rookie moaned.

That sweet ass pushed back again, Rook moaning the words out this time. "Too. Are too."

Bish tugged Jason over a little, giving his lovers room to play. Jason looked worried, but Bish nuzzled gently. "It's just playful. Not bad at all."

Rookie waved his ass at Knight again.

"See? He wants what Knight's doing."

"Why?"

Knight hummed. "Because it feels so good."

Rook nodded, smiled happily. "It *does*. So will your piercing, K."

"No." Knight swatted Rook again. Stubborn man.

"Yes! Yes! Yes!" Rook laughed, ass just wiggling and wagging in Knight's face.

Knight started laughing, too, then he tackled Rook, tumbling them over and over on the bed. Bish kept Jason out of the line of fire, keeping him sweet with touches. Knight and Rook ended up curled together, laughing and kissing.

"You see?" He kissed Jason then nuzzled him. "Although, I think the best way to learn is to do. And I'm just the one to do you." He slid his hand down to cover one of Jason's ass cheeks.

"Wh-what?" Jason stiffened, and Bish could feel the kid's heartbeat speed up.

"Spanking. It's fun, Jase. And I'm betting you'll love it." He let his hand smack Jason's body, just gently.

Rookie immediately moved closer, fingers sliding on Jason's skin. "You're going to love it, honey. I swear." That was their Rookie, always gentling Jason along, making sure their new boy had as much fun as anyone else.

He swatted again, humming under his breath.

Rookie pushed up against Jason's front and moaned. "Do that again, Bish."

He nodded and hit two more times, making sure the blows were solid, but not harsh. Jason moaned and Rookie echoed it, then kissed Jason. Knight scooted up behind Rook, spreading his ass.

"Fuck, this is good with four, isn't it, boys?"

Rook's agreement was muffled by Jason's mouth.

Knight winked at Bishop, teasing him, laughing at him. Knight could tease all he wanted, Bish was still throwing a piercing party and Knight was going to be the guest of honour. If his beautiful, pierced artist wasn't careful, he'd end up ringed all over.

He gave Jason a few more swats, watching his three lovers writhe together while he did. Knight was teasing Rookie's hole, Rook was sucking on Jason's tongue. He rubbed the tip of his prick over Jason's hole, then spanked him again.

"I…" Jason cried out, the sound muffled by Rook's lips.

He smacked that ass again and again, Rook rocking in the same rhythm, pushing Jason back against him. He was pretty sure Knight was fucking Rookie, too, driving into the man. It was a good idea. He found the lube and slicked up his fingers. The plug was easy to pull at and tug out.

Jason squeaked, pushed into Rookie's arms with a cry. Bish nuzzled the long, bare neck in front of him, licking Jason's skin as he slowly pushed two slick fingers into Jason's now empty hole.

"Gonna fuck you, baby boy, while Knight is fucking your Rookie."

Jason moaned for him, the sound echoed more loudly by Rook. Rook helped Jason spread and pushed that fine ass closer to him. He pulled his fingers out of Jason and slicked up his prick before pushing it against Jason's hole. He let Rook's movements push Jason right onto his cock.

Jason shook around Bish, his hole spasming. Rook whimpered, reaching out to touch Jason...to touch him even as Knight kept punching into their Rookie. Jason was slick, stretched, and took his cock like a pro.

Bish reached out himself, grabbing hold of Knight's shoulder and pulling them all close. Knight's cheek rubbed his hand, his artist smiling at him. A lot of guys never found one man to love and he had three. That made him three times lucky. Knight leant down and bit Rook's shoulder.

"Fuck." He ploughed into Jason, shoving him up against Rook.

They moved together, Knight never looking away from him. Bish pressed a kiss to Jason's shoulder, leaned to kiss Rook's shoulder as well, and then took Knight's mouth. Knight moaned into his lips, the sound hungry. He deepened the kiss, fucking Jason eagerly. It was like he was fucking all three of them. Rookie and Jason were devouring each other, both of them moving hard. He could feel every kiss, every motion around his prick.

Fucking amazing. The big bed was rocking, their sounds filling the air.

They moved together faster, harder—nothing but bodies and sex and it was amazing. Jason's body tightened around him, his hole squeezing hard.

"That's it, boy. So good." He let go, let their bodies move him.

Their boy responded so well to praise, the dear man needing to please.

"Hands on cocks," he muttered, sliding his hand down to Jason's and Rook's cocks.

Three hands met his. *Fuck, yes.* Just like that.

"Faster," he growled, and they all responded. The fucking, the jacking, the rocking—they all moved faster and harder...better.

Time to come, clean up, and order a fucking pizza.

"Come now. Now."

Jason shot and so did Rookie, Knight the only stubborn one. Bish met Knight's eyes and growled. Knight's eyes went wide, the dark irises reflecting his own face.

He came just after Knight did, filling Jason's ass. Fucking perfect. It was fucking perfect.

"Good boys," he muttered, reaching to pat each of them.

Rook hummed. "I want pizza. Lots of greasy, spicy pizza."

Knight laughed and Jason just cuddled in closer to Rook.

Stretching, Bish came out of Jason and put a kiss on the lovely shoulder. "I think we can make pizza happen."

"Spoilt brat," Knight teased, pushing away from Rook and already padding for the bathroom.

"You should go with him," Bish told Jason, giving the boy a slap on the ass. "Rookie and I will take care of the pizza."

"I... Okay." Poor Jase was still a bit leery of Knight, Bish thought. It would do the kid well to spend some more time with him.

When Jase got out of the bed, Bish drew Rook in close, giving his sweet lover a kiss. "So, you had a good day?"

Rookie laughed and nodded, nuzzling into him like Rook hadn't just come—hell, like he hadn't just spent the entire day coming, which Bish knew well Rook had.

"Horndog."

Rook nodded, perfectly happy with the accusation. "It's why you all love me."

"Only one of the reasons, Rookie."

A pleased smile bloomed across Rook's face, and Bish was kissed hard and deep.

"Okay, so how many pizzas am I buying?"

Chapter Four

The pre-dawn morning was perfect for jogging. Knight slipped out of the studio, where he'd spent the night working, and headed out onto the street. The sound of his feet slapping on the pavement kept him company, except on the parts where the snow was beginning to gather. The first hard snowfall of the season was supposed to hit later in the morning, but Knight was beginning to think it was coming sooner.

Three kilometres into his run, he knew the storm was early. He turned towards home, but only made it to Zva' before he had to stop. He slipped inside, glad they were already open, and his cell began to ring.

"Y...y-yeah?" Fuck, he was cold.

"K, where the fuck are you?" Bish sounded angry, which probably meant he was worried.

"At the c-c-coffee shop."

"Why are you stuttering? Are you okay? Have you seen the blizzard out there?"

"I'm just c-c-cold. It wasn't" — he beamed at Rick when a coffee was pushed into his hands — "snowing when I left."

"What are you wearing?"

Somehow that didn't sound as sexy as it usually did.

"Running clothes." A sweatshirt, shorts, and shoes. Bish was going to have a fit.

The growl on the phone said that was exactly what Bish was in the process of having. "Stay there." The phone went dead.

"Ah, fuck."

He sat, sipping his coffee, letting the heat thaw him.

It was nearly fifteen minutes before Bish came in the door, wrapped up like a mummy and carrying Knight's winter coat and boots.

"Bish." He went for a smile.

"You are going to catch your death out running in this weather wearing *that*."

His boots were dropped onto the ground in front of him, a hat, scarf and mitts pulled out of one of the sleeves of the coat Bish was carrying.

"I'll look silly in boots and shorts."

"So what do you suggest, K? Walking home like that?"

"I was going to run." He grabbed his coat.

"You did run — you're all sweaty. You're going to make yourself sick." Bish took a breath, helped him into the coat. "Sorry. I freaked out a bit when I saw the blizzard outside and you were nowhere to be found."

"It was early." He was shaky now, and tired. He'd worked all night. He wanted to go home.

Bish put his hat on, wrapped the scarf around his neck and got his hands into the mittens. "We're walking. The snow was too thick to drive." Bish's arm wrapped around him.

"Okay." He looked at Bish. "Okay. It's early for you to be awake."

Bish shrugged. "I had a feeling."

"Hey, guys." Rick came up, a pair of sweatpants in hand. "For the walk home, eh?"

"Thank you, Rick. I'd assumed he was wearing his running pants."

"Knight? That would be logical." He got a wink.

Bish snickered, arm tightening around him. "Come on, let's get these things on so we can get you home and warmed up properly."

"Please." He was suddenly exhausted, raw and shattered.

Bish got him dressed, got them moving, sheltering him from the storm when they went out. The walk to the house seemed endless and short, all at once.

Bish started stripping him the moment they got in. "Hot shower first."

"Okay." He was thinking through a fog.

"Did you sleep at all, babe?" Bish asked it like he knew the answer already.

Knight shook his head. "Was working."

"You should have come to bed when you were done."

"I needed to run." *Right?*

"You needed to sleep. You can always run later, baby."

Stripped down, he was led towards the big bathroom with the best shower. Bish got everything going and pushed him in. The hot shower beat down, creating steam almost immediately. Better than that, though, were Bish's hands moving over him. Knight moaned, leaning up into the hot spray.

Eventually Bish turned him, putting his hands on the tile. Two slick fingers slid into his ass, almost a part of the water as it beat down around him.

"Not cold there." No, in fact, those fingers were warm.

"I know." Bish pressed kisses over his shoulders, body pressing up against him as those fingers played, twisted, stretched, pushed deep.

He moaned and spread, a little bit lost.

"I've got you," growled Bishop, fingers pushing hard against his gland.

"Got me..." He shivered. "Oh, fuck. Right there."

"That's right. Not letting go either." Bish's fingers disappeared, the man's thick cock pressing against his hole.

"Promise?" He leaned into the stretch, the feeling familiar, right.

"I swear to God, Knight. Nothing's gonna stop me." Bish's prick kept moving into him, sinking in deeper and deeper.

"Fuck, yeah." He was flying, surrounded by heat.

Bish rumbled in reply, the sound vibrating against his back. Then his lover started to move, hips sawing back and forth. His body arched, rocking with Bishop's rhythm. Bish didn't say a word, just kept pushing into him over and over. Knight's eyes rolled back, sounds beginning to slip from him.

"Mmm..." Those rumbles of Bish's settled right in his balls.

"Bishop. Bish..." His.

Another grunt vibrated through him. Knight tried to squeeze, to grip Bishop tighter, make his lover crazy. Bishop was running the show, though, insisting on setting the rhythm. Stubborn ass. *Fine*, stubborn ass.

Bishop chuckled, as if he knew exactly what Knight was thinking.

"Laughing at me..."

"Nope." The next thrust hit his gland right on.

"Bish!" His cry rang out.

His lover stayed right there, banging on his gland over and over.

"Oh, fuck. Fuck. Harder. Harder, damn it."

Bish backed off, cock sliding all the way out before pushing slowly back in. Knight sobbed once, hungry, before he pushed back, demanding.

"Such a pushy boy."

"Fucking want you and I'm not a boy." Fuck, Bish made him ache.

"Sure you are. You're my boy, Knight." Bish hit his gland again with a good hard thrust. His answer was lost on a gasp.

Bish picked up speed and strength, fucking him with long, hard strokes. *Perfect. Fucking perfect.*

"Yes."

"Yes." Bish growled again and kept rocking, sending him flying.

His balls drew up and he groaned, body going tight.

"Not yet." Bish's hand grabbed his balls and tugged on them.

"Bishop! Fuck!" He slammed his fists against the tiles.

"I am fucking you."

Good and hard now, too, but not letting him come. Deep sounds poured out of him as his balls burned, throbbed, ached.

"Soon," murmured Bish, mouth sliding on his skin. "But only when I say."

"Bish… I ache."

"Builds character."

"Fucker."

"Your fucker." Bish moved harder, faster—just ploughing into him.

"Yes. Mine." He tried to reach for his cock, jack off.

Bish smacked his hand away. "And that's mine."

"I fucking need…" He was going to scream.

"You'll get what you need. You always do."

"I hate you." He didn't, but…

"No, you don't." Bish didn't stop thrusting.

"Uh-huh. Going to move to Hawaii all by myself."

"Someone isn't paying enough attention." Bish pulled right out, hands hard on Knight's hips.

"Bish! Bish, love, *please!*" *No. No fucking way...*

"If you're complaining as much as that, you're not paying enough attention."

He sobbed once, frustrated and tired and just pissed off. Bish's mouth latched onto his neck, suction strong as Bish started thrusting again.

"Gonna make you come and come and then I'm taking you to bed, Knight."

"Promise?" He gasped in a breath.

"I swear to fucking God, K."

"'kay." Also please. And yes.

"Gonna take care of you, baby." Bish started really fucking him again, pushing into him like Bish was going to fuck him right through the wall.

Knight groaned, body clenching, the world spinning around him, everything steamy and warm.

Bish let go of his balls, wrapped his hand instead around his prick and began tugging, moving him between cock and hand. "Okay, Knight. Okay, you come on my cock now."

"Now..." He groaned the word as Bishop's thumb dragged over the slit in his cock, tugging his orgasm out of him.

He clamped down on Bish's cock, making his lover moan, long and low, and fill him with heat.

The tears came, harsh and unexpected, tearing from him. *Jesus.* Bish stayed buried inside him, holding him there in the water. The storm passed quickly, leaving him empty...except for Bish.

Another kiss landed on his shoulder, then Bish slid out of him and turned off the water. "It's nap time for you."

"Nap time?" He felt like he was wrapped in cotton.

They stepped out of the water and Jason and Rookie were standing there—one with towels, one with huge mugs of hot chocolate.

He could hear the smile in Bish's voice as a mug was pushed into his hands and a towel wrapped around his shoulders. "When you spend all night working, you get to spend the morning napping. That's how it works."

Rookie nodded, kissed his cheek. "Jason and I are going to play in the kitchen and make scones. You go with Bish, hmm?"

"Are you sure he's all right?" Jason asked as he and Rookie left.

"Oh, yeah. He just needs to be reminded that human beings need sleep."

Bish chuckled as Rookie's voice faded away. "Come on."

"I'm okay. Really. Just working on the new pieces." Somehow there were always new pieces.

"I know, baby." Bish's arm was warm and heavy on his shoulders, leading him down the hall.

"It's going well. There'll be a show out of it." He was bleeding out onto the canvas, it felt like.

"Of course there will—you're brilliant." The words were sincere, he could feel that.

Then they were in the bedroom, the big bed made, the corner turned down for them.

"Uh-huh." Brilliant. That was him.

Bish grabbed his hot cocoa and put both mugs on the bedside table. Then his lover pushed him down onto the bed and followed, wrapping around him. *Oh.* Warm. Solid. His.

"Bish."

"Right here, Knight." Bish bit at his shoulder, then soothed the hurt with the hottest tongue. "We're not going anywhere."

"It's snowing. Hard."

"Yep." The licking turned into nuzzling.

He could feel Bishop's breath, seducing him, tempting him deeper and deeper.

"Love you, Knight. And I have you." He could feel the words *you're safe* with every breath Bish took.

Safe. Love. *Yeah...* He fell into dreams where the world was springtime.

"Is he okay? He didn't look okay." Jason shook his head. Knight was wicked, but Jason was sort of fascinated by the man and his clever, amazing mind.

"He will be, honey. Bishop knows what he needs, how to bring him back to the land of the living after he loses himself in his art." Rook brushed a hand over his back.

"Yeah?" Jason blinked and stretched. "I really should work out." Although playing in the kitchen with Rook sounded infinitely more fun.

Rook pouted and slid into his space, rubbing up against him. "Let's make scones and eat them in front of the fire — that's the best thing to do when it's blizzarding like this." Rook gave him a long look before adding, "We can talk about stuff."

"I like scones." He couldn't resist those eyes. "Did you print out the recipe?"

"I did. It's on the counter. I even paid attention and put the stick of butter in the freezer. We're supposed to grate it." Rook laughed. "Grating butter, isn't that a hoot?"

"No shit?" Jason chuckled and dared to touch Rook's cheek, stroke it. Rook nuzzled into his touch, eyes going soft and happy.

"I wouldn't lie to you. Especially not about food."

"You wouldn't." This whole situation was just... *Wow*. Who would have believed that only weeks ago he'd never been with a man and now... Now he was dangerously close to losing himself in one.

Rook beamed at him—that easy, ready smile addictive. "Okay. Kisses first, and then kissing. I mean blow jobs. No. Cooking. Kissing, blow jobs and cooking."

Jason cracked up, his laughter ringing out. "Horndog."

Rook tried to look offended and failed miserably. "I think the word you're looking for is corndog and we have some in the freezer."

"Ew. No. That's not healthy." Hot dogs were...awful.

That had Rook cracking up and the kiss that was pressed on him was full of the sound, of the happiness. They ended up leaning against the counter, wrapped up together, lips clinging. It happened with Rook. A lot.

Rook rubbed against him and slowly ended the kiss. "Wanna suck you."

He blinked then moaned. He loved when Rook said that. *Loved* it.

Rook slowly slid down to his knees, kissing and licking as he went.

"Rook..." His robe was opened, his body exposed.

"Uh-huh." Rook breathed on his cock.

"You're so...good..." At this. At kisses. At making him feel good.

Rook beamed up at him. "Love you too, honey." Then the man swallowed his cock whole.

Jason gasped, eyes wide as he watched his prick disappear. Rook pulled back again, Jason's glistening prick sliding from between his lips.

"Oh, God. Please." He reached down and stroked Rook's hair.

Rook pulled off long enough to say, "I love how you beg." Then Rook took him back down again.

His world spun and he held on to the edge of the counter. Rook's head bobbed, that mouth sliding up and down his prick. *Fuck. He... It... This... Damn.* The words floated through the air. The hum around his cock sent vibrations right to his balls.

Jason whimpered and shot. No matter how many times Rook did that to him — and it was often — it was always amazing.

Rook swallowed him down and cleaned his cock thoroughly, pulling off just before it became too much sensation. He was given a shit-eating grin, Rook looking so pleased.

"Yum!"

"Good morning." He blinked and swayed, his knees weak.

"It is!" Rook grabbed his ass playfully, then tied his robe back up. "Okay. Conversation and scones. I think it's about time we talked about safewords."

"I'll get the butter." *Safewords, huh?*

"The stick in the freezer, honey. We can take turns grating it, because that's got to be something everyone should do at least once in their life." Rook looked at the recipe and started pulling the other ingredients out.

Going by past experience, the cooking would happen with enthusiasm and a huge mess would be made, which Rook would laugh and shrug about and either he or Bish would clean up later. Rook was very hit or miss when it came to cooking — more miss than hit — but he had a lot of enthusiasm, like with everything he did.

Jason thought it was sort of incredibly adorable.

He found the butter and grabbed himself a banana on the way by.

"Oh, God, I love the way you eat those." Rook stopped what he was doing and set a hip against the counter, looking at him.

"Aren't we grating butter?" He handed the stick over and peeled the banana. "And they have lots of potassium."

"Uh-huh." Rook put the stick of butter in the bowl he'd taken out of the cupboard. "Let me watch you blow the banana first."

"I…" Now he was never going to be able to eat the damned thing.

Rook licked his lips and smiled.

"I can just eat it, right?"

"Uh-huh. Go for it."

Oh, thank God. He ate the banana, trying not to blush.

Rook moaned and sighed happily. "I do love watching you eat those…"

He snorted around the fruit in his mouth, stupid with happiness.

It was only when he was done that Rook sighed again and went back to fetching ingredients and measuring cups.

He moved behind Rook, hands on the man's shoulders. "You okay?"

"Mmm. I am, honey. I was just enjoying watching you. That feels good."

"Are we serious about piercing…things?"

Rook nodded. "Oh, yes." Rook turned and looped both arms around his waist. "They're not permanent and you'd look amazing with some pretty rings to play with."

"I don't know. I don't… I'm not sure I'm comfortable with that."

"I think we should definitely talk about safewords, honey. You need to know because that's the way you make anything stop."

"Okay. What's yours?" He liked that idea.

"Mine is 'guillotine' because there's no way I'd accidentally say that."

"Guillotine? Like off with his head?" *Seriously*?

Rook laughed and nodded. "Well, it has to be something easy to remember and that you wouldn't normally use. There's no way I'm going to say guillotine ever and not mean it as my safeword. And I'm hardly going to forget it, am I?"

"Right. Do Bishop and Knight have one?"

"Yep. Knight's is 'wonderland' and Bishop's is 'Alaska'."

He pondered that. "Have you ever used it?"

All the while, Rook cooked and he touched, watching the chaos.

Rook actually blushed. "You might have noticed I'm kind of a slut, right? Well, they've never done anything to me I wanted them to stop."

"No? If you did, would they be angry?" That was the real question.

"No! Not at all, honey. That's the point of a safeword. It's so you can stop everything if you have to. Sometimes…well, Knight especially, will say 'stop' and not mean it. What he means is 'don't you dare stop, Bish'. He needs to fight it, though. So Bish gives that to him. But, to make sure he's safe, there has to be a way for things to stop, for Bish—or me or whatever—to know that he actually means it this time."

Rook grabbed a cookie tray and lined it with parchment paper. "Now Bish—sometimes he needs to get Knight's attention, or mine if I'm off in 'oh-God-it's-good-and-I'm-not-paying-any-attention land' and he'll use his safeword and that's how we know he's being really serious and we need to stop and listen and talk about stuff. You would use yours if you needed everything to stop, and it would and nobody would be mad." Rook laughed. "Maybe a little frustrated and horny, but not mad, okay? I know you signed a contract that said we could do whatever we wanted to you as long as it wasn't permanent, but nobody wants to do anything to you that you truly don't want."

"I know that." He'd been here long enough to know that the contract was part of the kink, but that was it. He was here because he was fascinated.

They wanted him here.

"So are you going to pick a safeword?"

"I suppose. I just don't know what I want to pick." He rescued the bowl of dough — or was it batter? — as it tried to spill.

"Oh, nice catch!" Rook laughed and managed to knock the bag of flour with his elbow. It fell over and flour poured out onto the floor. "Oops!"

"You take this. I'll grab the broom." He chuckled and headed for the utility closet.

Rook took the bowl and began forming the scones and putting them on the tray. The oven beeped at them, letting them know it was at temperature.

"Do you think they'll turn out?" Rook asked. "We might have to go to the bakery."

"It's really coming down... I think we'll try them."

"Oh, I forgot about the snow." Rook crossed his fingers and put the scones into the oven. He even remembered to turn on the timer.

"Would you like eggs or something, too? Or just more hot cocoa?" Jason asked.

"I like the scrambled eggs you make."

Rook liked everything he made, it seemed.

Of course Jason wouldn't be bragging if he said he was the best cook in the house — he didn't exactly have a lot of competition. "Okay. Scrambled eggs it is."

Rook settled on one of the stools and put his chin in his hands, watching every move Jason made.

"So, why do you figure Knight is so…intense? Has he always been this way?" He grabbed half a dozen eggs, some milk, and a bowl.

"Uh-huh. He's an *artist*. They're all crazy. Van Gogh cut off his own ear, you know. Bish makes sure Knight doesn't lose it too badly. The biggest problem is he forgets to sleep. Lack of sleep makes everyone cranky."

"I guess so. It's unhealthy." He started cracking eggs.

"That's why Bish makes sure he sleeps. Before Bish, he never slept."

"Never? Wow. I bet he was psychotic."

"Uh-huh. For a while he did a lot of drugs. And he went through a period where he drank all the time." Rook smiled. "It's better now."

"Ah. Good. I'm glad." He didn't particularly *like* Knight, but he was intrigued by the man.

Rook beamed. "Me, too. I don't know what I would do without either of them. Or you, either."

"You'd have found someone else."

"But it's the three of you I care about, not someone else. You guys. Specifically."

"Yeah. I…I don't want other guys." He wanted them.

"Just us." Rook came over and hugged him hard.

"Just you."

Mostly Rook. Bish was a good friend and Knight excited him, but Rook… Rook's hug got tighter and the kiss that landed on his shoulder was soft, almost reverent.

He leaned against him, taking a second before he got a pan. He could feel Rook's smile against his shoulder. "Thank you." *For everything.*

"Mmm, you're welcome, honey." He got another kiss, this one to the side of his neck. "You still haven't picked a safeword. It's important that you have one."

He put the pan on the stove and looked at it for a long moment. "Is…is 'shotgun' okay?" He'd be able to remember that and he didn't think he'd ever say it by accident.

"It's perfect! I'll make sure everyone knows. Now make me eggs, I'm starving!"

"You got it."

Eggs it was.

Chapter Five

Rook poured wine for everyone and checked the clock. Ten minutes till piercer! He was looking forward to this. So much. He touched his nipples, looked down at them. Later tonight they'd be pierced. Knight was in the studio, ignoring them. Jason was in the shower, hiding. Bish was gloating.

"Are you going to drag Knight out of his studio before or after the guy shows up?"

Bish grinned. "Before. You going to get your boy?"

He nodded. "Guiches for both of them, right?" He'd thought about it and figured Jason would be happier with a piercing that was hidden — that would be theirs and theirs alone.

Bishop chuckled. "I'm getting Knight the full deal. I want that pretty cock pierced."

"Oh, God." He groaned and rubbed up against Bishop. "I love your brain."

Bish grabbed him. "Love you, Rookie. You ready to get those titties pierced?"

A shiver of excitement went through him. "I am!"

"Good. It's going to be so hot, touching them."

He gasped. "It is. I can't wait." He couldn't.

He shared a kiss with Bish, the wet sounds of it seductive and wonderful. Bish's fingers pinched and tugged his nipples, hard enough to make him moan.

"God, it's going to be wonderful, isn't it?" He grinned up at Bish. "You getting anything done?"

Bish shook his head. "I want to be in top form to drive Knight crazy. The last big painting was done last night."

"Really, really the last one?" Knight had been crazy working for weeks.

"Yes." Bish looked deadly serious. "Really, really the last one for the winter. He's ours until spring, damn it."

He kissed Bish hard. "Thank you for keeping him here with us, Bishie. I love you both."

"Love you, Rookie." Bish rubbed his cheekbone with one thick thumb. "I want you to go first, then the kid, then Knight last."

"I promise not to scream. Too much."

"You won't scream. You won't want to scare Jase."

Rook nodded. He knew. "I'll be brave, I swear."

"You are brave, Rookie." Bish made him feel ten thousand feet tall.

He gave his lover a long, hard kiss. "Let's go get our boys."

"Meet you here in five."

"It's a deal."

He headed for the bathroom to find Jason and get the party started. Jason was out of the shower, dressed in a loose pair of sweats and a huge sweater, standing in the bathroom, looking stunned.

He went over and slid his hands over Jason's shoulders. "Hey, honey."

"Hey." Jason looked at him, cheeks pale. "I don't know if I can do this."

"You can. You can do anything. I'm going first." He rubbed. "My nipples."

"Aren't you scared?"

Sweet, beautiful man.

He shook his head. "Excited. I am excited."

"Yeah? I just..." Jason ducked his head. "I don't know."

"Why don't you think you can do it?"

"Because I'll have to spread and... I just... That's private."

"It'll just be the four of us and the piercer. And he will never tell another soul what he sees."

"I guess."

"I would promise to distract you, but there will be a guy putting a needle through some sensitive bits and I'm guessing it's going to be a little hard to ignore, even with my considerable skills." He kept his tone light, teasing Jason gently.

"Yeah. I think so."

He rubbed against Jason, then took his lover's hand. "Come on. Bish and Knight will already be in the living room and we want to be all together when the piercer gets here."

"I... Okay. Okay, I guess."

He tugged and Jason followed.

Bish and Knight were waiting in the living room for them, Knight pacing in front of the window. Someone was even more wound up than Jason.

"...have work to do!"

"No, you finished last night. Annie picked up the pieces to frame." Bish sounded solid and firm.

"I'm going first," Rook told Knight, hoping to help defuse Knight's tantrum.

"I'm not doing this." Knight looked furious, scared, stressed, and exhausted. Rook would bet his entire fortune that, after tonight, the man stayed in bed for a couple of days.

He considered Knight for a long moment then went over and wrapped his arms around him, kissing him soundly just to get his attention. Knight leaned into his arms, pulled him in tight and held on. Oh, that was better. Rook snuggled them up close together and kept kissing.

The doorbell rang and Bish headed out of the room. Rook just held on. He held one hand out to Jason, fingers wrapping tightly when Jason's hand met his. There—he had them both, was giving them both his support and love. He drew Jason into their kiss, encouraging Jase to give Knight the attention he needed.

It didn't matter that Bish had gone to the door to let the piercer in—what mattered was that the three of them were kissing, making each other feel good.

Rook moaned happily.

A soft chuckle sounded. "They're beautiful, my friend."

"I know. I'm a very lucky man." Bish sounded so proud, and it made Rook preen.

"You are. Where do you want me to set up?"

Rook looked over and saw a lovely dark-skinned man with electric green eyes.

Bish gave him a smile and nodded towards the couch. "They'll sit together on the couch, support each other through the piercings."

"And what do you want done? I brought a selection of rings."

Rook parted from his lovers' lips and looped his arms through theirs, bringing them over to the couch. "I'm getting my nipples done!"

"Excellent. Do you all want matching rings?" He got a warm smile. "I'm Luke, by the way."

"Oh, matching rings…" Rook looked at Jason and at Knight, then over to Bish, giving them his best needy eyes. "Please?"

"Whatever you want, Rookie. Jason's getting a guiche and my Knight's getting nipples, cock, and guiche."

Luke whistled. "Impressive."

"I am not."

Rook rubbed up against Knight. "You know you are, K. Bishop said so."

"No."

Luke looked at Bishop. "We got a problem?"

Bishop shook his head. "He'll come around. Trust me."

Rook grinned and went over to the beautiful man. "I'm going first. Both nipples. You're going to take care of me, right?"

"I'll make it good. I'm the best."

Rook shivered, his nipples tightening up. "Where do you want me, Luke?" He gave Bish a wink.

"I brought my stuff. You just need to take off your shirt and settle."

Rook bounced and nodded, peeling off his shirt easily. Knight groaned and Jason made a soft sound like a sigh. He blew kisses at his lovers and settled between them. "You guys can help keep me still." He grabbed Jason's hand and squeezed tight.

Then he took Knight's hand, too. "I'm ready." He sure was—his nipples were already hard in anticipation and his cock was totally interested in the way the coming piercing was making him a little nervous and a lot excited.

"I can see that." Luke winked at him, then offered Bish a stunning smile. "I get to flirt, right?"

Bish's chuckle was warm and it made Rook's nipples go even tighter. "I do believe it's a requirement, Luke."

Rook nodded. "Just because we've all ordered doesn't mean we can't keep looking at the menu." He liked looking, it made the flavour of the 'meals' he had all the better.

"I'm one hell of a menu, pretty boy." Luke chuckled as he started unpacking—needles, a pen, a spray bottle.

Rook was suddenly distracted from the flirting by the stuff. Maybe he was a touch more nervous than he'd been to start with. He had to be strong, though. If he freaked out about just his nipples, Jason and Knight were never going to get their stuff done.

He licked his lips and managed a half flirt back, "You definitely are…"

Jason's hand tightened around his and Knight tried to let go altogether. Rook didn't let him. Knight was staying. They were doing this because Bish wanted them to. And because it was sexy. And hot.

He wriggled.

Luke met his eyes. "It's hot, pretty boy. I promise. There's a little burn and then a high."

He nodded, trusting the man Bish had brought into their home. "I'm ready. I'm so ready."

"I'm going to mark you first, make sure they're straight. I need you to make sure they're hard for me."

"I don't think that's going to be a problem." Everything about him was hard, from the curl of his toes to the way his fingers clung to his lovers'. He looked up into Bishop's eyes and the expression there took his breath away.

He was so loved.

The pen marked each side of each nipple, the little touch enough to make him shiver.

"It's cold," he whispered.

"They'll be hot in a second. How does it look, Bish?"

Rook puffed his chest out proudly, waiting for Bish's pronouncement.

"Perfect. They're going to be so hot, Rookie."

Knight frowned. "Let me look. I want them perfect, damn it."

Beaming, he turned to Knight, letting his artistic lover see.

Knight looked closely, head tilting. "Move the left side of the left nipple up, just a hair."

Luke wiped the ink away, re-marked, and Knight nodded.

Rook touched Knight's cheek. "For sure, K?" His voice was husky with need, his cock pushing against his sweats.

"I won't have you…ill-marked."

"My Knight." He kissed Knight softly, then grabbed his lover's hand again. "Okay, Luke. I'm approved. Let's do this."

"You got it." It didn't take long for Luke to take one nipple in a pair of forceps and tell him to breathe…then the needle was in, the antiseptic stinging.

His eyes went wide and he bit his bottom lip, hard, to keep from gasping. "Oh."

"Now the ring. You ready?" Luke didn't wait for him to answer, just tugged the needle out, pushed the ring in and one was done.

"Oh my God!" A shudder went through him and he nearly came.

"Rook?" Jason looked at him, eyes wide.

"I think the second one is going to make me come. Does that make me a slut?"

"No." Bish smiled. "Jase, kid. I want you to suck him."

"What?"

"Oh, yes, please. God, that would feel amazing."

"But…" Jason looked at Luke, who smiled.

"I've seen it, sweetheart. I've done it. I promise I won't be upset."

Rook stroked Jason's hair. "I'd love it if you did."

"F-for you, Rook." God, Jason looked at him like he was the centre of the earth. He fell in love with the man a little bit more.

Spreading his legs, he slid his hands through Jason's hair. Knight helped, easing his cock out of his sweats, but, for once, didn't say anything to make Jason wig.

"Gently," he murmured. "I'm already right there."

He pushed his chest out, offering his unpierced nipple to Luke as the pierced one throbbed in time with his heartbeat.

"You be still for me." Luke met his eyes.

"I will, I swear." His fingers tightened on Jason's head and he groaned as Jason's sweet tongue touched the tip of his prick.

That mouth took him, so gentle, and Luke grabbed his nipple with the forceps. *Oh, God. Oh, God.* He bit his lower lip and held tight to Jason's head and did his very best not to let the excitement and pleasure coursing through him make him move.

"Deep breath."

He sucked in a breath and the needle went in and he keened. He was going to come. Oh, God, he was. "Hurry. Hurry. Hurry."

"Here it comes."

Jason sucked and the ring tugged and Knight kissed his ear and…boom. He shot hard down Jason's throat, the keening sound still coming out of his throat. It was a perfect storm of *hot*.

"Oh, that was nice." Luke chuckled softly, and the sound wasn't mean, but fond and happy and warm.

Rook sank back, Knight right there to catch him as his sweet Jason licked and sucked and did his damndest to keep him hard.

"Nice is an understatement," he managed. "It was…well, orgasmic."

"Hell, yes. Who's next?"

Thank God Bish answered, because Rook was pretty sure he was melted.

"Jason's next. A guiche."

Jason swallowed hard around his cock and he groaned.

"It's *so* good, honey. Like nothing I've ever felt before." He slid his hands over Jason's head, along the broad shoulders.

Jason lifted his head, eyes meeting his, wide and scared.

Rook leaned in until their foreheads were pressing together. "I'll be right here the whole time. I'll hold you. And, if you hate it, tomorrow we can pull it out."

"Promise?"

"I swear, honey. Bish, tell him."

"Rook is right," put in Bish. "None of this needs to be permanent."

"What do I have to do?"

"The pretty man will tell us." Now that the utter intensity was gone, Rook felt able to flirt again.

"Have you shaved him?"

Jason's eyes went wider.

"I'll do it. I'll be so careful, honey."

"He can lean over the back of the sofa, and we'll shave him, then get it done."

"And that's given me such wicked ideas about shaving your pubes, honey." Rook kissed Jason, letting his delight and love show.

"Not like this, please."

"No, I mean in a few days. In the tub. With lots of licking and sucking and making love." Rook moved Jason, and Rook was proud to see Knight slide in close, offer support.

"You want me to do it, honey? Or you want Bish to do it while I kiss you?"

"I want you to kiss me."

He gave Jason his best smile. "I was hoping you'd say that." He gave Bish a quick kiss first. "Be gentle with the razor." Then he went around and settled in front of Jason, stroking the red cheeks before pressing their lips together.

Jason was a single breath from pure panic. He held Jason's eyes and put everything he had into that kiss, everything he felt for Jason. It was love, after all. Honest to God true love. He didn't know how he'd got so lucky. Through his kisses, he breathed his very self into Jason.

"Jesus, that's fine." Luke's voice sounded awed and Rook just ignored it. He slid his hands through Jason's hair, silently urging Jason to ignore it, too.

"Rook." There were tears in Jason's eyes, but Rook thought the panic was fading.

"You're going to be even more beautiful with it," he whispered.

"How are your nipples?"

"Throbbing. I'm hard again." He giggled softly. "I think I'm going to be horny all the time for a while."

"And this is different from usual how?" Bishop asked.

Jason actually smiled for him. He waved his middle finger back in Bish's general direction.

"Going to shave you now, kiddo." Bish sounded solid and sure and Rook figured it had to be giving Jason confidence.

"Bish has shaved me, honey. He's got a real good touch."

"Okay, Rook. Okay. I don't know about this."

"Why not? The hardest part is done—you're exposed. The ring is going to be amazing."

Bishop nodded, hand on Jason's ass. "It's going to feel so good."

"We won't be able to play with it for a while, but it'll be there. You'll be aware of it and it'll make everything *more*."

"More?" Jason reached for him, squeezed his fingers.

"Uh-huh. These nipple rings? They're making me hard just being there."

"They're pretty."

He preened, inordinately pleased by Jason's comment. "Thank you, honey."

Knight stood up, hand sliding over Jason's back. "You're doing good."

Rook beamed over at Knight. No matter what Knight wanted people to think, he was a sweetheart deep inside. Knight moved to pour himself a drink and Bishop started shaving, so Rook could focus on Jason.

"This is our ring to you, Jason. Our gift."

"Not that kind of ring, though."

"No, this one is special. Like you." He meant every word of it—he hoped Jason realised that.

Jason smiled, at least until Bishop backed off. "He's all yours, Luke."

"Right here, honey. You keep looking right at me."

"It's not bad, kid. I promise. I have four and a full ladder," Luke reassured gently.

"A ladder. Wow, that's like bars all the way up his cock." Rook kept holding Jason's gaze, though a small part of him wanted to look at Luke, to see if he could tell now that he knew the ladder was there.

"I won't do that." Jason stiffened as Luke marked the places where the holes would go.

Rook shook his head. "No. I don't want anything in your cock. It's perfect just the way it is."

"Unlike mine?" Knight growled.

The sound of Bish's hand hitting Knight's butt was loud.

Rook shook his head. It wasn't like that at all and Knight knew it. Still, he couldn't help but reassure his lover. "I believe the ring in your cock is for *your* pleasure, K. And mine when you fuck me with it. Besides, I know Bish only wants it done because he knows you want it, too." Bish never pushed either of them further than they could go and Knight needed so much.

He turned his attention back to Jason and smiled to let Jason know he was still right there.

"You ready?"

Jason shook his head. "No."

Then Jase gasped, his eyes huge. Rook grabbed hold of Jason's arms and held on tight, his mouth pressing to Jason's. He would help Jason through this, make it positive.

"There you go, sweet boy. It's done."

Jason moaned into his lips, looked at him. "Please. Please, Rook. Take me to your room?"

He looked over at Bish and his lover nodded, winked, one hand on Knight's lower back. "Come on, honey. I can't wait to see!"

Jason stood, grabbed his sweats and tugged them up, not looking at anyone.

Rook took his hand and squeezed it. "We'll see you guys back in the bedroom when you're done. I want to see Knight's new jewellery."

Then he tugged Jason down the hall, his own nipples throbbing with every step.

Chapter Six

Bish watched Rook lead Jason away. Their sweet Rook would take good care of Jason, ease the kid's nerves. He had a boy with nerves of his own to soothe.

"You ready, Knight?" he asked, hand drawing circles in the small of Knight's back.

"I'm not doing this."

"You need it, baby. You need to know I see you, that we all see you."

Knight shook his head, eyes wild. "You're out of your fucking mind."

He grabbed Knight and hauled him in close, kissing the words out of his mouth. They were going to do this — going to pierce his nips, his cock and behind those balls — then Bish was taking Knight to bed for days.

"We'll start with the cock." That was going to be the hardest of them.

"No."

Luke chuckled. "You had one eager one…"

"I did. Knight just wants me to convince him. Don't you, boy?" Bish saw Knight. He saw Knight every moment of the day.

"Not a fucking boy, you asshole."

"You're mine, Knight. Entirely."

"Fuck you."

He spun Knight around and peppered that sweet ass with some hard, sharp blows. "Respect, Knight. For yourself and for me."

"Bas...bastard."

"Your bastard." He could out-stubborn Knight. He did it all the damn time.

He stripped Knight's sweats off, sat on the sofa with Knight in his lap. "Do his prick first."

Luke looked at him. "I'm not doing it if he's not willing, man. I mean—I get it, if it's a game, but I need to know."

"Fair enough." Bish looked at his lover. "Knight?"

Knight looked at him, his eyes huge, wide.

"Luke needs to hear from you that you're willing to do this."

"I..." Knight glared at him, so pissed off, so fucking furious. "I hate you."

"No, you don't." He didn't believe that for a second. And if he truly thought Knight didn't want this, couldn't take it, he'd never have suggested it. His lover needed to be pushed, though, and pushed hard.

Knight looked at Luke, so angry. "My fucking safeword is 'wonderland'."

Bish rubbed Knight's back. "Good boy." Then he gave Luke a rueful grin. "I imagine that's what you needed to hear, hmm?"

"That's totally cool, man. Now he can fight all he wants. I hear that word, everything stops."

"Cool." He gave Knight a hard kiss. "All right, babe, sweats off so we can get the rest of this party started."

"I said no."

He grinned. God, he loved this game, loved pushing, loved that Knight trusted him. "I'm not going to ask again. You have five seconds before I tear them off."

Knight flipped him off.

He snorted and grabbed at the waistband, tugging the sweats down. Then he grabbed Knight's legs, spread his boy wide. "Do his cock first, then the guiche. Then we'll pierce his pretty nips."

Knight started fighting him.

"You want this done right, don't you?" He bit at Knight's shoulder. "You stay still when it starts."

"Not my cock, Bish. I'll scream."

"Then scream, K. Let us hear you."

Luke cleaned Knight's prick, touch light, gentle. "You ready?"

"No."

"He's ready. Do you need me to hold his prick?" Bish asked?

Luke shook his head. "You hold his hips and keep him from grabbing me."

"Put your arms on my hips, Knight."

Knight did as he was asked, proving to Bish that his boy was going to be with him on this, no matter what was coming out of his mouth.

He slid his hands through and around Knight's arms and grabbed his lover's hips. "Got you, K. I see you. I see every inch of you."

"Don't do this. I don't want it."

Luke cleaned the tip of Knight's cock, squeezed the tip, and grabbed a curled needle. "Okay, deep breath in."

"You might not want it, K, but I can feel how badly you need it."

Knight jerked, a sharp cry sounding, his boy fighting him hard.

"Breathe, K. You need to breathe for me and stay fucking still so this thing goes right where we want it."

"Please, Bish…" Knight gulped in panicked gasps of air.

"Here we go."

He watched the needle go in, and Knight keened.

"That's it, K. Let me hear you, baby. Let me hear every fucking sound."

"Oh, fuck. Oh, fuck…" Knight groaned as the ring went in, then Luke went immediately to the guiche. Knight was already shaved. Bish had done that this morning.

"The fucking is coming, babe. I'll give you everything you need."

"Never. Never letting you in again. You bastard." Knight groaned again as the guiche needle went in.

"Gonna do it when your piercings are done."

"Never again."

"You'd hate it if I never fucked you again."

"Hate you." Knight winced and tried to pull away as the ring went in. "Let me up. No more."

"You're staying right here and you're getting rings in your nipples." He squeezed Knight's hips hard. God, Knight was stunning—so brave, so strong, and his. "Here comes the nipples, baby."

"No…" Knight groaned, sobbing softly. "I hate you." Those nipples were hard and dark, so needy.

"No, you don't." He nipped at Knight's neck.

"Uh-huh."

"These should feel almost good, honey. You've got so many endorphins from the first two now." Luke smiled softly.

"You hear that? They're going to feel amazing." Bish leant forward, pushing Knight's chest out.

"Make sure they're not ugly."

"Baby, you couldn't do ugly if you fucking tried."

Luke smiled, the look gentle. "They'll be perfect. I swear."

"See, Knight, I brought you the best." He wouldn't let anyone touch Knight if they weren't at the top of their game.

"I want to go to bed. I'm so fucking wigged."

"Nipples first. We're going to do this right." He'd cleared his schedule for days.

Luke marked Knight, working quickly and quietly, and soon one of Knight's nipples was in the forceps.

"Here it comes, baby." He slid one hand forward, wrapping it around Knight's cock.

Knight whimpered and shook his head, but the sweet, pierced cock jerked, trying to fill in his hand.

"That's it. Let the wave carry you."

The needle went in and Knight moaned, his cock throbbing.

"Mmm. Yeah, baby. I've got you. I've got you."

"Promise me you'll make everyone go away and leave me alone for a while. Promise." Knight's voice was thick with so much need.

"It'll just be the four of us. For as long as you need."

The second nipple was grabbed and Knight groaned, fighting him.

He squeezed hard on Knight's cock. "Be still."

"No more."

Luke pushed the needle through and Knight screamed like the man was killing him.

Bish held on tight, face buried in Knight's neck to breathe his lover in. "Let it all out, K."

Knight stormed for him, screaming and releasing, then collapsing in his arms.

Luke grabbed his things, silent as a mouse and nodded to him, mouthing, *We'll settle up later – call me.*

He mouthed back, "*Thank you*," wrapping his arms around his lover, holding on, making sure Knight knew he was right there.

Luke disappeared, leaving him with his sobbing, shaken lover.

"I've got you," he promised Knight. "I'll always have you."

He lifted his lover and headed for his bedroom where they could hide, where he could touch.

The lights were on, the glow soft and gentle, and a leather-scented candle flickered on the nightstand. The covers had been turned back. Rook's touch was there, making the room warm and right, putting their lover right there with them in spirit, even though he wasn't there in body.

Bish put Knight in the centre of the bed and stripped quickly before wrapping around Knight again. Knight pulled away from him, then pushed close. *Sweet, needy man.*

He kissed the top of Knight's head. "I bet they're throbbing with your heartbeat."

"I want them out."

"Not going to happen, baby." He had Knight's wrists in one hand, fingers petting the lean belly.

"No?"

"No, baby. I like 'em and you need them." They were fucking stunning, actually.

"I can't believe you did this to me."

"Can't you?" He rolled them, putting Knight on his back, and straddled his lover's belly, holding the thin wrists up over Knight's head.

"No." Knight's eyes were so hungry, so needy and open for him.

"You can't believe that I saw you? That I saw what you needed and gave it to you?"

"My head hurts. I have work to do. I can't think."

He knew. He knew it. "You're not supposed to think."

Knight's eyes squeezed closed, so tight. Bish pressed their lips together, bent over his boy as he kissed Knight silly. God, he loved this fine, beautiful son of a bitch.

The kiss ended and he nibbled his way to Knight's ear. "I know you can feel your heartbeat in all four rings. You can feel them throbbing. So hot."

Knight whimpered and shook his head. That pretty pierced cock, though — it filled.

"You can't lie to me, baby."

"Bish…"

He hummed at the soft word, rocking Knight gently. "Right here, baby. Treating you right." He kept kissing, one long touch after another, until the tears stopped. "That's my boy. My fucking boy." He stroked Knight's hair. "I want to look."

"What if they're ugly?"

"Then I'll take them out. They aren't going to be ugly, though."

Knight looked so fucking tired, but those eyes were focused on him now. Present. He'd make Knight feel amazing, make him come, then he'd insist his lover sleep. The second his lover woke up, they'd do it again. And again.

"Hold on to the headboard." He was going to stretch Knight out and look his fill.

"What?"

He took Knight's hand, gently brought it up and eased it into a fur-lined cuff. Then he did the other one. "I said hold on to the headboard."

"You… I hate you." The words were almost gentle.

He kissed Knight softly. "Love you, too."

Then he shifted, moving to look at his boy. The sweet nipples were red and angry-looking, but his Knight's pretty cock looked amazing.

He wanted so much to play with the ring, but he knew better and didn't. He did put his hands on Knight's thighs and press. "Open up for me, baby. Let me see the guiche."

Those thighs spread for him, Knight beginning to relax, to melt for him.

"Oh, fuck." The ring there was like a little surprise gift.

"Is it okay?"

"It's fucking stunning, baby." He touched that ring, so carefully — the skin hot, stretched over the metal. "I can't wait to play."

"It burns."

He bet it did. "It's good, huh?" He slid his fingers around and around the ring.

Knight shrugged. "I don't know."

He snapped his fingers across the top of Knight's thighs.

"Bish!" A look of pure shock covered Knight's face.

"That's better. I don't want your shrugs and your 'I don't know's."

"It's the truth, you bastard! I don't know."

"Yes, you do."

Knight started fighting the cuffs, frowning mightily at him, cursing him.

He smacked Knight's thighs again. "Deep down, you know. And you can fight me all you want, but you know you crave the pain. You need it."

"Fucking moving out. Fucking finding a place in Mexico." Knight began to ramp up, heading back into that wild emotion.

He dove into Knight's rant, pushing his tongue into Knight's mouth. *Come on, baby, open up. Let me in, let me help you.*

He kept pressing, kept kissing, sliding his fingers down to grip Knight's hip. He moved his thumb, pressed in, nice and slow. There was going to be a bruise there. There and all over Knight's body. One bruise after another, painting the sweet skin. Gold rings and dark bruises to turn his artist into a piece of art himself.

Bish moved his grip to Knight's upper thigh, digging his thumb in there, too. Knight groaned, but pushed into the touch, into his thumb. He rolled it so his nail dug in as well.

"Bish... Easy. Please. No more sharpness, not today."

"Just the bruises, hmm?" He eased his nail back, letting his thumb make Knight ache gently.

"Please."

He rewarded Knight with a soft, easy kiss. He moved and pressed a spot near the bottom of Knight's ribs. Knight shifted, just slightly. Bish raised one of his eyebrows, his hand staying right where it was. Knight didn't respond, but didn't move again. Bish leaned in to bite at that tempting lower lip. Knight tried to pull away, shook his head.

He grabbed Knight's chin, letting his fingers dig in as he held it in place, taking the biting kiss he wanted. Knight growled, kissed him back for a few heartbeats, then pulled back. Bish followed, growling right back.

"Back off." Knight moaned, pressing his knee between his legs.

"Why? Because you're liking it?"

"Yes."

He offered a long kiss for Knight's honesty. "Sexy fucker."

"I don't feel sexy. I feel…shivery."

He licked Knight's lower lip and blew on the man's right nipple. *Yep. Shivery.* He pushed his thumb against Knight's collarbone and blew over the other nipple.

"No…" That nipple tightened, the ring shifting.

He wanted to play with it. It was the only drawback to piercing, really—the waiting. He let his tongue touch the tip—just barely, just enough to taste. It tasted amazing. His boy tasted so good. Knight swallowed hard, moving restlessly.

"Sweet love." Bish turned his head and bit the inside of Knight's thigh.

Knight moaned for him, opening his lips, tongue flicking out. Yeah, he had his boy's attention now. He licked where he'd bitten.

"Ass." Knight actually smiled.

"I've got one. You've got one, too." He pushed Knight's leg up and licked the man's ass.

Knight laughed for him and he smiled, then rubbed one cheek on that hot ass. While he was down there, he licked at Knight's hole. The tiny ring of muscles twitched and moved under his tongue. Humming, he licked again, his fingers digging into Knight's inner thighs.

"Bish. Yes. God, yes."

He could hear the cuff chains rattling. He spread Knight's legs wider to press a sucking kiss on that sweet little hole.

"I'm tired, Mouse. Like in my bones, you know? Like I can't breathe."

He could hear the weariness in Knight's voice as his lover voiced his private nickname, so deep it was almost sharp.

"I know, baby. Why do you think we had this little party, hmm?"

"Because you're evil and mean."

He laughed and pinched Knight's inner thigh. Knight squeaked, but there was laughter there — something Bish could work with. Knight needed more than anyone he'd ever met.

He grabbed the lube and slicked his fingers up, then pushed two into Knight without any fucking fanfare.

"Yes…" Knight's knees drew up, giving him more.

He curled his fingers, finding Knight's gland…right…

"Mouse!"

There. That was what he was looking for. He pegged it again, watching Knight's face. The look there was beginning to slide into bliss. He pushed in a third finger, stretching Knight as he kept working the little gland, not letting up for a moment. Soft moans started sounding, filling the air.

He kept the pressure up with his free hand, pushing his thumb into Knight's flesh to draw up marks. He loved painting his artist.

When every line of Knight's body was straining towards him, he let his fingers slide away, pushing his cock to that little hole. He was careful not to catch the guiche as he pressed in.

"Take your knees, baby." If Knight rolled himself up, it'd be easier to keep clear of the piercing.

Knight nodded, raised his knees and spread.

"Oh, fucking perfect." He pushed all the way in, nodding as his balls squished up against Knight's ass.

Knight moaned, toes curling. Hands on the backs of Knight's thighs, he helped his lover keep those legs up, and started humping. He could see the reflection of the light on Knight's nipple rings. That vision hit him right in the balls and he moved faster, harder.

"So beautiful." Knight was looking right at him.

"That'd be you, baby."

"Don't stop, okay?"

"Never." He pushed in harder.

Knight nodded, lips parting as they moved together. He worked his prick in and out, holding Knight's gaze. Knight's fingers wrapped around the cuff chains, using the tension to bear down against him.

"Yes! Fuck! Knight!" He jerked into Knight, his movements losing their finesse.

"My Mouse. Right... Oh, fuck. Right there."

"I know." He kept pegging Knight's gland, so fucking close he could taste it. He wasn't coming until Knight did, though. *Damn it.*

"Come on. Come on." Knight moaned, head tossing.

"You first, baby."

"Uhn..." Knight was trying to argue, Bish could tell. He grabbed Knight's prick around the middle and gave a few half-jacks, staying well away from the pretty ring shining at the top.

"Oh. Oh, Bish. What if...? What if I can't come?"

He snorted. "You can come."

Pushing in hard, he hit Knight's gland.

Knight arched, a sharp cry sounding. "Again!"

"Pushy." And he loved it. He nailed Knight's gland a few more times.

"Yes! Yes! Mouse, love!" Knight pulled furiously on the cuffs. "The tip. Please. Just once. Need it." Greedy, pushy, beautiful man.

Bishop let his hand move up along Knight's prick, then he very carefully pushed his thumb into Knight's slit. Knight screamed, and his spunk sprayed, back bowing impossibly. Bishop watched, even as his own body tightened, Knight's orgasm bringing about his own.

Perfect. Fucking perfect.

Knight came and came, body shuddering and shifting through every second of it. Bish kept moving his hips, kept nudging Knight's gland, making it last for both of them. By the time Knight relaxed, the man was open-mouthed, his eyes closed, totally lost in pleasure.

Bish rolled his hips a bit more and pulled out, collapsing next to Knight, one hand on the man's belly to keep them connected.

Knight moaned. "Love."

Yeah. Yeah. He nodded, patted Knight's belly. "Always."

Knight sighed, entire body relaxing, melting down into the mattress, cuffed hands lax.

Now Knight would sleep for hours and, when he woke, Bish would feed him, then love him into submission yet again, keeping the brilliant mind blown with pleasure until Knight was settled once again in his skin.

Chapter Seven

Knight slept for days.

Days.

And when he woke up, Bish was there to touch him, love him, and put him back to sleep. Occasionally there was something to tempt him to eat—homemade bread with caramelised butter, grilled asparagus tips wrapped in prosciutto, slivers of smoked salmon—but mostly he slept.

Finally his own stench had him pushing out of bed and staggering to the shower. Knight didn't look at his scraggly self in the mirrors, either—he just turned on the hot water. The sensation of the water against his nipple rings had him gasping. His cock jerked, began to swell, and the water hit his PA.

"Oh, fuck, look at you." Rook's voice was nearly a purr and he looked up to catch Rook licking his lips.

"I was dirty." He felt a little giddy.

"You look edible. God, that jewellery is pretty on you." Rook's eyes were fastened to his nipples.

"Thank you. How's Jase?"

"About as freaked out about the piercings as you are." Rook pushed his own chest out. "I love mine."

"They look amazing. Can I touch?"

"Just a little and don't tug. I wish they didn't take so long to heal." Rook grinned at him and stepped closer.

"I won't." He reached out, just barely brushed one fingertip over one ring.

Rook's eyes glazed over and he moaned, his whole body jerking. "Oh, fuck. Knight."

"Not for a few weeks."

Rook chuckled and pressed in close. "Perv," Rook said happily.

"Uh-huh." He rested one cheek against Rook's shoulder.

Rook slid his arms around his waist, the two of them standing together in the shower. Knight kissed Rook's jaw, neck—just relaxing. Eventually, Rook grabbed the shampoo and began washing his hair, massaging his scalp.

"Oh, God. Rookie..." He groaned, head falling forward.

Rook just kept massaging, stroking his head and making him feel good all the way through.

"So good. So good, Rookie." He sighed and stretched, the smile undeniable.

"You know I'll always take care of you, K."

"You been fucking Jase through the mattress?"

"Yep. And Bish has been making you sleep."

"Uh-huh. Forever."

Rook giggled. "Or five days, which I realise is even longer."

"Aeons. I've probably lost my talents."

Rook laughed. "Baloney."

"You don't think?"

"You have more talent in your big toe than most people have all their lives." Rook kissed him softly. "Nothing will ever change that."

What made it perfect was that Rook believed that, honestly.

The hands on his head moved down, lazily working his shoulders.

"I missed you the last few days." He leaned hard. He needed Bish, but no one made him happy like Rook.

"Me, too. And I'm here now."

"You are." He took another kiss, long and lazy. "Thank you."

"My pleasure, K." And Rook meant that honestly, too.

Grabbing the soap, Rook continued to touch him, slick fingers gliding on his skin like magic.

"Fuck, I love your touch. I want to feel you."

"How do you want me? Name it."

"Yes." He smiled and it felt normal, easy, for the first time in months. "But right now I want you to touch me and let me feel your magic."

Rook melted against him, smiling as he pressed their lips together. He cupped Rook's face, letting himself lick the water off Rookie's lips. Rook's fingers danced over his skin, stroking him like he was precious. He moaned, drinking Rook's joy.

Staying away from his nipples, Rook still teased him, circling his areola.

"Do yours ache?"

"All the damn time. Makes me fucking horny!" Like Rookie needed a reason.

"I want to suck them, see what you do."

Rook shuddered. "Oh, fuck, yes."

That made him smile. "Want to tug them, twist a little."

Rook nodded hard. "Yes. Yes."

"Soon, hmm?" Soon he'd be able to drive Rookie nuts.

"Uh-huh. I can't wait."

Rook's mouth met his—this kiss needier. He fucked Rook's lips as he moaned softly. Rook rubbed up against him, all hot and bothered now.

"Easy." He shifted his pierced cock over, moaning deep in his throat.

Rook's eyes went wide. "Sorry, K."

"Don't be." He wasn't.

Rook cuddled up, "Does it hurt to come?"

"God, no." He whispered in Rookie's ear, "It's so fucking good. Don't tell Bish."

Rook laughed for him, mouth pressing against his. "You're so bad!"

"Love you, Rookie." He laughed, too—the sound bubbling out of him.

Rook beamed at him. "Love you, too, K." Then Rook laughed again. "I love it when we get to wallow in it."

"Fuck, yes."

Rook's fingers went back to their exploration, slick with soap and rubbing all over his body. It was soothing and arousing at the same time. His cock was full and hard, the ring throbbing. Rook's hand wandered down to his package, cupping his balls. When the fingertips brushed his guiche, he jumped.

"Oh, God. You're so sexy, K. So damn sexy."

He felt sexy. Sensual. Fine. God, he hated it when Bish was right.

Rook's hold moved to the base of his prick, his lover being really careful.

"Gonna make me shoot?" He wanted that, bone deep.

"You fucking know it."

"Thank God." Knight rested against Rook, his hands circling Rook's hips.

"No, thank me."

He chuckled, kissed Rook's jaw. "Thank you."

Rookie grinned again, his fingers so delicate as they moved up and down his prick.

"Oh, damn." His toes curled.

"Your face when you're wanting makes me so hard."

"Everything makes you hard."

Rook stuck out his tongue. "Don't ruin the romance, K."

He cracked up, laughing deep and hard. Rook got his attention back lickety-split, thumb pressing against the tip of his cock, careful not to touch the ring.

Knight's eyes crossed. "Fuck. Rookie."

"I can, if you want me to." Rook slid his tongue along Knight's lower lip.

"Mmm." He could handle that. In fact, he was sort of incredibly for that idea.

"Oh, fuck yes. Turn around, K. I'll take care of you."

He turned, hands on the tile, pushing his ass out towards Rook, shaking it side to side. Rook's laughter warmed him — the hands on his ass were even better.

"God, I love your ass."

"Is it nice and round?" He knew better. It was lean and tight.

"It's fucking perfect." Rook slapped him gently.

"Hey!" Rook wasn't allowed to do that.

Rook giggled, then rubbed up against him. "How am I supposed to resist this ass, hmm?"

"Butthead. No spanking. You have Jase for that." Like Rook would ever swat Jason.

Rook snorted. "Jase doesn't like it like you do." One of Rook's fingers probed his ass.

"No? You… Oh, just like that, Rookie."

"Nobody likes it like you do." Rook crooked his finger, finding Knight's gland.

"Nobody?" He went up on tiptoe, eyes rolling.

Rook's kisses slid along his spine as the finger inside him disappeared. It came back a moment later, slick, pushing in easily. *Hell, yes. Just like that.* God, he needed.

Another finger pushed in and Rook found his gland again, pegging it before coming back and pegging it again. Knight rested his head on his hands, leaned in and sighed softly. Each kiss, each breath that slid over the skin of his back said Rook loved him.

They should all get together tonight—be together...be a family.

Rook's fingers disappeared, then the hard head of Rook's prick pushed against him, pushed into him. He moved back into it, breathing out as he made room for Rook's cock. Groaning, long and low, Rook kept working in until Knight felt the cradle of Rook's hips against his ass. Rook kissed his spine, then laid his cheek against it.

"Love this, K. Love feeling you around me." Rook hummed the words out.

They stayed like that for a long moment, Rook filling him, resting against him. Then his Rookie began to move. He rode him slow and easy, moving on that pretty cock, his toes curled. He heard the noises Rook made, each one for him, warm and good and sexy.

This was easier than Bish—like breathing, to let Rook love him. Rook reached around, wrapping long fingers around his prick.

"Yeah, Rookie. That's sweet."

"Uh-huh. I've got you." Sweet kisses slid over his back as that hand slid over his cock, Rook's rhythm getting faster.

"Got me." He moaned softly, feeling his eyelashes brush his arms.

"Always." Rook shifted and hit his gland.

"Rookie!" Oh, hell yes.

"Yes!" Rook sounded fierce and hit him there again, the slow, easy glides giving way to hard, needy thrusts.

He called out, needing Rook, needing this. Rook kept pushing into him, giving him everything. Every time Rook slammed in, the heavy balls nudged his guiche, making him shiver. Rook's hand slid forward on his cock, nudging the ring on his prick. Spunk shot from him, his entire body shuddering violently as he came.

"Knight!" Rook called his name, jerking inside him.

"Rookie..." He moaned happily, settled in his bones.

"My Knight."

"My Knight." Bishop's voice was low, husky. "I brought a plug for him, Rookie, and I ordered Chinese."

He felt Rookie's smile against his back. "And Jason?"

Bish chuckled. "Putting Knight's favourite movie in the DVD player."

"Are there blankets on the couch?" They loved cuddling together on the huge sectional.

"Of course there are." Bish showed him the plug before sliding it down his back where Rookie took it.

"I didn't say you could plug me." He was relaxed enough that he didn't even tense.

Rook giggled, the plug hard but warm against his ass.

"Laughing at me!" He squeezed Rook's cock with his ass.

Rookie groaned softly. "Nope. I never laugh *at* you, K."

"No? You sure?" He kept clenching then relaxing, over and over.

"Fuck!" Rook panted, one hand wrapping around his hip and holding on tight.

Bishop laughed softly. "Talented boy. Fucking live for your ass, Knight."

"So wicked, Knight." Rook kissed his spine again. "We're going to turn into prunes. Happy, well-fucked prunes, but still prunes."

"Vanity, vanity." Despite the words, he stepped forward to let Rook slide out. The press of the plug surprised him—he'd thought he could avoid it, what with Bish not being the one having it in hand.

Rookie was right there, though—pushing it in, locking his seed inside him. Knight's eyes rolled a little, his heart slamming in his chest. Rook didn't back away, just seated the plug, then hugged him close, body pressing against his back.

"Come on, you two. Dry off. I brought you sweats." Bishop was licking his lips, smiling. "And there's a chocolate cake for dessert."

"Damn. Did Jason make it?" Jason had turned out to be a far better cook than any of them.

"I ordered it in."

Oh, hell yes.

"Oh!" Rook patted his ass and gave him another soft kiss to his spine. "That means it's that really amazing one from Diniso's. See you guys there!"

He chuckled as Rook grabbed a towel and bounced off, calling for Jason. Knight turned off the water and moved into the open towel Bish was holding for him.

"You're looking easy in your skin." Bish began to towel him off, hands patting him through the terrycloth.

"I slept for a hundred weeks."

Bish snorted. "Give or take a hundred weeks."

"Uh-huh." He leaned into those amazing muscles. "Forever."

"Long enough for now." Bish wrapped the towel around him. "Now come on. They're saving room for us under the covers *and* cake."

"Sounds perfect."

It really did. Chicken lo mein and cake.

"That's because it is." Bish ran a finger along his lower lip and they headed for the living room and their lovers.

Chapter Eight

Jason headed downstairs to the gym at six a.m., needing a workout in the worst way. He'd missed three days last week, and he was getting lazy. He touched the heat up a little, turned the music on and started warming up.

Footsteps sounded on the stairs and in a moment Bish had joined him. "Hey, looks like I'm not the only early bird."

"Morning, Bish." He nodded, smiled, and turned the treadmill up.

"Morning, baby boy." Bish's hand landed on his ass.

His footsteps stumbled, his rhythm lost.

"Careful," murmured Bish.

"Yeah. Yeah." He nodded, focused on the run again. No focusing on Bishop. None.

And it worked, until Bishop set up next to him, shirt off, biking right there beside him.

Asshole. Beautiful man. Muscled beast.

Like Bish could hear him, the man turned and smiled. Jason felt his cheeks heat and his balls draw up.

"We could move to the bench. Spot each other." The words sounded so dirty coming out of Bish's mouth.

"Sure. Sure, if you're warmed up."

"I'm getting there."

"Yeah, me too." *Like whoa.*

Bish's smile was definitely wicked. The man got off the bike and bent, right there in front of him, to pick up his shirt. He licked his lips, almost reaching for that fine ass. Then Bish stood and turned around, smiling at him knowingly.

"You lifting first or am I?" he asked, trying to ignore the husky tone in his own voice.

"Go ahead."

"Okay."

Bish followed him to the bench and helped him set the weights up. Jason lay back, humming as he grabbed the bar.

Bish stood at his head, all those chest muscles gleaming. The man was ripped...and half hard.

Sexy. Really fucking sexy.

"Good job. Keep it up."

Jason did five more reps, then rested.

Bish's hand slid over his where it was wrapped around the bar, squeezed. "How's the jewellery this morning?"

"I didn't notice it." He'd tried to ignore it.

Bish chuckled and said softly, "Liar."

"Am not."

Bish moved slowly around the bench, sitting on the end and leaning in, reaching between his spread legs.

"B-bishop?" *Oh, God.* "I need to do another set."

His hand kept moving and just barely nudged the ring between his legs.

"Oh, fuck." His toes curled.

"So how's the jewellery this morning?" he repeated.

"Fine. Fine." Hot. Aching just the barest bit.

"It's fucking sexy, Jase. How does it feel when you're getting fucked?"

"Aren't we supposed to be working out?"

"The equipment isn't going anywhere, baby boy."

Bish's hands landed on his thighs then began rubbing slowly up and down them, the touches deep and slow. His cock began to fill.

"It makes me hard, baby. Knowing it's there."

He looked up at Bish, an ache building in him. They were each different, but Bish made him feel…

Leaning in, Bish derailed his thoughts with a kiss that stormed his defences. One huge hand cupped his cock and balls and squeezed, just enough to make his breath hiccup.

"I think we'd both be happier this morning if we bench-pressed each other."

"Bench-pressed…" His eyes rolled.

Bish laughed, the sound deep and sexy. "Hey, we can't let Rookie be the only one allowed to make sex puns."

"He's good at it." *Sort of amaz… Oh, fuck.* Bish rolled his balls and his hips tilted.

"He is. I'm the one with you now." The next kiss stole his breath completely.

He cried out into Bishop's lips. Bish rubbed against him, letting him feel all those amazing muscles as they pressed him into the bench. He tried to let go of the bar, but his fingers were clenched tight.

Bish's hands slid along his sides, digging in so they didn't tickle. So he could feel them. On the trip down, his sweats were peeled away, baring him. Bish's body was hot and sweaty above his, the man's sweats disappearing at the same time his own did.

"Keep your hands on the bar, baby."

"What?" *Oh, fuck.*

"Do it or I'll spank your sweet little ass until it's red." Bish's eyes were dead serious.

He groaned, but held on.

Bish grinned at him. "I was kind of hoping you'd let go."

He chuckled softly, body heating. "I'm not"—*a brat*—"difficult like Knight."

"Doesn't mean you can't enjoy a good spanking now and then." Bish slid fingers across his nipples.

They drew up tight and he shook his head. "No spanking…"

"I don't know… I think it turns you on." Bending, Bish licked at his nipples this time, then bit the right one.

"Bish!" He twisted, his pecs shaking.

Bish licked where he'd bitten, fingers sliding to wrap around his waist. The sting became a warm, dull heat. A delicious ache.

"Taste good, baby boy. Sweet."

"Didn't sweat enough…" *Sweet*.

"Sweated just enough." Bish licked a line along his collarbone.

Oh. Oh, that tickled. He grabbed Bishop's shoulders, shivering. "Tickles!"

"You let go of the bar."

"Uh-uh." He grabbed it quickly.

Bish laughed. "Are you really trying to deny it?"

"Uh-huh." He didn't want a spanking.

"Sweet baby." Bush's mouth closed over his again.

He wasn't so sweet, was he?

He opened, body arching up into Bish's. Bish tongue-fucked his mouth—hard and fast, just like he knew it would be when Bish started fucking his ass. Bish pushed him into the bench, pressing him tight. The fingers of one hand slid over his right nipple, pinching and stroking by turns. He found the rhythm, eyes closed, and focused on Bish. Every touch sent him flying higher. He wrapped around Bish, his ass sticking to the bench.

"Want you."

He could tell — Bish's prick was wet at the tip and rubbing against his hole.

"Uh-huh." He could agree to that.

Bish pushed, the head of his cock pushing, stretching him. He groaned. Bish was thicker than the others, his cock fat and wide.

"So fucking tight." It didn't sound like a complaint.

Bish scooped his legs up, tilting him back and pushing deeper. The next thrust hit his gland.

"Oh…" His eyes rolled, his fingers digging into Bish's biceps.

"Look at that — I found it first try." Bish pulled back and pushed forward, hitting it again.

"Uh… Uh-huh." *Oh, fuck.*

The first try…and the second — third and fourth, too.

"Bish…" He couldn't think, he couldn't breathe. All he could do was arch and beg for more.

Bish held his gaze and kept fucking him, filling him over and over. The man was a machine, driving into him, pushing deeper and deeper. He was hard and leaking from it — and not a touch to his cock. Bish's body kept nudging his piercing, making him ache. Then Bish found his nipple, his thumb stroking across it. He moaned. God, he wanted Bish. He wanted them all.

Bish slid that hand down to wrap around his prick.

"Yes." He needed that touch.

"Needy man. Beautiful, studly, needy man." Bish's words were like another caress.

"Thank you." He felt like a million bucks.

Then Bish found his gland again, nailing it hard. His eyes flew open, his cock throbbing. *Oh. Oh, fuck.* Bish nodded at him, looking pleased, looking hot as fuck. He needed more, needed it again. Bish gave it to him, too, punching hard into him. He gasped, eyes rolling, body gripping...

"Fuck, yes. Just like that, baby boy."

"Again? Please?"

"Mmm. Do love it when you beg." Bish pushed into him again, smacking right into his gland.

"Yes..." He felt that in his bones.

"Yes," Bish repeated the word back at him, hips picking up speed, hand working his cock now.

Everything inside him went tight and red hot and desperate.

"Fucking gorgeous. Fucking ours." Each word came with another thrust, Bish working him hard.

Oh, God. Please. Yes.

"Come on, baby boy. Show me." Bish hit his gland bang on — hard, perfect. "Show me."

"Show you..." He bucked and shot, crying out.

"Fuck yes!" Bish jerked and filled him with heat deep inside.

"Bishop." He moaned, cock jerking weakly at the heat inside him.

"Right here, Jason." Bishop kissed him — this time softer, but no less in control.

Jason blinked, muscles loose and shaky.

Bish stayed buried inside him, hands on his skin. His muscles jumped and jerked, loving Bish's touch.

"I think this is my favourite kind of working out."

"Good. Good ab work."

Bish laughed, nodded. Strong fingers slid on his abs. "And you've got the best abs."

He flexed, grinning as that made Bish moan.

"Sexy man."

His hole clenched around Bish's cock.

"Fuck." Bish moaned again, pushing in hard.

Oh. Oh. His shoulders left the bench, his fingertips dug in. So Bish did it again.

"Bish!" The bench creaked.

"Right here." Bish rolled his hips and pushed in again. "In you."

"Yes. Yes." He had come more in the last few months...

Bish's hand found his prick again, wrapping around it. "Hard for me again."

"Never got soft." These men were magic.

"I know. Stud."

He shook his head.

"You are." Bish squeezed his prick and pushed in again.

Jase's eyes crossed, his toes curling.

"Stud, stud, stud. My stud. Our stud."

He was flying. Flying. Bish moved slowly but surely, keeping him going.

"I knew someone was having orgasms without me." Rook moaned, stumbling into the gym, naked and hard.

"Two someones," Bish corrected, holding a hand out to Rook.

Rookie came to them, touching them both. Bish pulled Rook into a kiss, then turned Rook's mouth to Jason.

"Morning." Jason moaned as Rook took his lips, tongue pushing in to taste him. Rookie's kiss did the same thing it always did—melted him, turned him into putty.

"Want your mouth, honey. Want you to suck me." Rookie licked at his lips, smiling at him.

"Yes. Facing me so I can see that huge cock of yours sliding between his lips." Bish slammed in hard as he spoke, making Jason cry out.

Rookie gave him another kiss, then straddled his head, prick touching his lips. *Oh, fuck. Oh, fuck.* Rook's scent surrounded him, heady and strong, making him shake.

"Feed it to him, Rookie. He loves it."

"He's a sweet cocksucker." How could that not sound like an insult? It didn't, though. The way Rookie said it, it sounded like the biggest compliment ever. It sounded like…need.

Rook pushed into his mouth, slowly, carefully easing the thick length into him.

"So pretty, Jason. Love the way your lips look on my cock." Rook groaned for him, the sound pure sex.

"You're fucking magic together." Bish's thrusts matched Rook's rhythm, both cocks pushing into him at the same time.

He cried out, swallowing hard, his entire body on fire.

"Oh, God, that feels good, Jase." Rook moved a little faster, Bish matching him stroke for stroke.

Rook's balls were soft, hot on his face.

Bish and Rook both moaned and he could hear them kissing, the sounds wet and sexy. His prick throbbed, the tip aching and sore. Then Bish's body nudged his guiche and everything lit up from that point outward. He took Rook down to the root, swallowing convulsively as he shot.

"Oh fuck!" Rookie's moan was sweet, the feeling necessary to Jason as his throat was flooded with salty heat.

"Pretty baby—love to watch him suck." Bish gripped his hips solidly enough to bruise. Then the man fucked him, hard and quick for half a dozen strokes.

"I love to feel him suck. And to watch your face as you come, Bish."

Bish grunted and more heat filled him. *Crazy.*

Rookie pulled out of his mouth and bent to give him an upside-down kiss.

"Now we need to go shower."

Bish was right, they were...well-used.

"Absolutely. It smells like a cat house in here. Freaks." Knight was in running clothes, bundled up for the snow.

Rook laughed and launched himself at the man, squealing when his naked flesh hit Knight. "Fuck! Cold!" Knight chuckled, pressing closer. Rook popped him in the arm, but there was a huge grin on Rook's face. "Come shower with us — we'll warm you up and catch you up at the same time."

Bish gave them an indulgent grin before leaning in to give Jase a soft kiss. "Thanks for the workout, baby boy."

"Good morning, Bishop." He couldn't stop smiling. This was ridiculous.

Wonderful.

Bish nodded and slid out of him before standing and holding one hand out to him, the other to Rook and Knight, who came in eagerly.

Then the four of them started making their way to the shower. The way Rook was looking at Knight, they probably weren't going to make it without a few stops along the way, but that was okay.

In fact, it was more than okay.

Chapter Nine

Rook banged his foot against the door. "Come on, I have no hands!" Well, he had hands but they were full. Very full.

He had supper from the Greek place and desserts from the bakery. Three bottles of wine and a bag full of fun adult games that they'd just got in at the store. He'd already told Bish they were having a night of food and wine and games all together. It was Bishop's job to make sure Knight didn't get wrapped up in something else before they got started.

He shivered as several snowflakes landed on the back of his neck and he banged the door again. He was going to start pouting soon and that was no way to begin the evening.

"Rookie?" The door flew open and there was Knight, laughing, breathless. "I thought I heard you!"

God, he hadn't seen Knight so relaxed and happy in months.

"You did! Let me in, it's fucking freezing out here." He held out his arms, encouraging Knight to take something — anything.

Knight grabbed bags, helping him in. "Christ, it's frigid. Did you order this weather? Is there something yummy in here?"

"Did I order the weather? Like I have that kind of power. Although...if we're having a night inside, it's nice and cosy if it's cold outside. And of course there's yummy stuff in there. I went to Mykonos Beach." He closed the door behind him and pursed his lips for a kiss.

"Mmm." Knight smiled for him and kissed him happily. Lord, what had Bish done to make Knight so mellow? Whatever it was, Bish should probably do it again.

"So, is everyone ready for a night of food and games?"

"Sure. Jason's cleaning up the front room. Bishop's pulling out pillows to sit on."

"Perfect." He leaned into Knight and took another kiss. "I have octopus in one of those bags."

"Mmm. You are made of win. You know I love octopus."

"I know. I think I got everyone's favourite."

He followed Knight into the living room, grinning at the scene. There was a fire in the fireplace, candles, pillows and plates and glasses. Jason and Bish were both in pyjama bottoms, Jason also wearing a T-shirt. God, they were studs, both of them. Rook took a minute to look his fill before putting down his bags and stripping out of his winter gear.

Knight headed for the wet bar. "Red or white?"

"Red, please, K." He stripped all the way down, grinning at Jason's wide eyes. "Pyjama bottoms?"

Laughing, Bish tossed his favourite pair at him.

"Thanks, beautiful." He tugged them on, the soft material comfortable.

He took the wine from Knight along with a kiss, then sat on the floor by the coffee table, pulling containers out of the bags. "I hope everyone is hungry."

Jason sat. "I'm starving. It smells amazing."

He leaned into Jason. "Give me a kiss hello first, honey." One muscled arm wrapped around him and his dear, happy boy offered him a slow, burning kiss. He moaned softly as their lips parted, absolutely melted. "Thank you."

"My turn." Bish turned his face and took his mouth in a hard, sure kiss.

Where Jason had melted him, Bish made him ache. Next he needed his Knight—his fiery, sensitive artist. Knight was right there to kiss him as Bish's mouth left his. When that kiss was over, Rook sighed happily. "It's going to be such a fun evening."

Knight settled across two pillows, head in Bishop's lap. "Feed me an olive?"

Laughing happily, Rook lay down in Jason's lap. "Me, too?"

Jason looked shocked for a moment, then brushed his hair from his eyes and fed him an olive. The salt filled his mouth, reminding him of his lovers' cum, and he chewed, grinning up at Jason.

Jason smiled down at him. "You look happy."

"I am, honey. Like really, really." So happy it was almost scary. How could he not be? He was with the three men he loved and adored who loved and adored him back. "Are you?"

Jason nodded, traced his bottom lip. "Been a good day."

"Cool." He grabbed at Jason's finger with his lips, sucking on it, tongue stroking the pad.

He loved how Jason's cock filled, throbbed against his face. He rubbed his cheek against it, smiling and losing Jason's finger at the expression on Jason's face. God, he was stupid in love with this man.

"Up, boys," Bish demanded. "Olives are one thing, but you're both going to choke to death if you eat lying down like this."

Jason laughed as Knight grumbled, but they both sat up and he passed containers of everyone's favourites to them. They cuddled together, sharing and laughing, Knight keeping the wine glasses full.

When the meal was over, every last crumb of the desserts he'd bought gone, Bish leaned in and kissed him. "That was lovely, Rookie. Thanks."

"You're welcome, Bish." The kiss was enough to make him dizzy. When it ended he was caught staring adoringly up at Bish. That earned him a smile and a nudge.

"You haven't emptied the last bag and it has the store logo on it. What naughtiness have you brought us?"

"Oh! Games!"

"Games?" Jason looked at him, eyes confused. "Like Monopoly?"

Grinning, he shook his head. "Sexopoly is one of them. But that's just naughty Monopoly. The better games are the ones that get you to do stuff."

"Do stuff?" Knight laughed. "We're already close to naked, Rookie."

"You mean you're already a sure thing?" he teased.

"I mean strip poker is a quick game."

"So you don't want to try sexy Truth or Dare? Or Taboo? Or Scattergories?"

Jason started laughing and Knight's grin went evil. "Truth or Dare? I'm in."

"Good." He beamed at Knight, smiled at Jason and looked over at Bish, who just grinned and shook his head. Bish didn't say no, though.

"Truth or Dare?" he asked Knight.

"Truth." Knight sipped his wine, leant back against Bish.

"What did Bish do to you today that's put you in such a good mood?"

Knight pinked, eyes widening. "I… What?"

"You are in a *fantastic* mood. Come on—what did he do?"

"He made me waffles and then we took a shower and…played."

"Did you get to play with them too, honey?" he asked Jason.

Jason shook his head. "I was napping this afternoon. Being lazy."

"Getting ready for tonight." Rook waggled his eyebrows.

Knight nodded, winking at Jason. "We'll keep him busy."

Rook slid his hand along Jason's thigh, smiling. "Your turn to ask the question, K."

Knight leaned up, kissed Bishop's chin. "Truth or Dare?"

"Dare."

Rook shivered as Bishop gave his answer.

"Hmm…" Knight hummed. "Should I dare you to strip me with your teeth or to give Jase a blow?"

Bish growled a little and Rook bounced on his ass.

Knight grinned. "Strip me. I'll save the blowjob for next time."

"Damn." Rook pouted in Knight's general direction, but it wasn't a real pout.

"With my teeth?" Bish looked at Knight. "Really?"

"Uh-huh. After all, it's just sweats and briefs." Knight grinned evilly. "And no biting."

"You're wearing briefs?" Rook pouted. "I'm disappointed. I'm not the only one going commando, am I?"

"I have boxers on." Jason was so modest.

"We'll fix that soon enough, honey." He leaned into Jason, settling against lovely muscles so he could watch the Bish and Knight show.

Knight stretched out, toes wiggling, teasing Bishop. That was dangerous.

"You're going to pay for that," Bish noted softly.

"Hmm?" Knight's eyelashes fluttered.

Bish chuckled and leaned in, teeth wrapping around the top of Knight's sweats. Knight sucked in, abs rippling.

"Oh, that's pretty. Isn't that pretty, Jason?"

Jason nodded, fingers on Rook's side. "Almost as pretty as yours."

He tore his gaze away from Knight and Bish to smile up at Jason. "Thank you, honey." He pushed their lips together, taking a soft kiss. He could get lost in those kisses, in the way that Jason pressed close to him.

Then Knight moaned and he glanced over, pushing harder into Jason as Knight's hard prick popped free of his sweatpants. Bishop eased the sweats down, tugging and grumbling as Knight wiggled.

When he finally got them off, he pounced on Knight and growled. "I will pay you back."

Rook was pretty sure Knight was going to enjoy every second of it, too.

Knight wrapped around Bish and hummed. "You're warm."

"Uh-huh." Bish kissed Knight, then turned to him. "My turn. Rook—Truth or Dare?"

Rook grinned. "Dare!"

"Surprise, surprise." Knight laughed softly. "Dare him to do a strip tease."

"I could do that!"

Bish laughed and swatted Knight's ass. "It's *my* dare." Bish rolled his eyes. "But go ahead, Rookie. Give us your best show."

"Is there going to be awful porn music?" Jason's soft-spoken joke made Rook cackle.

"Boom chicka bow wow!" He rolled his hips as he sang it.

They all applauded, laughing with him—loving him.

"Come on. Help me out with the music now!"

"Dance with him, Jase. He looks lonely." Knight turned the iPad up, the low music that had been playing in the background all evening filling the room.

"Oh, good idea!" He turned and held his hands out to Jason, swaying to the music now, putting a sexy little oomph in his hip movements.

Jason stood and took his hand, moving with him. It took a second, but then Jason relaxed and started dancing and Rook's mouth went dry. *Look at that...* He was going to take forever to take his pyjama bottoms off. *Forever.*

He met Jason's eyes and smiled at his lover, putting a little something extra in the next roll of his hips. Jason hummed, hand on Rook's butt, moving him like a Chippendales dancer.

"He's a natural, Bish." Knight sounded stunned.

Rook wasn't going to say a word—he didn't want to break the spell. Jason was focused on him and the music, and suddenly it wasn't all about the dare—it was about them. He moved in close, his hips sliding against Jason's, one of his legs between Jason's. Jason was half hard, his eyelids heavy.

He slid his free hand over Jason's chest, fingers playing with the lovely muscles. Cut and warm, Jason was a living wet dream sliding against him. He found

Jason's lips with his tongue, tracing them, slipping his tongue between them. His lover hummed for him, opening for their kiss. He pressed closer to Jason, their bodies barely moving now.

"Rook..." Jason moaned for him, kissing him happily, honestly, openly.

He gave up all pretence of trying to dance, wrapping his arms around Jason's neck and giving their kisses his full attention.

"You're getting distracted, Rookie," Knight pointed out.

"Nothing wrong with a little distraction."

"Nothing at all." Jason drew him closer, wrapped around him.

Laughing happily, he took another kiss, letting himself melt into Jason's body.

"Aren't we playing a game?" Was Knight actually pouting?

"I'm still wearing my bottoms, K." He wriggled his ass in Knight's direction.

"You're supposed to be stripping, Rookie." Someone swatted his butt.

"You just want me naked."

Bishop's laughter filled the room. "We're human, Rookie."

He shook his ass at Bish and Knight, pleased with Bish's answer.

"Help me take them off?" he asked Jason.

"Mmm-hmm." Jason eased the pyjama bottoms down.

"Mmm. You're getting good at that, honey."

Jason pulled him close, hiding him from the others.

He stroked his hand through Jason's hair. "I'm not shy."

"I know. I am."

He smiled at Jason and took another kiss. "Let me strip, honey, and then it can be your turn."

"You're pretty naked, Rook."

He looked down at himself and laughed. "You're right, honey. That makes it your turn. Truth or Dare?"

"Truth?"

Poor, nervous baby doll.

"Hmm... What's your favourite position with each of us?"

"I. I..." Jason went bright red. "I like... You mean fucking?"

He nodded eagerly, stroking Jason's cheek with his hand. "It's okay—you can keep looking at just me while you tell us."

Jason's eyes were hot, burning. "I like when...when Bishop takes me in the mornings, downstairs."

Rook moaned, a shudder of desire going through him. "Oh, I like that, too."

"Knight uses...uses the plugs." Jason stepped closer.

"You like it when he does that, hmm?" Their sweet Jason was a very kinky boy beneath that layer of shyness.

"I..." Jason nodded.

Rook still moved against Jason, though now it was less dancing and more humping. "What about me, honey?"

"I like it best when..." Jason leaned close, whispering so softly, "...when it's just you and me together at night. Making...making love."

"Oh, honey." He kissed Jason hard as a reward, not even caring that the others hadn't heard—they'd heard what Jason liked with each of them and that was good enough.

He drew Jason back onto the sofa, wrapping them both together in a blanket, ignoring the fond looks from Bish and Knight.

After a bit of canoodling, he nudged Jason. "Your turn, honey."

Jason looked right at him. "Truth or Dare?"

"For you, I'll pick truth."

"Are you... What do you like best?"

"I like it when we're all here together enjoying each other." It was the first thing that popped into his head and it was true. "Is that what you meant?"

Jason nodded, offering him a bittersweet smile. "It is."

He pushed Jason's hair off his face. "The three of you make me so happy. I'm the luckiest man in the world."

Jason kissed his cheek, his temple. Rook hummed happily, tilting his head back to offer Jason anything he wanted.

"Stop basking, Rookie. It's your turn." Knight was getting testy.

He rolled his eyes and smiled at Knight. "Truth or Dare, big boy."

"Dare."

Oh, hooray.

"I want to watch you sucking Bish off."

Knight chuckled. "Like that's a hardship."

"Dares don't have to be a hardship." He just wanted to have fun.

Knight crawled over to Bishop. "Whip it out, stud muffin."

Rook burst out laughing.

Bish shook his head, though. "No, I think you should get it out. With your mouth."

"It's not your choice, man. Rookie dared me to suck." Knight was laughing, fingers on Bishop's belly.

Bish shot him a look and Rook shrugged. Knight was right—he hadn't been specific.

"You know you're cruising, don't you, Knight?" Bishop was growling now.

"I'm just playing, Bishop, don't snarl."

"I'm pretty sure you like it when I snarl." Bish spread his legs for Knight, though.

"Maybe." Knight nosed Bish's belly, humming softly.

Bish made a happy noise, dropping a hand to Knight's head, stroking it. Rook settled in with his head on Jason's shoulder, enjoying the show as they all got back into the swing of it. Jason leaned into him, cuddling in the comforter. He rubbed Jason's belly, watching as Knight fished out Bishop's prick.

"Pretty motherfucker." Knight nuzzled the tip of Bish's cock.

"Not as pretty as Rookie and Jason."

Knight hummed. "Perfect."

"Flatterer."

Rook could tell Bish was pleased, though.

Knight shrugged, then swallowed Bishop down like a master.

"Fuck!" Bish jerked, prick pushing into Knight's throat, and Rook groaned at the sight.

Knight pulled hard, giving Bishop no quarter.

"Look at that. Knight really goes for it, doesn't he?"

Jason nodded, eyes moving around the room, trying not to stare.

"You're allowed to look, honey. In fact, it's kind of expected."

"I know. I just... It's hard."

He groped in Jason's crotch, finding his lover's hard cock. "Mmm. It is."

Jason jerked. "Rook!"

"Don't be shy now." He pushed his hand into Jason's sweats.

"I know. I try not to be."

"You just need a little distraction." And he was just the right distraction. He leaned in and kissed Jason.

The soft, sweet lips parted for him, letting him in. God, he loved kissing. And kissing Jason was particularly sweet. Jason cupped his cheek, tracing his cheekbone with his thumb. Rook hummed, deepening the kiss, his hand beginning to move on Jason's prick.

Bishop was groaning, growling deep as Knight's head bobbed. Between the kiss and the sounds, it was intoxicating.

Jason's hips shifted, his cock beginning to leak. Rook shifted to straddle him.

"Rook…" Jason moaned into his lips.

"Right here, honey." His hand kept moving up and down along the sweet, heated flesh.

"K! Fucking shit!" Bishop slammed up into Knight, driving hard.

Rook moaned and rocked against Jason.

Jason grunted into his lips. "Crazy. We're all crazy."

He shook his head. "No, honey. We're just all right where we're meant to be." This was heaven, and it was theirs.

Bish cried out and Rook looked over in time to watch Knight swallowing convulsively, taking Bish's cum in. *There. Fuck, yes.* That was so pretty.

He moaned happily and offered Jason another soft kiss. Jason drew him close, relaxing against him. He rubbed idly, watching as Knight cleaned Bish up until Bish pulled Knight up along his body to give the man a hard kiss. They were so sexy together. Knight fit against Bish perfectly, tanned skin and pale complementing each other.

He reached out to touch Knight's thigh and sighed happily at the connection between the four of them.

It was Knight's turn, but he wasn't in any hurry to prompt the man. They could keep playing when one of them got restless. Rook was willing to bet it would be Knight himself.

Knight and Bishop kept kissing, mouths moving slowly.

"Pretty, aren't they?"

"They are." Jason nodded, nuzzled him.

He nuzzled right back, wriggling his ass, too.

Knight chuckled softly. "Little perv."

"No way — I'm a *huge* perv."

Knight's grin widened. "Yes. You remember when you let Bish fuck you in the movie theatre?"

"Oh, God. I do! God, that was something." The fear of being caught had made everything bigger somehow.

Bishop snorted. "Or when Knight did the naked dance in the fountain in the moonlight?"

Rook put his head back and laughed. "He nearly got arrested for that!"

"I didn't. I even got a cop to pose with me."

"You did. That was almost as amazing as you dancing in there to begin with."

"You guys are nuts." Jason just shook his head.

He giggled. "Probably."

Bishop grabbed Knight's balls and rolled them. "Absolutely."

Rook grinned. "It's Knight's turn."

"Mmm. Truth or Dare, kid."

Jason groaned. "D…dare." Oh, their Jason was such a brave boy.

Knight's eyebrow arched. "Let Bishop fist you."

Jason went pale. "What? No."

Rook gasped, his prick jerking where it pressed against Jason's body. "Oh, God."

"No." Jason frowned. "No, that's part of the deal. No injury. No."

"Oh, it won't hurt you, honey. Bish'll be careful. He'll make it wonderful." Rook smiled, remembering having Bish's hand in him. It had been amazing.

Jason shook his head. "No."

"He did it to me, Jason, and I promise—it didn't hurt. It was one of the most amazing experiences I've ever had."

"No." Jason stood up, shook his head. "Pick something else."

"You won't even try, honey?"

"I… I'm going to the restroom. I'll be right back."

"No, honey. Talk to us. Talk to *me*."

"I'll be right back." Jason headed out of the room, arms around his middle.

Rook whimpered, looking to Bish and Knight.

Knight rolled his eyes. "Jesus Christ."

"Stop that," Rook admonished. "He's young and innocent."

"He's a baby. Bishop wouldn't hurt him. Ever."

"I know that, and you know that. But it's a *huge* thing, K. Don't be mean about it."

"Go talk to him, Rookie." Bish kissed the top of his head. "Work your magic and get him back into the room. Even if he won't do it, hmm?"

"Yeah. He doesn't have to. He should know that. We haven't forced him to do anything." He nodded and kissed Bish, then Knight. "Love you guys."

"We love you, Rookie." Knight met his eyes. "But don't forget, the kid's in love with you."

"I love him, too. I'll go get him, bring him back. Maybe we can show him how good it can be instead of asking him to take the leap and do it."

He headed for the bathroom. The door was open, Jason not in there. He headed down the hallway to Jason's room, the closed door.

Leaning against it, Rook knocked. "Honey? Let me in, please." He needed to hold Jason, to remind Jason this was about loving each other and having fun.

"I'm just finding another pair of sweats. These weren't comfortable."

"I'm coming in." He opened the door.

Jason was in a heavy sweatsuit and socks, his cheeks bright red. "Hey. I'm not sure I want to play anymore tonight."

"Oh, honey, I'm sorry. You know we'd never hurt you, never push you too far, right? You could have just safeworded and we'd have stopped immediately. It's important to remember both those things." He went over and wrapped his arms around Jason's waist. "And it's even more important to remember that we love you. That *I* love you."

"Yeah." Jason didn't lean into him. "I think I'm going to go to bed early tonight, Rook. In here. I'm really tired."

"Knight wants to show you what it's like. Having Bish's hand inside him. He wants you to come watch, to share it, so you know it wasn't a terrible thing he was daring you to do." He pressed a soft kiss to Jason's lips. "Please, honey? We were having such a good evening."

"I... I don't know." Jason would give in, though, Rook knew it.

"No one wants you to do anything scary. Just come and watch. Watch Knight's face as Bish holds him like that. I think it'll help you understand." He stroked Jason's back, wishing it was skin he was touching but accepting that it wasn't. "We won't even make you change back into your pyjama bottoms," he teased gently.

"Okay. For you."

"Thank you, honey. I know this is hard for you and I know how much it means that you'll do it." Rook pressed their lips together again, more breathing with Jason than kissing him.

"Yeah." Jason stood up. "Let's go. I need a glass of water."

"Water sounds good." He took Jason's hand and squeezed it. "I do love you, Jason."

"Thanks, Rook."

He beamed at Jason and tugged him out of the room and down the hall to the kitchen. Grabbing four bottles of water out of the fridge, he passed two to Jason to carry. Jason was quiet, following along. The guys had cleaned up the food and turned down the lights.

Rook offered over his two bottles of water and settled on the couch, patting the spot beside him for Jason.

"You okay, kiddo?" Knight offered Jason a smile.

"Yeah, I'm cool."

Bish went one further, coming over and giving Jason's shoulders a rub, kissing him lightly. Jason stayed stiff for a second, then slowly relaxed.

"Are you and Knight gonna show us the fisting?" Rook asked.

Bish nodded. "We'd like to. It's something good and loving. It's not hard or harsh at all." The last was directed at Jason and Rook squeezed his hand to let Jason know he wasn't alone here.

"You don't have to. I mean, not just for show."

"I don't think Bish and Knight are doing this just for show. They both love it, right, guys?"

Knight snorted. "I said I wasn't going to bottom with Jason here."

"Oh, please, Knight." Bish rolled his eyes. "You've done practically nothing but since he got here. And he still thinks you're an amazing stud."

Rook chuckled. "That's because Knight *is* an amazing stud. Who knows what he likes."

"I don't know why there has to be so much worry." Jason shook his head. "I don't think badly of any of you."

"It's just you took off…"

"I… I don't want to do that. Ever."

Rook patted Jason's hand. He had a feeling Jason would eventually change his mind, but there was no point in trying to get there tonight. "We'll just watch."

"You can go be with them. I'll watch. It's cool."

Rook watched as Knight and Bish got rid of the coffee table and set up blankets and pillows in front of the couch they were sitting on.

"I'm not sure they need me. Guys? You want me to do anything?"

Bish grinned wolfishly. "I have lube and a well-cleaned-out sexpot."

"No wonder Knight is in such a good mood!" He laughed and cuddled in with Jason. "We can both watch, honey."

Jason nodded but hid his face. Rook kissed the top of Jason's head and turned to watch his lovers.

Bish laid out the big jar of lube and settled next to Knight. He'd placed Knight so that Jason and Rook had a great view. They were going to blow their sweet baby boy's mind. Knight's too. That was as much thought as he spared for anyone else, though. All his focus would be on Knight now.

Knight was watching him, eyes serious, quiet. He rested for a moment, his hands on Knight's splayed knees, meeting Knight's gaze.

"You want this, Mouse?"

Bish smiled, the nickname warming him all the way through. "You know I do."

"Yeah. Yeah, I know."

"I don't even have to ask if you want this, I know you do."

"Maybe." Little tease.

He chuckled, tickled the insides of Knight's thighs. Knight spread for him, the heavy, bare balls drawing up. All of Knight was joining in, offering that hole to him. He touched the tiny hole, traced it. *So fucking pretty.* Humming, he rubbed the wrinkled flesh.

"Talk to me, Bish."

"You want me to tell you what I'm about to do? How I'm going to start small. With my pinky finger and slowly add fingers."

"I want you to talk to me, to be here with me."

"Always, babe. You know that. You're always on my mind and in my heart." He lubed up his hand, pushing his little finger into that tight hole.

Knight reached up, cupped his jaw. He nuzzled into the touch, fucking Knight with one little finger. Knight moved lazily, dancing to the music from the radio.

"You are so fucking stunning, Knight." He slipped a second finger in.

Knight chuckled, body gripping him.

"It's no joke, man."

"No, it's not," murmured Rookie.

"I'm the artist. I get to say who's stunning."

"Okay, then, who's stunning?" Rook asked.

Bish slipped in a third finger, nice and easy.

"You three. Studs, all of you."

That had Rook laughing softly. "Well, Bish and Jason for sure. I'm a little too lean to be called a stud."

Knight looked at Rookie. "I love you, dork. You're perfect."

Rook bounced up and kissed Knight. "You're so good to me." Then he settled back on the couch with Jason and waved his hand. "Carry on."

Bish chuckled. "I am." He nudged Knight's gland to prove it.

Knight's lips parted and his beautiful man groaned. Rook made a happy little noise and Bish did it again, fingers nudging that bit of flesh hard.

"Oh, fuck. Bish. Bish, right there."

"I know, baby." Bish tagged that spot a few more times, sending Knight flying, opening him up and getting him ready for the next finger.

Bishop heard Jason and Rook both moan.

He slid out of Knight and lubed up all his fingers, curling them slightly as he put them back at Knight's hole. Four first, and then he'd tuck his thumb against his palm and push his whole hand into Knight's body, connecting them in that very special, very intimate way.

Knight groaned, his body fighting him. "I don't know…"

"You know, Knight. You know you want my hand. You want me to feel your pulse in my palm, in my own body. You holding me tight as I hold you."

Knight shook his head, eyes rolling. "You keep saying things."

Knight didn't want Jason to see him vulnerable — Bish knew it.

"You asked me to talk to you, so I'm talking. I'm telling you how stunning you are, how brave and strong. How you let me make you fly." He slowly pushed four fingers into Knight's body.

"Only you." The words were soft, barely given breath.

"I know. You're something special, Knight." He kept pushing until his fingers touched Knight's gland, moving over the little bit of flesh.

Knight keened softly, cheeks flushed, and all Bishop knew was his lover, this perfect man, and his need.

"So fucking tight, babe. So perfect. God."

"Full." Knight's hips rolled up, body taking him just the barest bit deeper.

"Not completely full, though. You'll take my whole hand. You'll hold me tight inside you."

"Full of you." Knight's body rippled around his fingers, muscles fluttering.

"Mmm. Oh, yes." He moved his fingers in and out then stretched them a little, loosening Knight up, getting his body ready.

He added lube, slicking the way, slowly shifting deeper and deeper. Next, he curled his thumb into his palm and kept pushing, Knight's body slowly but surely stretching to accommodate him.

"Can you feel it? Feel how I'm filling you up."

"How could I not? You're everywhere." Knight was panting now, fingers opening and closing.

"I am. Filling you up. Holding you in my hand. I can feel your heart beating."

"Mouse…"

He heard Jason's soft whisper, Rook's answer, but he ignored them. His world was Knight.

"I'm right here. Inside you." His hand pushed completely into Knight's body and he moaned. "Oh, fuck, yes."

"Mouse…" Knight arched, body fighting to make room for him.

He moved with Knight, careful not to stretch the man any more than he already was. "I have you. I goddamn fucking have you." In the palm of his fucking hand. *God fucking damn.* "Forever."

He could feel each heartbeat.

He met Knight's gaze and held it, breathing with his lover, the connection between them so strong, so palpable, he was sure it was visible. He took a deep breath, encouraging Knight to do the same. Then he took another breath and began to move his hand inside Knight's body. He slowly closed his fingers into a fist, then moved it in a circle, then forward and back in little increments.

"You're mine, Knight. My heartbeat." He couldn't think of a better way to say I love you. He moved his hand some more, the tightness holding him in, demanding he stay.

Knight nodded, his breathing beginning to hitch.

"You need to come for me." Release some of the pressure.

"I can't. It's too big." Knight always said that.

"You can. You will." He wrapped his free hand around Knight's prick, thumb and forefinger squeezing the tip, moving the ring buried there.

"No..." Knight's shoulders left the sofa. "Oh, fuck. Mouse. Just like that."

"Like this?" He stroked up and down once, moved his hand inside so his knuckles brushed Knight's gland. Then he did it again.

Knight convulsed, spunk spraying up on that flat, perfect belly. Two moans joined his, Rook and Jason noisy in their appreciation.

"Good boy, Knight."

Knight whimpered softly, cock not flagging a bit. He continued to move his hand inside Knight's body and leant forward to tongue the slit.

"My hot motherfucking boy." He whispered the words against Knight's cock. Then he took it in, tongue playing with the slit and moving the ring back and forth

"Your boy!" Knight's toes curled, fingers tangling in his hair.

He hummed around Knight's prick and sucked harder. Wild sounds poured down over him, desperate and needy. He took Knight in all the way, swallowing around the tip. His hand wasn't still, easing slowly but rhythmically inside Knight's body. He could feel those muscles jerking and bumping around him.

His own prick was hard as a diamond, the trust and intimacy between them more arousing than the physical.

Knight blinked at him, lips parted, hungry.

He swallowed around Knight's prick again, then pulled back far enough to press his tongue into the slit. His sweet pain-slut loved that burn—the sting, the ache. His hand was beginning to ache, but he'd see Knight come again before letting go of this heartbeat.

Knight reached down, fingers touching his arm where it disappeared into his body. That was right, they were joined together…right there.

Rook cried out, the sound deep and wild.

Bish let his teeth just graze Knight's skin. Spunk filled his mouth, Knight sobbing for him. He swallowed it down, pulling his hand out while he did.

Knight was crying hard, undone, needing him more than ever. He cleaned them both up, then drew Knight into his lap, rocking him, focusing only on his lover. A bottle of water was pressed into his hand, a blanket wrapped around them.

"Thanks, Rookie." He made Knight drink, kissing the man's face, catching each tear.

Rook rubbed his shoulders. "Call out if you need anything."

"We will. You love on the kid. I'm keeping my K with me."

"Thank you for sharing. Love you both."

One last squeeze and he and his Knight were alone.

"So big, Mouse. That's so big."

"It's the biggest thing ever. And you are so brave, so beautiful."

"Tell me we can stay like this forever."

"We can stay like this forever." It was true enough for right this moment.

"Okay. I believe you."

"Good boy." His boy.

"Love you, Mouse. Rookie needs to be careful — the kid's in love with him."

"You don't think it's mutual?"

"I think Rook loves him, yeah, but Jase… Jason is *in* love."

"And you think Rookie's going to hurt him?" Bish thought it made everything easier, the love they all shared.

"Not on purpose, ever. But… You know what it's like, that first man you're in love with. When Jason realises that Rookie's not going to commit like that…"

"Hey, he committed to us, babe. Full on."

Knight nodded. "Maybe I'm just paranoid. You know how I get."

"The truth is you're a softie inside and you worry about the people you care about." Knight hid a lot behind his crazy artist persona.

"Bullshit." Knight flipped him off.

He kissed Knight's forehead. "Don't worry. I won't spill your secret."

"You'd better not."

"You know I wouldn't." He kissed Knight's nose and then his lips. "Now weren't we supposed to be afterglowing?"

"Uh-huh. Cuddling and staying warm." Knight laughed, looking young.

"You got it, babe."

Knight kissed his jaw. "Love you, asshole."

"And I love all of you, even your asshole."

Knight's laughter was the neatest thing he'd ever heard. Ever.

Jason wasn't the only one in love and Bish knew it. He also believed it was a good thing.

He held on to Knight, settling in for the long haul.

Chapter Ten

Jason worked out an hour earlier than normal, then left a note saying he was going for a walk. He didn't want to do this anymore. He just had to figure out how to tell them. It had been one thing when they'd just been fucking, but now... Now he was in love and stupid over a man who was in love with two other men.

His cell phone started ringing about an hour into his walk. He looked at the screen, not sure if he could talk to anyone right now. It was Rook.

He sighed, thought about just letting it ring, then answered. "Hey."

"Hey, honey! It's Rook."

"Good morning, Rook. How're you?"

"I'm good. Missing you, though. Where are you, honey?"

"I needed a walk."

"I hope you dressed warmly. I don't want you getting a cold."

"I'm okay, I have my coat on."

"Are you going to be home soon?"

"I thought I'd take myself to breakfast, maybe to the library."

"And I take it you don't want company?" He thought he could hear a pout in Rook's voice.

"I...I was having a think, Rook." He always wanted Rook's company.

"So do you want to talk about it? I could meet you somewhere for breakfast..."

"Okay. Okay, yeah." He'd just tell Rook he was giving notice. Moving out. Finding a life where he wasn't making a huge mistake with his heart.

"How about Zva'? In twenty minutes?"

"Okay." Okay. Yeah. He could do that.

"Awesome!" Rook sounded so happy at his agreement. "See you then, honey."

He swore he heard a kiss blown at him, then the line went dead.

Jason sighed, stopped and looked out over the water. What was he going to do? How could he let go of Rook? Could he walk away from the only person he'd ever loved?

He didn't know, but he was pretty sure he needed to try. He just really didn't want to.

* * * *

Rook was already there when he got to the coffee house, chatting and laughing with the owners behind the counter. Jason almost just walked away. Rook turned before he could decide, though, his smile getting wider when he caught sight of him.

"Hey." *Oh, God.*

Rook came right over and kissed him. "Morning, honey. That'll be a real kiss when we get home. What do you want for breakfast?"

"Just coffee, I think." His stomach was in knots.

"Not hungry?" Rook frowned at him. "Are you okay, honey?"

"I... I think... No, Rook. I'm not. Can we sit down?"

"Of course we can." Rook waved at the guys at the counter. "Just two coffees, boys." Then Rook led him to the comfy seats in the corner of the nearly empty coffee house.

"I'm sorry." He sat and folded his hands together. *You can do this, Jason. You can. It's best for everyone just to walk away.*

Rook reached over, wrapped a hand around both of his and squeezed. "You're scaring me. What's wrong?"

"I think... I'm going to have to move out, Rook. I have to go." He let himself hold on to Rook a second, his heart breaking.

Rook's face fell—he looked devastated. "What?" There was barely any sound behind the word.

"I can't... I can't do this. I-I'm not the right guy to do this and not fuck everything up at the end, I'm sorry."

"No. No. No. You're the perfect guy. Absolutely perfect. Is this because of the fisting? Honey, we'd never hurt you, never push you to do something you don't want to. You have to know that. I promise."

"No. No, it's not that. It's..." It was because Rook's perfect life was two other men and then him and he wanted to be...special.

"It's what? Please, honey, you have to tell me so I can fix it because I don't want to even think of life without you. I love you, honey."

"But I'm in love with you, Rook. I didn't try to, but I fell. I'm sorry."

"Oh. Oh, Jason." Rook smiled at him, looking so happy. "Don't be sorry. That's so wonderful!"

"It's not. I... I just can't live there, knowing that I'm in love with you. I need to go."

"I don't understand how loving me means you have to leave."

His cheeks burned and he couldn't meet Rook's eyes. "I... When we were playing Truth or Dare...that's when I knew. You don't feel the same about me. It's okay. I get it, but... I want to be something more." Was he even making sense?

"Jason. I love you. This isn't the first time I've said it. I don't understand."

"You love me, but you're not in love with me, huh? I love Bish and Knight, sure, but I'm *in* love with you."

Rook leaned in. "Then how come you don't want to stay with me?"

He shook his head. "Because I want to be special."

"But you *are* special. No one else is my honey — no one else is you."

"I'm not. I wish I was." He looked up when his coffee arrived. "Thank you."

"What do you mean you're not? You are! I love you! I... I don't understand." Rook kept saying that.

"I'm sorry." He was a bad person, but... He didn't know how to make himself clear.

"I can't let you go, honey. Please, it would break my heart."

"I..." How could he do that? Hurt the man he loved?

"Come back home with me. Please." Rook's fingers stroked his wrist, and all he wanted was to go with Rook — to go home. To touch.

Rook stood, reaching a hand out to him.

He stood, taking Rook's fingers. "This is a mistake, Rook." He couldn't deny Rook, though.

Rook shook his head. "No. No, it isn't. I swear it isn't. Oh, please, honey, come on home."

"I'm stupid in love with you." Didn't Rook understand?

Rook smiled. "And I'm in love with you, honey."

They were moving, somehow—walking towards the door then out into the snow. Rook shivered and hunched into his coat but didn't let go of Jason's hand.

"I'm sorry." He was. He didn't want to hurt anyone.

"Hush." Rook hurried along.

"I am. I didn't intend to…" He wrapped around Rook, protecting the man from the cold. Rook leaned into him. "I have you." He did, stupid or not.

"Thank you, honey."

It didn't take long to get home, the two of them pushing through the door and out of the cold. The house was quiet, still—Knight and Bishop still hidden away.

They went to Rookie's room. Rook closed the door and led Jason over to the window seat. He sat, still in his coat and boots.

Rook wrapped both arms around him and held him close. "I don't want to let you go. Not ever."

"It's really impossible to break up with you when you're so close." And everything he wanted.

"I don't want you to break up with me." Rookie leaned in.

"But…" He looked up, made the mistake of looking into Rook's eyes.

"I don't." Rook pressed their mouths together.

The kiss was soft, slow, and made his toes curl. It went on and on. Rook's kisses were always like this—wonderful and breathtaking. They made him feel amazing, stupid and dizzy.

Rook's fingers slid over his coat, began to undo his buttons.

"Rook…" This was a mistake.

"I love you, honey. I don't know how else to tell you so I'm trying to show you just how much." Rook cupped his face, eyes glistening, and kissed him again, tongue sliding on his. He could feel the love and care in that kiss—he could.

Jason closed his eyes, trying so hard to think.

Rook's fingers returned to their job, opening his coat and pushing it off his shoulders. One kiss melted into another, then another—Rook not letting him think. He didn't rush to make Jason naked once his coat was off, only kissing him and kissing him and kissing him.

Jason was shaking and shivering, achingly hard and hot.

Rook met his eyes. "I love you, honey." Then the kisses began again.

How could he fight this?

Tracing his face, Rook's fingers warmed his skin. Tears slipped from his eyes, wetting Rook's fingers. Whimpering, Rook deepened the kisses, pressing closer to him. His hands landed on Rook's hips, circling them. Rook groaned into his mouth, tongue tracing his teeth, tickling his gums.

How was he going to…? *Oh, God. So sweet.*

Shifting, Rook slid out of his jacket and straddled Jason's lap. He moaned in his lover's lips, loving how Rook fit against him. Their bodies moved together, almost clicked in place. Rook's hands stroked through his hair, tilting his head so their kiss could deepen. His own prick was hard, Rook's pressing against it as the man began to rock against him.

This was crazy. Absolutely crazy.

"I love you, Jason. I have almost since the first day I brought you home."

"I don't know what to do." That had been his life, for the last few months.

"You let me love you, Jason. Because I do and I won't hurt you." Rook cupped his face. "Trust me."

"Trust you…" He had. From the beginning.

Rook nodded. "Trust me, honey. I'm not letting you go. Not ever. Trust me."

"You have Bish and Knight. You don't need me."

"What?" Rook shook his head. "No. I have Bish and Knight and I love them, but they aren't you. I need you, too, honey. You're not just some guy we picked to join us. Not anymore, not since..." Rook shrugged. "You've been special from the start."

His cheeks heated. "I just... No one's ever been like you." *Ever.*

"Oh, honey, thank you. And I'm not going anywhere. Why would you leave?"

"I keep trying to explain." And failing miserably.

"You seem to think I'm going to hurt you because you're in love with me. But that's just makes you even more precious to me."

"I just don't want this to be bad."

"Has it been?"

"No." He was too stupid to explain.

"Then why assume it will be in the future?" Rook looked honestly perplexed.

"Because I want to be, like...yours. Like really yours."

"What's stopping you from knowing that you already are?"

"I'm not. I'm all of yours."

"So you just want to be mine and not Bish's and Knight's too? Isn't having more people love you better?"

"I'm too fucking dumb to do this, to explain. It doesn't matter." It just didn't matter anymore.

"Of course it matters! You matter." Rook hugged him. "I want you to be happy. I want you to be in love and loved and to know that you're my Jason."

"Am I? Yours?"

"Oh, yes. Yes, you are." Rook met his eyes, deadly serious. "You are."

"I love you, Rook." *And you're a guy and you love two other guys.*

"And I love you, Jason," Rook swallowed and continued softly, "more than anything."

"You... You don't have to say it." *If you don't mean it.*

"I don't say things I don't mean." Rook pouted. "You should know that by now."

"I do. I do know. I..." He swallowed again. "Say it again?"

"I love you, Jason." Rook kissed him, stole his breath. "I love you more than anything."

He cried out and pushed into Rook, the kiss going deep and hard. Rook held him and that magical mouth opened to him, Rook sucking on his tongue as it slipped in. Jason groaned, pushing closer, hungry for him. Rook made a happy noise, body still rubbing against him.

This was what he needed, who he needed, right here.

"Love you, honey. Love you. Love you." Each word was punctuated with another kiss.

"Love. Love, Rook. Oh, God. I didn't think I could..."

"Didn't think you could what, honey?"

"Fall in love. Especially with a man."

"A life without love would be so sad, honey."

"Yeah." He could believe that. It was what he was scared of in the end.

"Then thank God we found you and you came to us."

"Really, that's... Thank Knight."

Rook laughed. "Knight is going to love that you compared him to God."

"Laughing at me." He chuckled, and it felt so good.

"With you, honey. Never at you." Rook's lips slid over his, hips rolling again.

"With me. I want you. I want to make love."

"Oh, yes, please."

Rook slid off his lap and grabbed his hands, pulling him back towards the bed. They settled together, side by side, reaching for each other. Rook started with more of his amazing kisses, tongue sliding along his lips before pushing into his mouth. He opened up, sliding his fingers over Rook's side. Rook moaned for him, nice and sweet. He took one soft kiss after another, their lips clinging.

Rook began working on his shirt, teasing it up over his hips. He sucked his abs in, his ass tightening.

"God, I love your skin, honey." Rook traced his muscles, touched his nipples.

"Love..." His balls drew up, the ring behind them throbbing.

"That's right. Love. So much of it." Rook's fingertips danced over his nipples.

The touch made his nipples ache, draw up tight. Humming, Rook moved to take the right one into his mouth.

"Rook..." He arched, pushing into that hungry mouth.

Tongue flicking over his nipple, Rook sucked and licked and sent him flying high. His fingers brushed over Rook's head, encouraging the pleasure to continue. Rook hummed and moved to the other nipple, fingers dancing on his ribs.

"Don't tickle, now." He did chuckle, though, his worry trying to fade.

"Just loving on you."

"I want you to. I want to love on you, too."

"Yes, please. Touch me. Love me. Make me fly like only you can."

The words were exactly what he needed to hear and he rolled atop Rook, covering his beautiful body with his own. Rook arched up against him, moaning and rubbing.

"Need you." He took Rook's mouth as his cock slid alongside his lover's.

"Yes. Please, honey. I want you."

He nodded, wrapping a hand around one of Rook's legs, drawing it up. It slid around his waist, opening Rook up to him.

"Can I?" He rocked down, cock hard and leaking.

"Please, Jase." Rook's other leg came up and wrapped around him as well.

"I... Slick?" God, he wanted in—he wanted to feel Rook all around him.

"I got it." Rook arched beneath him, reaching for the tube on the bedside table.

Jason moaned as the motion rubbed Rook all along him. Rook's hand was trembling as he passed the lube.

"I won't hurt you." Ever.

"It's excitement, not fear, honey." Rook's smile rocked him.

"Oh, good. Good, because I want it to be amazing."

"Me, too." Rook leaned up and kissed him, tongue slipping into his mouth.

He took the lube—only dropping it twice as the kiss made him dizzy—and tried to get his fingers slick.

Rook let one leg drop from his waist, shifting so he could get a hand between them. "Can't wait to feel you inside me."

"Want to. Want to know." His hand was shaking and he hid it in another kiss.

Rook grabbed his hand as they kissed and brought it to that hot hole. Tight and tiny, Rook's body took him, squeezing his finger, and Jason moaned into Rook's lips. Rook's sweet whimper answered him and the lovely body bucked beneath his touch.

"So pretty. So hot." He moved his finger in and out, fucking Rook slowly.

"Oh, Jason, you make me feel like the only man in the world."

"You are." *The one that matters.*

Rook's mouth closed over his again, the kiss long and heady. One finger became two and Jason loved how Rook moaned, bucking up into him.

"More, honey. Please."

"More…" He added more slick, pushing in a third finger, and watched Rook's lips part.

"Jason…please. I want you."

He nodded. "You're ready?" He slicked his cock with a trembling hand.

"Always ready for you. Come on."

He looked down, placed the tip of his cock at the tiny hole and pushed, so carefully, Rook's body taking him.

"Mmm. I won't break, I promise." Rook's hand landed on his ass, tugging hard, and half his cock disappeared inside a perfect heat. Rook squeezed, then bucked, taking him in deeper.

"Rook!" His body knew what it needed, what to do, and he pushed in hard.

Rook's other leg came up to wrap back around his waist, keeping him from pulling out too far. His hips moved restlessly, his rhythm hard and deep, body aching with pleasure. Rook was an enthusiastic partner, rocking up into him.

"Feels so…" So much bigger than good.

"Uh-huh. I know." Rook pulled him into another kiss, body pushing up to meet his over and over.

He let himself stop worrying and start just feeling—loving Rook. Moans and whimpers filled his mouth, Rook so responsive.

"I love you." More than he knew he could.

"And I love you, Jason."

He pushed in deep, eyes crossing. *Good*.

"More, honey. Please. I want to feel you when we're finished."

"Close. So close." He balanced on one hand and reached for Rook's cock.

"Yes!" Rook arched into his hand and drove back onto his prick.

Fuck—look at his lover, look at that.

"More," Rook demanded, his eyes hot, intense.

"More." His tightened his fingers, squeezed.

"Yes. Oh, Jason." Rook's eyes widened and his back bowed, spunk flying from his cock.

He cried out, his body jerking convulsively as he drove into Rook, pushing harder. Rook's whole body pulled at him, trying to hold him deep inside.

"Gonna…" He shot, the room going silver around the edges.

Rook kept holding on to him, fingers trailing along his spine. Every touch made the pleasure keep going. When Rook took his mouth and added those intoxicating kisses to the mix, he nearly lost his breath altogether.

It was perfect.

The kiss ended, Rook taking a deep shaky breath. "I love you, honey."

He nodded, kissed the corner of Rook's mouth. "Love. So much."

"Which means everything is going to be just fine, honey. More than fine, even."

"You think?" He wanted to believe.

"With everything in my heart. And I have a really, really big heart, Jason."

"You do." That he knew.

"Then trust me. Stay with me."

He nodded, took a deep, shaky breath. "I can do that." He could.

With Rook's help, he would.

He just had to trust that it wouldn't leave him with a broken heart.

About the Author

Often referred to as "Space Cowboy" and "Gangsta of Love" while still striving for the moniker of "Maurice", Sean Michael spends his days surfing, smutting, organising his immense gourd collection and fantasizing about one day retiring on a small secluded island peopled entirely by horseshoe crabs. While collecting vast amounts of vintage gay pulp novels and mood rings, Sean whiles away the hours between dropping the f-bomb and pursuing the kama sutra by channelling the long lost spirit of John Wayne and singing along with the soundtrack to "Chicago".

A long-time writer of complicated haiku, currently Sean is attempting to learn the advanced arts of plate spinning and soap carving sex toys.

Barring any of that? He'll stick with writing his stories, thanks, and rubbing pretty bodies together to see if they spark.

Sean Michael loves to hear from readers. You can find his contact information, website details and author profile page at http://www.total-e-bound.com.

Total-E-Bound Publishing

www.total-e-bound.com

Take a look at our exciting range of literagasmic™
erotic romance titles and discover pure quality
at Total-E-Bound.